ALL THAT I DREAD

A K-9 SEARCH AND RESCUE STORY

LINDA J. WHITE

Cover design: June Padgett, Bright Eye Designs

First Printing, May 2019

Printed in the United States of America

White, Linda J. 1949-

All That I Dread/ Linda J. White

ISBN-13 978-0-9912212-6-4 Paperback

ISBN-13 978-0-9912212-7-1 ebook

For Becky,
whose encouragement, enthusiasm, and help
have kept me going

Amid thoughts from visions of the night, when deep sleep falls on men,

dread came upon me, and trembling, which made all my bones shake.

— JOB 4:13-14

1

SUDDENLY, the ground gave way under my feet. Welcome to my life.

I slid partway down the ditch on slippery Virginia red clay. My dog kept going. I could hear him crashing through the forest. I forced myself to my feet, grabbed a root, and pulled myself up the slope. Which way had he gone?

Luke answered the question for me. He came racing back through the woods barking, jumped up, and planted two big feet on my chest. I stumbled back, my arms windmilling.

Emily put her hand in the middle of my back and shoved me forward. "Go, go!"

"Thanks," I cried and raced after my large German shepherd.

The subject of our search was an "elderly man who had wandered off from a home nearby." Actually, he was a search-and-rescue dog handler named Nathan Tanner. I didn't know much about him, only that he was the training director of the volunteer SAR group I wanted to join.

When I caught up to my dog, I found him dancing around the guy.

"Okay now, play, play!" Emily instructed.

I jerked the Kong out of my pocket. "Good dog! Good Luke." I threw the toy for him, admiring his body, his athleticism, his grace. His black-and-gold coat gleamed in the sunlight filtering through the trees. Pride filled my heart.

Three more tosses and I ended the game. "Good dog, good Luke! Enough, now." I shoved the toy back in my pocket and held up my hands. Luke waited a moment, then turned and found a stick to harass.

I looked at the others, trying not to grin. My dog had worked it!

"They performed really well as a team," Emily said, looking at Nathan. Sweat beaded her brow. The 75-degree day carried with it a boatload of humidity.

The man brushed his clothes off, twigs and leaves fluttering to the ground. I profiled him, old habits dying hard. He stood about five feet eight, maybe a hundred and sixty pounds, mid-forties, with thick, dark-brown hair that matched his full beard. He had the most striking blue eyes I had ever seen. Did he wear colored contacts?

When he spoke, I detected a soft southern accent. "The dog did find me, true enough." Nathan cocked his head. "He's part-trained, you say?"

I tore my attention off his eyes to respond. "His prior owner started working with him, but I have no idea how far he got." A clinical description of a much more complex situation.

Nate pulled a toothpick out of his shirt pocket and stuck it in his mouth. "Why is it you want to do this?"

I raised my eyebrows. What difference did it make to him? "Luke's a big dog. He's too smart and has too much energy to just hang out. He needs a purpose, a real job." And so do I, I wanted to add. Investigating divorcing couples just wasn't cutting it.

"He's big for you."

"I'm stronger than I look."

Emily chimed in. "He almost knocked her flat back into a ditch. He needs a new indication."

"That was his indication? To jump on his handler?" Nate shook his head. "That'll never do."

"No big deal. I can train him to do something different." Luke trotted over and nudged my hand. I stroked his head and scratched him behind the ears and around his neck, while I kept my eyes on Nate. The dog leaned against me. He'd been doing that lately. I didn't know why.

Nate stared at the dog, then lifted his gaze. "Ever had a dog before, Jessica?"

I met those blue eyes straight on, raising my chin. "When I was younger, I had an Aussie. We competed in agility." Images of joyful, happy Finn flashed in my head. "He was the top-ranked agility dog in the nation in my freshman year of college."

The skin around Nate's eyes softened a little. A good sign. So I continued. "I know how to train for obedience and agility. I've just never done search and rescue before."

"How long you had him?" Nate gestured toward Luke, who had moved away and found another stick.

"Six months." I pulled a water bottle off my belt and took a long drink, my mouth suddenly dry.

"And he's how old?"

"Two and a half."

Nate shook his head, frowning. "We do a lot of work in the woods. You got to deal with ticks, mosquitoes, snakes, hills, rocks, swamps, nasty weather, cold, heat."

"Sounds great!" I smiled. "I live in the country. I run mountain-trail races. I'm used to all that."

"Once in a while, we have an urban search. There you've got concrete, heat, noise, fumes, and sometimes folks who aren't happy to see us."

"Raised in the city. So no problem."

"Now and then we spend the night out in the woods, by ourselves, in makeshift shelters ..."

"I did that in Girl Scouts!"

"... sittin' over a dead body."

My heart hit my chest wall with a thud. I searched for a quick comeback. I had nothing. "Part of the job," I said finally. It sounded weak, even to me.

Then I remembered something I'd read on the Battlefield Search and Rescue website. "Don't you have different teams? Live search teams and cadaver teams?"

Nate paused a moment before he agreed that yes, they did. I straightened my back.

He took a deep breath. "Look, if you want to give this a try, I won't stop you. I'll give you the forms when we get back. But here's the thing: When I look at you, I see a big, half-trained, rowdy dog and a small woman."

I opened my mouth to retort, but that guy talked right through my reaction.

"I'm sorry that's not PC, but I'm tellin' you what I see. Maybe you can do this. Maybe you cain't. We'll find out soon enough."

2

WHY WAS Nathan Tanner so negative? I had no idea, but I'd faced plenty of discrimination from men before and he wasn't going to stop me. No way.

Emily volunteered to help me prepare for the initial tests. Her own dog—a border collie named Flash—had cut his foot on a search and was on injured reserve for a while. An elementary school teacher, she had time to work with me in the late afternoon. Honestly, I was happy she volunteered and not Nathan.

We began on a cloudy, cool Thursday in September. I knew from reading that Battlefield Search and Rescue volunteers worked everything from lost kids to wandering adults. They also searched for human remains buried underground or in lakes or left in remote areas. Crime victims, suicides, lost souls—all eventually became dust and ashes, but the remarkable noses of the dogs could still sniff them out.

"A dog has about two-hundred million olfactory receptors in his nose," Emily told me, "compared to about six million in a human's. A dog can smell a teaspoon of sugar in a million gallons of water—enough to fill two Olympic-sized pools."

Wow.

Ten thousand other facts followed, all of which fed my interest, and I scribbled them in the small, black, Moleskine notebook I always carried in my back pocket. There was more to SAR than I'd realized—more training, more equipment, more details, more of a time commitment. Still, the thought of working with Luke and finding some lost kid or wandering dementia patient fired me up. My life needed to count for something. My father had taught me that.

However, I needed to watch one thing—overworking. When I get my mind on something, I pursue it. But with dogs, you get too serious, and they'll shut down. With them, it's all about play. Make it fun. Good boy, good boy!

So I limited myself to two training periods a day, and I kept them short. My methodology worked. Within two weeks, Luke had passed the initial tests—heeling on leash, ten-minute stay, recall, and aggression evaluation. That gave us official candidate status! Now, we had one year to complete all the challenges to become operational. That was the rule.

Emily said our next task was to retrain Luke's indication that he'd found the victim we'd been searching for. She suggested I teach him to grab a long, braided-cotton tug toy tied to my belt. It turned out to be much better than having his eighty pounds jumping on me. After a couple of weeks, he nearly had that down. Plus, he was getting pretty good at searching out a cotton ball soaked in birch oil that I hid in increasingly difficult places.

While I worked with Luke, Emily trained me. She showed me how to puff a little baby powder in the air to find the wind direction, how to follow a topographic map and use a GPS, how to map out a search plan and chart features that had been searched. She demonstrated how to pack for the field, how to use the handheld radio to stay in touch with the base, and most importantly, she instructed me on safety and crime-scene preservation.

That I already knew, but I took notes anyway.

There was so much to learn, but I loved it. Finally, something besides adulterous husbands and runaway wives occupied my mind.

Sometimes, when we worked on weekends with the Battlefield group, I would see Nate watching us across the field, a black-and-white springer spaniel at his side. He seemed to be studying us, arms crossed. It looked to me like he was perpetually frowning.

"What's his story?" I asked Emily one day when we were packing up.

"You should ask him, Jess," she replied. "He's an interesting guy."

Interesting?

We worked hard, Luke and I. He seemed to know how to handle my OCD. When I pushed him too far, he'd stop and simply look at me, like, "Whaaat?" while panting, a silly grin on his face. I'd make him do something simple—a down or a sit-stay—to "assert my authority." But then I'd play with him, grabbing him, roughhousing with him on the ground, play-chasing him, until both of us were de-stressed. We slept well on those nights.

After two months of twice-weekly coaching sessions plus weekend work with the team, Emily approached me. "Hey, I told Nathan you're doing really well. He wants to try a dry run. Would you be up for that?"

I shrugged. "Sure, I guess."

"I think he wants to catch anything you guys are doing wrong before it becomes entrenched."

"He doesn't trust you?"

Emily laughed. "He's the training director. Plus, he knows more than all the rest of us put together."

"Okay. What's the plan?"

"Just the three of us somewhere up north, plus a search subject Luke hasn't met. He's going to check with a park to see if they'll let us use the area. I'll let you know when he has it figured out. Probably be on some weekend soon."

I thought about that as I got ready for bed that night. Were we ready for a test? What would Nate say if Luke messed up? If I messed up?

It didn't matter, I told myself, setting my jaw. We had ten more months to complete the necessary exercises. And if I needed to, I'd take every minute of that, regardless of what Nate said.

But something disturbed my sleep that night. I woke to a pounding heart and Luke standing at my bedside, licking my hand. "What, buddy?" I sat up, petting him as he nudged me with his nose. I checked my watch—4:14 a.m. I forced my mind into the present. What day was it? What did I have to do?

I got up, went to the bathroom, and downed a glass of water. Finally, my heart slowed to a normal rhythm. I searched my mind for any fragment of a dream but found nothing. Part of me was thankful for that.

By the time I returned, Luke had flopped back down on his favorite part of the rug. He followed me with his eyes, not lifting his head, watching as I crawled back into bed. "I know, it's not time to get up," I said. "Sorry, buddy."

I snuggled down into the covers and soon heard Luke's soft snoring, but sleep eluded me. So frustrating. Finally, at five-thirty, I gave up. I rose and put on running clothes. By the time I tied my shoes, Luke stood at the door, dancing in anticipation.

I stepped out into the Virginia fall morning and inhaled the brisk, fresh air. A thousand stars drew my eyes upward. A question emerged from somewhere deep in my soul. *Why?*

I didn't want to think about it. So I shook it off and began running.

The rhythmic pounding of my feet and the comfortable cadence of my heart settled me. I loved my beautiful dog running beside me, his strong body so in tune with mine. Running forced me to focus on the trail. Dreams and questions got left behind.

I ran the half mile down the driveway and turned left onto the shoulder of the narrow country lane on which we lived. I kept

Luke on a leash for this part of the trip because of the occasional car that passed by. Less than five minutes later, I diverted onto the path my landlord Bruce and I had cut through his forest.

Bruce had been my first client. My discovery of the double life his soon-to-be ex-wife was living saved him a bundle in the divorce. When he found out I was looking for a place to live, he offered me his downstairs, and I gratefully accepted.

After settling in, I began running on the country roads around the house. But Bruce was a runner, too, and when I suggested we cut paths through his twenty-six acres of woods, he thought it was a great idea.

Once I turned and entered the tree line, I let Luke off leash. He happily watered a few bushes and sniffed around. In fact, he disappeared momentarily, but it wasn't long before he ran at my side again, choosing to be with me.

Honestly, he was better than a guy.

We ran three loops—about five miles—then returned home. Luke collapsed on the floor while I showered. As I finished, I heard my phone signal a text.

Prince William Forest Park Thursday morning. Meet at Greenway Walmart 0700.

Thursday! Much sooner than I expected. I took a big breath and texted Emily back: *Will do.*

3

On Thursday morning I drove toward the Walmart parking lot. I had stayed up late the night before, reading the notes I'd made in my Moleskine and double-checking my pack. I also worked with Luke a little.

The outside temperature gauge on my Jeep's dashboard read twenty-eight degrees. No matter. I had dressed in layers—good, Under Armour leggings and a long-sleeved tactical shirt—under my other clothes. I'd add my North Face parka when I got out of the car.

I threaded my way through the lot and spotted Emily standing next to Nate's old, red Chevy Tahoe. I pulled over to it and rolled down my window. A woman I didn't know was sitting in the back.

"All set?" Nate asked.

"Yes." I almost added "sir."

"Be a thirty-minute drive or thereabouts," he said, his breath frosty. "Don't be lettin' the dog out 'til I tell you."

"I won't."

Nate had gotten permission, Emily had told me in a long e-mail, to hold the exercise in a remote corner of sprawling Prince

William Forest Park in Northern Virginia about thirty miles south of Washington. Not far, really, from my mother's home. It was an easy drive, up Route 29 past Culpeper and into Fauquier County, then over back roads. I'd checked it out on Google maps, but still I followed Nate closely.

The training director led me past the park headquarters to a remote area. As I pulled my Jeep off the road in the place he indicated, I saw the unfamiliar woman get out of the back of his Tahoe and dash into the woods. Our search subject, no doubt.

Luke stood up in his crate, tail banging the sides, anticipating his release. But I held off, guessing Nate would want the woman's scent to dissipate a bit before I let him out.

I slid out of my front seat, slipped on my parka, and stretched. "Did you take off school for this?" I asked Emily. My mentor was removing gear from Nate's Tahoe.

Emily shook her head. "It's Veterans Day."

I'd forgotten. My eye caught Nate nearby, fixing his bootlaces. "Are you a vet, Nate?" I realized I hardly knew this guy and yet so much of my future with SAR was in his hands.

He nodded, turning those blue eyes toward me. "Three tours in Iraq, one and a half in Afghanistan." He shrugged on a black backpack. As he did, his collar stretched open, and for the first time, I saw what looked like a burn scar on the side of his neck. "Let Luke out to relieve himself," he said, "and then Emily will brief you."

That burn scar told a story, I knew, and it triggered my curiosity. Still, it would have to wait. I released Luke from his crate. He jumped down, shook himself, then began watering every bush in the area. Soon he came back to me, his tail wagging, so beautiful he made me smile.

"You are such a good boy! Are you ready to work?" I tapped his left shoulder, then his right as he shifted his weight. It was a game we'd invented, a dance of sorts, and it never failed to lift my spirits. When I looked up, Nate was watching us.

"Ready?" he asked.

"Just about." A little shimmer went through me. Fear? Anxiety?

Whatever. I shook it off and put Luke's SAR vest on him. His golden-brown eyes lit up, and he barked twice. "Good dog." I slid my hands into black-leather gloves, pulled a blue-knit hat down over my hair, and shrugged on my pack. "Ready," I said to Nate.

"Let's have our briefing over here." I joined him and Emily in a cluster next to Nate's car. I was the searcher, Nate would play a police officer accompanying me, and Emily was base commander.

"We believe," Emily said, setting up the fictitious problem, "that a woman may be in these woods. She is forty-three, five feet nine, dark hair. She may be lost, and her family thinks she may be suicidal."

I nodded. "Is she armed?" I knew that was a good question. Out of the corner of my eye, I checked for Nate's approval. His face remained impassive.

"A handgun is missing from the home." Emily gestured toward a non-existent dwelling. Then she handed me a portion of a topographic map. "Your sector is here," she said, indicating an area marked off with green highlighter. "If you find the suspect, don't approach. Let the officer call the shots. Got it?"

"Yes," I said. "Where's the next closest team?" A team nearby could distract my dog.

"You're by yourself," Emily responded. "When you're ready, you can go."

"Radio check?"

"Good call."

We confirmed we had good radio contact, then I studied the map in my hand. I felt Nate's eyes on me, or at least I thought I did.

I chose a target—a creek about a mile away. I circled some

features of interest—an abandoned shack, a drainage ditch, a fence. Then I grabbed the small container of baby powder out of my pack, puffed it in the air, noted the wind direction, and set a back-and-forth course. Using my compass, I established my bearings and found a closer target toward which I would walk to keep myself on track.

What had I forgotten? Ah, to set a waypoint on the GPS in my pocket, a mark showing my starting location.

Emily whispered, "You'll do fine!"

Was my anxiety so obvious?

I moved toward the woods, told Luke to sit, and checked my map and compass. "Good boy, good boy!" I said, rubbing his neck. I unhooked his leash and gestured. "Seek!" I told him. "Seek, seek!"

My handsome dog took off, his long stride swallowing the ten yards between us and the woods in a few swift moves. I ran after him, glancing down at my compass and trying to pay attention to my footing at the same time.

Ahead, I could hear Luke working. While tracking dogs are trained to sniff human scent on an object and then track that person, Luke was an air-scent dog. His task was to find any human, so he began by making wide sweeps across the search area.

Back and forth, back and forth through the woods we went. I knew Nate was behind me, but I remained focused ahead. A quarter mile in, I found the old hunting shack. Instinctively, I stayed back and asked Luke to search it.

The dog did not alert. Still, I approached the shed carefully and checked it myself. "Good boy!" I said, confirming his lack of interest. I thumped Luke's side. "Now, seek!"

We pressed on until I saw the creek, the edge of our search sector. Luke happily lapped up creek water. I called him back to me and poured some water from my pack into his collapsible bowl. While he drank, I used the baby powder and set my next course, still crisscrossing against the wind. "Good boy. Seek!" I sent Luke off to the east.

I had to run through a swampy area that soaked my boots. Push through brambles that tore at my 5.11 cargo pants. Fight off cobwebs. But Luke was on to something, and when I saw him racing back, when he grabbed the tug on my belt, it was all worth it.

"Good boy!" My investigator brain kicked in. Follow the dog. Carefully. Who knows what a suicidal woman might do?

I walked forward, using trees for cover. Luke came back and tugged again. *Hurry up,* he seemed to say. But I wouldn't hurry. I would not be caught by surprise. Not again.

Ahead, I saw Luke race toward a fallen log, then come back. This time, I made him stay. I turned to Nate.

"Go ahead."

I shouted, "Carol! Carol Putnam!" A hand emerged from behind the log.

"Okay," Nate said. "Follow me."

We moved forward. Carol Putnam stood up, grinning.

"Good boy, good boy," I said, clapping Luke on the side. I pulled his favorite toy, a small rubber ball, out of my pocket and threw it for him. "Good boy." My heart was racing. Success!

"Five more minutes and I would have had to find another hiding place," Carol said, trying to remove something from the back of her neck. "I feel like I'm covered in bugs. Nate, help me!"

He pulled her collar down a little and brushed away some leaf parts. "No bugs. Too cold for 'em," he reported.

Carol shivered. "I saw beetles working on that log. I was sure they'd crawled down my shirt." She looked at me and stuck out her hand. "Hi, I'm Carol."

"I'm Jess, Jessica Chamberlain. And that's Luke." I shook her hand and gestured toward my dog.

"Good job. If you'd just run up to me, I was ready to say, 'Bang, I shot you,' but you did it right. Nice!"

My heart pounded with pride. "How long were you lying there?"

"Fifteen or twenty minutes. I'll tell you what, though—Luke is intimidating. No way was I going to take off running!"

"I'm mighty grateful for your help this morning, Carol." Nate said. Then he turned those searchlight eyes on me. "Let's debrief."

Debrief?

I felt like a kid listening as her teacher started going over the correct answers to a test. My stomach tightened, and my back stiffened.

He started by asking me questions. Which way was the wind blowing? Why did I choose the intermediate targets that I did? What did Luke's behavior around the hunting cabin tell me?

On and on it went, until, after about ten minutes, he nodded and said, "You did good. Better'n I expected to be honest." Then he glanced around. "Where's the dog?"

The dog? I looked around. "He was just over there." I pointed to some brush, then I whistled. "Luke!"

I expected to see his head bob up from behind some bush. Or hear leaves rustling as he raced toward me. "Luke! Luke! Here, boy!" Had he run off after something? I felt anxiety creeping up my back. I glanced at Nate. He was studying me. Great.

Suddenly hot, I unzipped my parka. Then I heard a bark, way off. A surge of relief flashed through me. "Luke!" I called and I followed it with my loudest whistle, but to no avail. "I'd better go get him," I said to Nate, forcing a smile. "Maybe he got tangled up in something."

Nate nodded. His silence fell on me like a judge's gavel.

I jogged toward the bark I'd heard, pushing through the underbrush, stepping over logs. I tried to remember. Had the map shown a fence line? Barbed wire? What could Luke have gotten into? And after doing such a great job on the search. "Luke! Luke!"

I picked up my pace as Luke barked again. Why wasn't he coming? Was he hurt?

After pushing through a swampy area filled with brambles, I saw him lying down on a little rise, his tail sweeping the ground. Had he hurt his leg? "Luke, buddy, what's up?" He remained where he was, tongue lolling, tail wagging.

The smell hit me about ten feet from my dog, sending shock waves through me. "Phew!" I blew air out of my nose, then covered it with my arm. Something really stunk— something dead. Was it a deer? Is that what he'd found?

My throat closed up. I forced myself forward because Luke wasn't budging. "Hey, buddy!" I said, drawing near to my dog. "What's going on?"

My hand reached out to grab Luke's collar. My limbs felt like they were filled with concrete. My dread grew with every breath. I snapped on his leash, my eyes fixed on my dog, but as I straightened up, my gaze fell on an open area right behind him. A foot— a dusky-gray human foot in a pretty, gold sandal—lay on the leaves.

I gasped, involuntarily drawing in more death-saturated air, stale and nasty. I turned away, gagging, and squeezed my eyes shut. Then, putting my forearm over my mouth, I made myself turn back and look again.

There, in the little clearing, lay the partially decomposed body of a young woman, her body sinking into the earth, her eyes sightless, her hair spread like a halo on the ground. As I looked, wide-eyed, breathing in death, a yellow poplar leaf drifted down, down, down and landed on the young woman's chest.

4

STOMACH ACID BURNED MY THROAT. I yelled for Nate, then remembered my radio. Emily, still in base commander mode, could barely understand me when I said, "Send Nate."

With Luke on leash, I moved away from the body to wait. I leaned against the rough bark of an oak tree, pressing my face against it as if it would anchor me in the storm swirling inside. Trying to calm down, I closed my eyes for a second, but that didn't help at all. All I could see were the girl's dead, empty eyes.

Already the questions tumbled through my brain. Who was the young woman? Who left her here? Was it a murder, a suicide, an accident? What?

Luke leaned against my legs. Poor guy. He'd not been rewarded at all. I dropped down and hugged him. "Good boy, good boy." He licked my face, as if his slobber would heal my brokenness. I buried my face in his fur.

"What's wrong?" Nate asked, breathless from his run through the woods.

I stood and motioned toward the clearing, my mind numb. "A body."

Nate's eyes widened, then narrowed. He moved toward where

I pointed, then stopped and squatted down, resting his elbows on his knees, considering the scene.

I bit my lip against the tears that brimmed in my eyes. Part of me wanted to follow him. It would have been the professional thing to do.

Nate returned. I tried to read his face. I couldn't. "He found this?" He gestured toward Luke.

"He was lying near the body, wagging his tail and barking. He didn't move until I released him."

"So he works both ways." Nate shook his head. "Live finds and human remains. Well, I'll be. That's unusual."

I started to take a deep breath, then stopped as a breeze blew the cadaver-laden air toward me. A tremor ran through me. The girl was so young. Not much older than my sister Brooke. Who cut her life short?

Nate seemed to read my thoughts. He took my elbow. "You come away now over here. Sit down on this here fallen oak, and I'll call it in." His voice was soft, calming, and I yielded to it.

I pulled off my pack and sat down. Luke moved close, nudging me with his big nose. I petted his head and neck, rubbing my hand through his thick coat, trying to lose myself in Luke's golden-brown eyes. Then I leaned down and rested my head on his, inhaling the scent of his fur, feeling the guard hairs, his undercoat. He nuzzled my ear.

Nate walked back to the body, his cell phone to his ear. I saw him pull his GPS out of his pocket, and I knew he was reading off numbers, the latitude and longitude that defined our location.

Nate returned and sat down next to me, swinging his pack to the ground as he did. He unzipped a pocket and withdrew a small container of Vicks, uncapped it, and offered it to me. "It helps," he said.

Yes, I know, I wanted to say. *I know, I know!* But I remained silent. I took a little and dabbed it under my nose.

I started to move Luke on the other side of me, but to my

surprise, he sniffed Nate, then nudged his hand, begging for attention.

"Must have been a shock, finding her," Nate said as he rubbed Luke behind the ears. "You okay?"

"Yes." The lie caught in my throat, and I had to clear it to speak again. "Who'd you call?"

"The park ranger. She'll call 911." Nate stroked Luke between the eyes. "This here's federal property though. Eventually, it'll be the FBI in charge."

My dog was mesmerized. Nate seemed to know exactly how to touch him.

"This your first body?" he asked, turning toward me.

How was I supposed to answer that? I decided to simply shrug and hope it would end there. I really didn't want to go into all of it. Not here, not now.

Thankfully, Nate didn't pursue it. Instead, he tugged open the Velcro on the leg pocket of his cargo pants and pulled out a pipe. "Don't you worry," he said, reacting to my stare. "I don't smoke it."

Nate put the empty pipe in his mouth and drew on it. "Started this when I was seventeen. My girlfriend thought it was cool. This pipe," he took it out of his mouth and gestured with it, "this pipe's been all over the world with me. LeJeune. Iraq. Afghanistan. Germany. San An-tone." He drew on it again. "It's good company."

"You were in the Marine Corps."

"Yep. Quit smokin' once I got to Iraq. Couldn't get good pipe tobacco and didn't need to add smoke to all the dust I was breathin'. Still, I like my pipe."

As he spoke, he rubbed Luke's neck. I caught a glimpse of a tattoo on his left forearm. It looked like it might be an anchor.

Nate turned toward me. "It'll be a while afore they get here."

"Okay."

He stretched his legs out. The leaves on the ground before us were a tapestry of color—browns, yellow, orange, and an occasional red. "Where you from?" he asked me.

"New York."

"What brought you down here?"

"My stepfather's job, initially."

"Where do you work?"

"I have my own business. I do legal work for lawyers around central Virginia." I needed to change the focus before we went too far down that path. "Are you from around here?"

Nate drew on his pipe. "The mountains. Born and raised. So close to West Virginia if I rolled out of bed the wrong way I woulda been a hick."

I couldn't help but smile.

Nate started talking about growing up, and the dogs he'd had —bird dogs and beagles and feists—

"What's a feist?" I asked, interrupting.

Nate grinned. "Yeah, you are a Yankee," he teased. "A feist is a terrier-type dog, small, short-coated. We used 'em for rats, squirrels, that kind of thing."

"Like a Jack Russell?"

"More like a fox terrier, but sometimes a Jack Russell gets mixed in." He looked at me. "In the mountains, you use what you got." He knocked his empty pipe against his boot and put it back in his cargo pocket. "My favorite dog, though, was a black-and-white springer. That dog would retrieve until you made her quit. Slept in my bed, she did." Then he turned to me. "Tell me about your Aussie."

The sudden redirection made me pause, but I recovered quickly. "His name was Finn. I got him as a puppy when I was thirteen, a gift from my uncle." Remembering that little ball of white, gray, and black fur put a smile on my face. "I was super excited. My mom insisted I take him to obedience classes, and I met a woman there who did agility. It looked like a lot of fun, so after we got through the basics, we started that."

"Good fit, then."

"I was competitive, and Finn was smart and fast."

"So, this agility—what does the dog have to do?"

I started to explain about the jumps, the tunnel, the weaves, and in the middle of it, I realized what Nate had done— completely distracted me from the half-decayed body that lay just fifty feet away. He had eased my stress, gently and compassionately. A rush of gratitude closed my throat. Maybe I'd been wrong about him.

While we were talking, Luke raised his head, alerting to the sound of people coming through the woods. He sat up as sheriff's deputies, a detective, and the park ranger, guided by Carol, arrived.

"The ME is on the way. I'll go back and bring him here," she said to Nate.

The men circled up. I hung back, using Luke as an excuse. Did I know any of these officers?

Nate explained what we'd been doing and how we'd found the body. One of the deputies stared at me like he was trying to place me. I noticed he was the only one of the group who didn't move to take a closer look of the body.

Fifteen minutes later, the medical examiner arrived along with his team. His eyes lit up when he saw Nate. "I should have known it was you! Dragging me through these woods on my day off."

Nate grinned. "Doc, you know you can't resist a body." He turned to me, putting his hand on my shoulder somewhat protectively. "This here's Jessica Chamberlain. Her dog found the victim. Jess, this is Dr. Henry Shipman. Doc."

Doc looked at me, narrowing his eyes. I felt like he was taking both my pulse and my blood pressure with his gaze. "Hello, young lady. Why are you hanging out with this mope?" He bobbed his head toward Nate. When I didn't respond immediately, he moved on. "Well, where is she?"

"Over here." Nate turned to me. "Put Luke on a down-stay and come with us." He called the sheriff's deputy to join us.

I followed them over to the body, my feet heavy, crunching through the dry leaves. I focused on the men to distract myself. Doc stood just an inch or two taller than Nate, but he must have outweighed him by thirty pounds or more. He was built thick, like a wrestler. Completely bald, the ME was clean-shaven except for a long, gray, handlebar mustache. Very dramatic. He talked the entire time we were walking. The sheriff's deputy was an older man, clean-cut and gray-haired, trim and fit.

The ME turned to me. "How'd you find her?" His eyes were like an eagle's.

I fought through the web of emotion that suddenly engulfed me and recounted the story. Exactly. Every detail. Like I was a witness in a courtroom.

I knew what I was doing.

"No chance the dog disturbed the body?" the ME asked.

I hesitated. "He'd been here a while before I caught up to him, but honestly, I think he just laid down, right here, and waited for me."

"HRD dog then," the deputy said.

I glanced at Nate. "Both live and cadaver." I should have been proud to say that. I wasn't. In fact, it made my head spin.

Doc ducked under the crime-scene tape. I had watched a medical examiner do a preliminary review before. Tension tightened my back.

After bending over the victim, probing here and there with a tongue depressor held in his gloved hands, Doc stood upright, tossed the tongue depressor in a trash bag held by one of his assistants, and walked back to us.

"Female, early twenties," Doc said. "My early call is strangulation about two weeks ago. Neck is broken. Body's pretty degraded overall. I'll know more when I get her back to the morgue." He removed his gloves with two snaps. "She's small, maybe five feet one or two, and light. Easy to kill."

"Not killed here, right?" the deputy asked.

Doc nodded. "I think she was dumped." He scanned the area. "Somebody went to a lot of effort to dispose of her body. Wonder why he didn't just bury her? Or dump her near the road?" He turned, looking at the trees. "My guess is he knows the woods." He narrowed his eyes at Nate. "You walking me out?"

Before Nate could reply, there was an explosion of loud barking. My heart jumped. I whipped around toward my dog. A tall, dark-haired man dressed incongruously in a business suit strode toward us.

The FBI had arrived.

5

I QUICKLY MOVED to contain Luke, thankful he had limited his reaction to barking.

Frankly, I was happy for the excuse to move away from the body—away from the smell, away from the empty eyes, away from the ugliness of death.

I stayed with Luke while the men huddled. Mr. FBI provided such a contrast to Nate. Four inches taller. Clean-shaven. Navy-blue suit stretched tightly across his broad back. Black leather oxfords. No topcoat. Totally out of place.

He introduced himself as Special Agent Scott Cooper. He barely glanced in my direction as Nate explained how we'd found the body. His tone when he spoke was take-charge—"Listen to me. I'm the big gun."

Men like that set my teeth on edge.

Cooper asked the sheriff's deputy to assign someone to take a statement from me and Nate. Then he told Doc, "I'm calling in the Evidence Response Team."

The ME frowned. It would hang his crew up for hours. But there was no arguing with Mr. FBI.

Soon, Nate and I were free to go. We walked back through the

woods without speaking, threading our way through the brambles and fallen trees, the dry leaves and undergrowth, with Nate
in the lead. With every yard, I tried to scrub the images that
gripped me—the body, the haloed hair, the eyes.

Despite my efforts, my brain betrayed me, refusing to let the
mystery go. Did the victim see the attack coming? Did she fight?
Did fear grip her? Did she reach a point when she knew she
would die? Did she despair then, or keep fighting? Did she call
out for a loved one when death drew near?

Lost in my imaginings, I inhaled sharply and stumbled. Nate
turned at the sound and caught me. Our eyes met.

"Thanks," I mumbled. He hesitated and for a second I was
afraid a question would follow. "Tree root."

Nate nodded and glanced down. There was no root. My face
grew hot. He didn't say anything.

Three minutes later we emerged from the woods. Five
minutes later, I had Luke in his crate and my pack stowed. Nate
talked to Emily near his car. I know they assumed I'd come and
say goodbye.

They were wrong. I got in my car and pulled out, waving as I
went, ignoring the surprise on their faces.

I drove a mile away from Nate and Emily until I was well out
of sight. Then I pulled off the road, jumped out of the Jeep, and
threw up over and over in the grass. I could hear Luke moving
restlessly in his crate. My tears fell on my boots. I turned my face
to the sky.

I just wanted to help people and now this?

Why did I have to find a body?

Death was stalking me.

6

ON MY WAY HOME, I stopped at the dog wash and scrubbed Luke down, thankful that Emily had suggested I keep shampoo, towels, and a brush for him in the car. She had learned that trick after Flash had an unfortunate encounter with a skunk on a search.

When I got home, I threw all my clothes in the wash and took a shower, scrubbing my skin until it was pink. Drying off, my basement apartment felt chilly. I could not get warm.

So, after putting on my usual nighttime clothes, I wrapped up in a quilt, collapsed on the couch, and vegged out, streaming reruns of *Parks and Rec* on Netflix while I drank hot tea. When dinnertime came around, I didn't feel like eating. Luke chowed down as usual. Like all dogs, he lived in the moment. Lucky guy.

Tired but not sleepy, I turned to work, pretending that finding the secret bank accounts of someone's soon-to-be ex-husband was enough to push death out of my mind. It wasn't. I woke up three times that night, restless and scared.

Maybe SAR wasn't for me after all.

The next day, Emily called. Then Nate. I ignored them both. When Emily texted me the location of this weekend's SAR group meet-up, I texted back I couldn't attend. I was going to see my mother. Which wasn't true, but I soon made it so.

I worked until four on Friday, then threw an overnight bag in the Jeep, put Luke in his crate, and drove ninety minutes to Burke, where my mother and stepfather live. When I'd called my mom, I'd found out my stepfather was out of town. It was a good time to visit.

I tried to time it so I'd arrive just after my mother, who maintained fairly regular hours in her government job. But when I pulled up to the two-story colonial, my mother's car was still gone, the house locked up tight.

No problem. I looked under the doormat and found the key. Would they ever learn?

Mom arrived half an hour later. "Jess?" I heard her call.

Luke erupted in barking and headed for the front door. Thankfully, I caught his collar. "Enough!"

My mom stared at him, her face tight. "Well, I certainly didn't expect that."

"Sorry, Mom. He doesn't bite."

"If you say so." She put her black-leather business tote on the hall tree just inside the door and hung her coat on one of the hooks, moving stiffly as if braced for another outburst from Luke.

Why had I thought coming here was a good idea? I needed to fix this. "Luke, down." The dog dropped to the floor. "Stay."

I hugged my mom. "I'm sorry. He is loud."

"Loud and scary. I need some tea." She moved toward the kitchen. "Earl Grey?" she called over her shoulder.

I followed her meekly. "Here, you sit, I'll make it." I filled the kettle, pulled two mugs out of the cabinet, and found the teabags. "Hope you don't mind that I broke in."

"No. But I'd forgotten about the dog."

I decided to skip lightly over that comment. "You guys really should find a better place to hide your key."

Mom dismissed that thought with a wave. "Your sister is

always forgetting hers. Or losing it. We had to do something easy."

I heard Luke whine. "I'm going to let him up," I said. "He'll sniff you, but he's fine, really." The kettle was still heating. I released Luke from his down-stay. He came into the kitchen, sniffed Mom, then laid down with a thump.

"There, see? He's pretty chill." I poured the water into the mugs and placed them on the kitchen table. "So, how's Frank?" My stepfather's Department of Defense job frequently took him out of town.

"Busy." Mom tried a sip of tea, but I could tell by the way she grimaced it was still too hot.

"Tell me about Brooke." My half sister was always good for a diversion. Always.

My question started a ten-minute trip down Half Sister Lane. Brooke, a sophomore at a small college about two hours away, "absolutely loves college," Mom reported, although "the girls in the dorm are so immature." Still, "Even with all the drama, Brooke's thriving. Although she's changed her major again."

"To what this time?" In my mind I calculated the increased tuition costs for lost credits.

Another dismissive wave. "Communications? I don't know if that's the current one or the last one."

I tried to connect. Honest. But I'd been gone from home for over ten years. Now it seemed even longer.

My mom's eyes fell on the scar on my right wrist. I braced myself. She set her tea down. "And how are you doing? I've been so worried about you. You look so thin."

"I'm fine, Mom." I withdrew my hand. "That guy," I nodded toward Luke, "keeps me running."

"Are you happy?"

"Of course! I like what I'm doing, and Luke is a lot of fun."

"I never really understood what happened with Mitch."

I laughed. Even I thought it sounded forced. "Dogs are so

much easier than men. Speaking of which..." I stood, leaned over, and kissed Mom's cheek. "Thank you for driving me to all those agility trials. What a pain! I was telling somebody about it the other day." I didn't tell her that somebody was Nate and we were sitting over a dead body.

"I never understood your obsession with that dog. But I wanted to support you."

"And I appreciate it."

Mom rose. "I thought we'd go out to dinner." She checked her watch. "What would you like? Thai? American? Italian?"

"I'm happy with anything. But do you mind if I grab something from my room?"

"Of course not."

"I'll be back in a sec."

Luke followed me as I climbed the stairs to the second-floor bedroom I'd occupied as a teenager. Walking into the room made me catch my breath. Nothing had changed. My pictures still hung on the wall. Shelves held the agility trophies I'd won with Finn, as well as soccer and swimming awards and academic honors. The gray, black, and white quilt—colors from Finn's coat, and a touch of pink for me—that my aunt had made for me when I graduated from high school still covered my old bed.

I picked up a picture of Finn and traced the outline of his body. Finn saved me at a time when I really needed saving.

I replaced the picture and rummaged through drawers until I found what had drawn me—an old wooden box. I pulled it out, set it on the desk, and opened it. I hadn't looked at it in many years. I pulled out each object—an NYPD badge wrapped with a black elastic band, a grainy photograph, a folded program from a 9/11 memorial service, and an old pipe.

I ran my finger down the smooth briarwood of the pipe and sniffed its bowl, smelling the remnants of decades-old tobacco. I wondered if Nate had ever blown smoke rings for a little girl, or if a child had ever watched, fascinated, while he added fresh tobacco and tamped it down. I wondered if anyone had ever grown used to the smell of his pipe—and missed it now.

As I pondered these thoughts, a sound from the first floor made Luke jump to his feet. Before I could stop him, he went racing downstairs barking. I grabbed the box and followed him, shouting.

"Jess!" her mother cried out, panic sharpening her voice.

Then I heard someone else. "Oh my gosh, a dog!"

Brooke? I got downstairs just in time to see my half sister drop to her knees and throw her arms around Luke's neck. "And who are you?"

Thankfully, Luke was wagging his tail and accepting the attention.

"Brooke!" I yelled. "You shouldn't approach a dog like that."

"Aww, he is so cute!" She scratched Luke under the chin.

"What are you doing home? What a surprise!" my mom said.

Brooke grinned. Even I had to admit she had a million-dollar smile. All that orthodontic work. "You said my big sis was coming home, and I wanted to see her!"

I had inherited my father's coloring, his sandy hair and green eyes, and his athletic build. Brooke was the spitting image of our mother, short and slight, blonde and blue-eyed. She wore her hair long and straight, parted down the middle, and faded, ripped jeans along with a long, flowery tunic top. Put flowers in her hair and the '60s hippie look would be complete.

Brooke rose, "I'll be right back!" She giggled. "I gotta go, bad!"

Luke started to follow her. I called him back.

"Might as well let him go. Clearly, she doesn't have a problem with him." My mother shrugged.

So I released him and watched Luke disappear upstairs. "Why didn't you ever get her a dog?"

Mom rolled her eyes. "She wanted one, believe me. But we didn't think she'd have the discipline to care for it." She hesitated. "Besides, we aren't really dog people."

The gulf widened.

"I can't believe she drove home," Mom said.

"Impulsive as ever." I instantly regretted my judgmental attitude.

Mom's look withered me. "She misses you. It's been over a year, Jess. Fifteen months at least. You didn't even spend Christmas with us last year."

I bit my lip. "I've been busy, that's all. Moving, starting this business. So much to do." Truth was I'd spent Christmas alone in my basement apartment, watching old movies and sipping hot chocolate. But she didn't need to know that.

Overhead, the sound of scrambling feet in the second-floor hallway threatened to drown out our conversation. "Brooke's throwing a ball down the hall for the dog. Is that okay with you?"

"I guess so." Mom stared at the box I held in my hand.

"Just some things from my room I wanted to keep at my place."

She nodded. "Well, I'm hungry. We need to get going. Where will you put the dog when we go to dinner?" The implication was obvious—not in the house.

"He can stay in my Jeep." I whistled for Luke, who came scrambling down the stairs. I leashed him and took him out in the backyard so he could empty his bladder. Then I opened up the back of the Jeep and told him to kennel up. Luke jumped in. As I closed the crate door, my eyes fell on my overnight bag.

Maybe not.

BROOKE SEEMED SO YOUNG. But then, she was just eighteen. Twelve years separated us. I should cut her some slack, I reminded myself.

I'd been surprised when Mom remarried so soon after my father died and shocked when a baby came along almost right away. But it wasn't until much later when I'd accidentally stumbled on some papers of my mother's that I realized Brooke was either the first eight-pound preemie ever, or there'd been some fooling around. I hoped it was after my father died.

At Brooke's suggestion, which bordered on insistence, we went to a Japanese restaurant. I stared at the menu, trying to decide what my stomach could handle. Brooke pushed us to try "something different."

Everything was different. Everything in my life, anyway.

I settled on grilled miso salmon, a selection Brooke thought was ridiculous. She coached Mom on what to order, then selected dumpling soup and a variety of sushi, including sea urchin and eel, for herself. She tried to make me sample them.

Raw seafood? No way.

Mom, sensing everyone's discomfort, asked Brooke about college.

What followed could have populated a laundry list of Things Not to Do. Parties. Late nights. Casual dates.

Brooke cleaned it up for Mom, but I knew how to translate her words into reality—alcohol, hookups, and all-night parties. And as I looked into the face of my young, blonde half sister, all I could see was another young blonde, lying on the ground, a yellow leaf drifting onto her chest.

"What classes are you taking?" I asked, hoping to shift the conversation.

Brooke rattled off some of the standards, but she was more interested in the dog, and switched the subject again. "Mom said you're doing search and rescue? That's cool!"

"Yes, well, we're trying it. Luke is already partially trained."

"So, like, what do you search for? Kids? Puppies?"

"Humans."

"Dead or alive?" Brooke laughed. "Oh, man, that's lit!"

A few minutes later, when Mom left to use the restroom, I confronted my sister. "Brooke, what do you think you're doing?"

"What?"

"Drinking. Parties. Hooking up. That's risky behavior!"

Brooke rolled her eyes "When did you get so old?"

"I'm not that old. Look, you may think you're just having fun, but that's how college women get in trouble."

"Pregnant? I'm not that stupid."

Tension tightened my jaw. "Not pregnant. Abducted. Killed. Predators take advantage of women who are drunk. They look for them."

Brook waved her hand like she was dissipating smoke. "I know how to stay safe."

"Apparently, you don't!" My eyes shifted beyond Brooke. My mother was returning.

Brooke glanced over her shoulder. "Don't you dare say a thing."

I bit my lip.

Mom returned and glanced at both of us, then smoothed her hair and forced a smile. "So, I thought maybe we could go to the outlets tomorrow. Wouldn't that be fun?"

I took a deep breath. "I'm sorry. I need to go home tonight."

"Tonight? Oh, dear. I thought we'd have a little more time with you."

"Next time, Mom. I'm sorry. I got a text and, uh, I need to go."

Across the table, Brooke grinned broadly. There'd been no text. I had just lied like a teenager, and my little sister knew it.

7

A COLD RAIN fell as I drove home. My tires hissed on the wet asphalt, and lights from the strip malls and convenience stores gleamed. I was glad for the dark. It matched my thoughts.

This part of Fairfax County was the "good" part. Back in the day, I'd been told I was lucky to get assigned here. But there are no good parts. Not in Fairfax County, not anywhere.

I found that out the hard way.

I flipped on the radio, trying to distract myself, but my mind is stubborn and soon I was thinking again. Why had I been so uncomfortable with my mother and half sister? They were really the only family I had left, except for my stepfather, my uncle, and a couple of cousins.

In mandatory counseling, the psychologist had talked about the "dangers of isolating." Was that what I was doing?

If so, I'd been doing it half my life.

Luke moved in his crate and whined. I glanced in the rearview mirror. "About an hour to go, buddy." I heard his body thump down in resignation.

I turned south on US 29 and made my way through Centerville and Manassas. My uncle, a Civil War buff, had told me one time that the word "Manassas" came from the Bible—a Hebrew word meaning "to forget."

I wished I could.

I MANAGED to ignore phone calls from Nate, Emily, and my mother for a couple of weeks. I kept busy, working cases and running with Luke. Occasionally, he'd sniff the pack where I kept our SAR gear, and once he even pawed at it. I stowed it in my closet after that.

I tried to make up for the absence of SAR with running. Maybe I'd run a half-marathon in the spring.

Then I got a call from Nate followed by a long text.

FBI id'd the body, a 24-year-old woman from Pa. Her mom wants to see where she was found and meet the folks and the dog who found her. Can you come tomorrow at 10 a.m.?

I slammed my phone down on the couch as a gray fear flashed through me. No. No way. It wasn't my problem. I texted back that I had to work.

But it was my problem, and I knew it. My phone burned a hole in my back pocket all day until I admitted I couldn't just walk away. The grieving mother deserved some closure. And Luke and I could help provide it.

I got up early the next morning and did a long run to calm my nerves, then showered and dressed. Luke got excited as soon as he saw me pull out our SAR pack. How could I admit to him that I didn't have the courage for this job he loved?

Clouds had rolled in overnight—thick, gray, heavy clouds. The dashboard thermometer read thirty degrees. Snow wasn't predicted, but I knew well that weather forecasts in Virginia were a roll of the dice.

Ninety minutes later, I pulled off the road in western Prince William Forest Park. Nate's Tahoe was the only other vehicle there. I braced myself for his judgment.

As I got out of the Jeep, Nate emerged from the woods, his springer spaniel Sprite dashing ahead of him. He acknowledged me with a nod. "Thank you for coming."

Those blue eyes. I imagined them searching corners of my soul even I didn't know existed. I took a deep breath, surprised at how shaky I was. "So what's the story?" I tried to exude confidence. I know I failed.

"The young woman you found, her name's Faith Caldwell. 'Sposed to get married next year. Came down from up north to meet a friend. Goin' dress shopping in Richmond. Pulled off 95 to get coffee and that's the last anybody saw of her."

"Do they have security footage?" My mouth felt like a desert. I swigged water from my Yeti.

Nate nodded. "From the coffee shop."

"What about her car?"

Nate shrugged. "Don't know." He gestured toward the Jeep. "Why don't you let the dog out before they come? I'll put Sprite up."

Luke dashed around happily, sniffing and watering the bushes. I leashed him up, put on his vest, and stuffed his ball in my pocket just as a big black Suburban came down the road.

Special Agent Scott Cooper got out of the driver's seat. Once again, I was struck by his good looks. This time he was wearing 5.11 cargo pants, boots, and a dark-blue North Face jacket. He looked almost attractive. Almost.

Cooper opened the back door of the Suburban and extended his hand to help a woman step out. Another woman sat in front. Turning to us, he said, "This is Elizabeth Caldwell, Faith's mother."

"Ma'am," Nate said, extending his hand. "We're sorry about your daughter."

"Thank you." Mrs. Caldwell tucked her bobbed blonde hair behind her ears and pulled on a Penn State baseball cap. Her hiking boots looked well worn. A bright blue L.L. Bean parka topped her khakis. She was no stranger to the woods.

Then her eyes lit on Luke. "Oh, is this the dog? May I pet him?"

"Yes, ma'am," I said, following Nate's polite lead. "This is Luke." I told Luke to sit. Mrs. Caldwell approached him, let him sniff her, and then began to pet him. This mom knew her way around dogs.

Mrs. Caldwell rubbed Luke behind both ears. "Oh, you are so beautiful!" She looked up at me. "It's so fitting that a dog found Faith. She loved dogs her whole life." She straightened up. "I'm told you're a volunteer."

"That's right." I hoped no one noticed the catch in my voice.

"Well, thank you. I'd like to find out more about what you do." Mrs. Caldwell turned to Cooper. "Can I see the spot now?"

Cooper nodded toward Nathan, who said, "Come along this way, ma'am. We'll show you." He looked straight at me. "Jess?"

"Coming."

While we were talking, another woman emerged from the Suburban. She joined us, quietly introducing herself to me as Special Agent Alice Lopez. "You go ahead. I'll follow," she said to me.

A third agent stayed behind at the vehicles. It was a reminder to me that, when it came to bad guys, you couldn't be too careful.

Like I needed that reminder.

Mrs. Caldwell walked side-by-side with Nate, and every now and then he'd gently take her elbow and help her over a log or through the underbrush. I could tell they were talking and could imagine that soft southern accent calming the grieving mother. Maybe he was explaining about SAR. I hoped so. Cooper followed them, and I trailed behind him.

A lot had changed in the woods in three weeks. About 80 percent of the leaves had fallen off the trees. The ones that remained were brown, unmoving on this still, cold day. I knew from experience many of them would hang on until spring's new growth sent them falling onto the forest floor.

Someone had marked the path, applying red spray paint on trees like a trail of blood. When I saw it a tremor ran through me. "C'mon, boy," I said, as if Luke were the one who needed encouragement.

My tension grew with each step. Twenty minutes later, we reached the spot. Nate caught my eye and gestured to keep Luke back. The dog was already alerting, sniffing the air, his nostrils flaring. The smell of human remains lasts a long, long time.

I was only too happy to keep my distance. I distracted my dog with a toy.

Nate squatted next to Mrs. Caldwell on the little rise, and gestured, pointing out exactly where Faith had been found. Although I was too far away to hear their conversation, it appeared that Mrs. Caldwell was asking Nate questions. She kept fingering something around her neck. A necklace maybe.

Cooper stood back a little. He was letting Nate give the answers and for a take-charge kind of guy, I found that odd. Maybe he was as uncomfortable with death as I was.

Mrs. Caldwell looked up toward the sky, and I wondered if she might be trying to imagine her daughter's last view of this world. Had they told her Faith was dead when she was dumped here?

My throat tightened, struck by Mrs. Caldwell's courage. She'd come alone, no husband, no son, no sister to support her. I wondered if her family, like mine, couldn't face trauma.

Luke nudged me. *Why are we just standing here?* he seemed to say. I ruffled his coat, grateful he'd interrupted my thoughts. "Okay, buddy."

When I looked up again, I had to catch my breath. Big puffy flakes of snow, a curtain of beauty, descended over the clearing. Nate looked up at the sky too. Mrs. Caldwell held out her hand to catch a flake. They looked like they were caught in a snow globe.

Scott Cooper turned and walked back toward me, his hands jammed in his jacket pockets. I expected him to move past me to where Alice, the other agent, stood guard. But no, he walked toward me.

"Great," he said. "Now it's snowing."

It's crazy that I noticed his eyes. They were blue, like Nate's, but not as bright, not as lively, and once again I wondered if Nate wore contacts. "It's lovely," I said.

Cooper shrugged. "Snow around here is a pain."

"Where are you from?"

"Denver."

"You ski?"

Cooper nodded. "Tried it around here. You can't really ski on ice."

Just then Mrs. Caldwell and Nate turned and moved away from the small rise. Relief surged through me.

"Ready?" Cooper asked as they approached.

"Yes, thank you," Mrs. Caldwell replied. She petted my dog. "Luke, the healer," she said softly.

I glanced at Nate, wondering what she meant, but he didn't react.

We walked back through the woods, following the red trail, Nate again in the lead with Mrs. Caldwell, me taking extra care not to trip. When we got to the road, Mrs. Caldwell turned. "I want to thank you all for bringing me here, for helping find some closure. What happened to Faith," her voice caught in her throat, "shouldn't happen to anyone's daughter. But thank you for finding her." She patted Luke again. "Especially you."

As Mrs. Caldwell shook my hand, I noticed the necklace she'd been fingering was a small gold cross on a gold chain. She continued saying goodbye. When she got to Nate, she hugged him. Then she climbed into the black Suburban and Cooper drove off.

"Can I take you out to lunch?" Nate asked me when everyone

had left.

"No, sorry. I've got to run." I tapped the back of my Jeep and Luke jumped up and entered his crate. I secured the door and dropped the tailgate. When I turned, Nate was still standing there.

"Findin' this girl was hard on you." He cocked his head, inviting a response.

"What? No! I didn't know her."

"You haven't been around, not to practice, not to the bonfire. People askin' about you."

"I've got other things to do, all right?" I walked to the driver's door and got in. "Work's been really busy. Besides, I'm not sure SAR is right for me." Good grief. I sounded like a pharmaceutical commercial.

Nate followed. "Thank you for coming. For what it's worth, I think you and Luke have made a good team."

I started the car, forcing a small smile. "Thanks." I jerked the Jeep into reverse and backed onto the road. When I put it in drive, I realized it had stopped snowing.

THAT NIGHT, the dream came back. I woke up in a sweat, my heart slamming against my ribcage, fear screaming through my veins. I gasped and sat straight up in bed. Luke jumped halfway up and began nudging me.

My recurring dream was more distinct this time, the gray and white and black swirls forming shapes. I heard screams, then the screech of tires, rising and rising. As always, in the end, it was the eyes, the dead eyes that woke me up.

I turned to my dog. "Good Luke, good boy." I willed my heart to settle down. I got up, went to the bathroom, and paced until it did.

This is why I can't do SAR. Seeing one body, one dead body, had triggered the dream again.

8

KEEP BUSY. That was my command to myself over the next week. Run. Lift. Work.

So I ran in the woods, lifted the kettle bells and weights in my apartment, and worked. Hard.

My current job was the case of a 48-year-old man who'd skipped out on his family after winning $1.2 million in the state lottery.

By working fourteen-hour days, it took me less than a week to find the dude, who'd run off to Las Vegas with a woman he'd met online. The lawyer I worked for called and told me I'd located him before he'd run through his new fortune. His family would have Christmas after all.

Pumped, I answered the next call before noticing it was Nate. The sound of his voice made my heart thump with fear. I almost hung up.

"Jess, I need you. And Luke. We got a little boy missing down in Westmoreland."

I caught the urgency in his voice. My heart hardened. Why was he bothering me? "So call out the team."

"Most of 'em's gone someplace for Christmas."

"Luke and I aren't operational."

"I know that. I've gotten an exception for you, long as you work with me." He paused, as if gathering his patience. "Jess, it's an emergency. Sheriff's dogs been lookin' for this boy for six hours. Night's fallin' and the weather's turning. It's forty now, and a cold rain's coming down. Do you know the chances of that boy surviving the night?"

I walked over to my window and looked out. The late afternoon sun lay obscured by clouds, and although it wasn't raining yet where I was, I knew it could start any minute. "So use Sprite."

"Cain't. She's an HRD dog."

"I can't believe you don't have a second dog." A classic middle-school technique, blame shifting.

Silence.

"Your pack's ready, right?" he said.

Luke stood staring at me, wagging his tail. Could he hear Nate's voice?

I murmured a yes to Nate's question.

"I need you. This kid needs you."

Luke barked.

"I wouldn't be asking if it weren't life and death."

Something in me triggered. "All right, all right. Text me where to meet you."

TWENTY MINUTES later I guided my Jeep toward a rendezvous with the state police on US 29. Nate said I'd be given a lights-and-sirens police escort to Westmoreland State Park. He seemed to assume I'd be comfortable driving 80 mph on rain-slick roads.

I was.

I'd been to Westmoreland before. It lay right by the Potomac River. Wooded hills, deep ravines, and a few boggy places would be the challenges. And cliffs. Those steep cliffs right next to the river. We'd searched for fossils there once on a high-school field trip.

Would a three-year-old know to stay away from the cliffs?

Why had I decided to respond to Nate's callout? I mean, in my mind, I was done with SAR. Finding that body unearthed too much in me that I'd rather lie buried.

But this search wasn't for a body; it was for a kid. A little boy. The kind of kid I used to babysit.

My father taught me to run toward danger, not away from it. To help whenever I could.

I gripped the wheel. "This one's for you, Dad."

I showed up on the scene less than ninety minutes later, threading my way through the cluster of emergency vehicles and the rain-soaked searchers huddled around them. Nate's eyes brightened when he saw me.

"Thank you," he said, nodding. "I b'lieve you two might make the difference."

Together we met with the incident commander. The boy's home was next to the park, he told us, and the family took many walks in the woods. The mom, who was pregnant, had fallen asleep. She awakened to find the five-year-old still watching TV and the three-year-old missing. The family dog, a beagle, came walking out of the woods alone, fifteen minutes later, while she was still searching for her son. That's when she called 911.

Despite my resistance, as the story unfolded my heart became fully engaged. When he left the house, the little towheaded boy had on inside clothes—a long-sleeved T-shirt and sweatpants. Now darkness had fallen, and the rain continued. I imagined little Joey Washburn shivering in the cold. How long could he survive? Urgency rose in me.

Looking over the topographic maps, the search commander sketched out the areas they'd covered.

"Wait, the most likely areas have been searched, right?"

"True enough," Nate told me.

"What about this area?" I pointed to the map.

"Didn't seem like a three-year-old would go that route."

"Maybe we should try?" I said.

The two men agreed and outlined an area for Luke to check. "I'll be your walker," Nate said when he finally looked up from the map.

And my coach, I thought, because I don't really know what I'm doing. I went back to the Jeep, tugged on my lighted visor, and let Luke out of his crate. He watered the bushes and exploded with joy when I pulled out his SAR vest. "Good boy, good boy. We've got to find this kid. And it's not going to be easy."

I could feel the eyes of the other emergency responders on me. Muddy, wet, and tired, they were looking to us for hope.

Luke practically danced over to where Nate entered data in his GPS. "Somebody's excited," he said with a grin. Then he showed me the map, encased in plastic. "This here's going to be hard goin'." He pointed to a place about two hundred yards or so in from where we were starting. "A deep drainage that no doubt has water in the bottom."

"And hard up the other side." I took a deep breath and met Nate's eyes. "Let's do this thing."

"Bring Luke over here and let him go then."

I moved toward the spot Nate had entered as our launch point. I checked for wind and found none. Just a lot of rain. I made Luke heel, then removed his leash. "Seek, seek!" My excited dog took off.

Chasing Luke through the woods in daylight was one thing. Doing it on a cold, dark, rainy night was something else again. I used both my lighted visor and my good flashlight, but I still stumbled at times.

I found myself distracted by the shadows of trees that swung around as I moved. More than once, I saw a dead stump and thought it was a little boy. When we got to the ravine, I nearly fell down it before I realized I was at the edge.

Casting my light forward, I saw Luke racing up and down the ravine looking for a scent. Suddenly, he stopped and looked at me. "Seek, seek!" I called out, gesturing toward the other side. He took off, scrambling up the far side, and disappeared into the woods.

"Does he have something?" Nate asked.

"I'm not sure." I worried that we'd end up stumbling around on a cold dark night for nothing.

I made my way down into the ravine and up the other side. I heard Nate right behind me. The clay was slick under my feet. More than once I slipped, and he had to catch me.

When we reached the top Nate said, "Stop. Let me set a waypoint and take a bearing." He looked up after a moment. "Better call him back. We're not too far from those cliffs."

Rain dripped off my visor. Nate and I were both covered in mud. He was looking at a map encased in plastic and still had to wipe it off now and then. Whatever marks he'd made were smearing.

I whistled for Luke who came bounding back. The rain didn't seem to bother him at all. I poured some water into his portable bowl and let him drink, then finished the bottle myself. After all this, what if we found the kid dead? *Please, no. No, no, no.*

"Best leash him up," Nate said, gesturing toward Luke. He shined his flashlight on the map and held it out so I could see it. "Cliffs are ten, maybe fifteen yards away. With all this rain, they could be crumbling."

I pulled a thirty-foot lead out of my pack and clipped it on Luke's harness.

"Let's give it another half hour," Nate said, "then regroup."

We worked Luke on leash right up to the cliffs. In several places, Nate even got down on his belly and shone his flashlight over the edge, searching for a little blond-haired boy. I wanted to hang onto his legs. Once, the edge crumbled under his hand, sending him scurrying backward.

"Nothing," he said.

I think both of us were discouraged at that point. I know I was.

We'd covered the sector we'd been assigned. "Should we go back?"

Nate cocked his head. "We go back, that's it for this little boy. Nobody else coming out here tonight."

I didn't want to quit. I was wet, tired, and frustrated, but I didn't want to quit. We knocked around some ideas, but nothing fit until I asked, "What about that ravine? What if the boy stumbled into it and started walking downhill?"

"Then he'd be on the beach down there, but they searched that good, according to the sheriff."

"But a little kid like that, he might not make it all the way to the beach. And it was hard for us to make it out of that ditch. I don't think he could have. I remember my little sister at that age. She certainly wouldn't have had the strength to climb up that steep wall."

Nate shifted his weight. "So what are you thinking?"

"Let's go back to the ravine using a different path. Then let's search in the bottom, downhill, going toward the river. I can let Luke go down there in the bottom. I trust him."

"We could start here," Nate said, pointing to the map, "and work our way down. It's gonna be hard."

"I know. But I think we should do it." Luke stood near us. I could see he was ready to go again. "Look, Nate, I won't be able to sleep if we leave without checking that ravine."

My passion forced a grin to his face. "I call that good prey drive."

I laughed for the first time in months.

He dropped his head. I noticed his eyes were closed. I swear, he was praying. Who was I working with? Tim Tebow? Then he looked up, took a deep breath, and said, "Okay, we'll do it." He dug into his pocket and pulled out a protein bar that combined dried fruit, nuts, and chocolate. "We're going to need some energy." He handed it to me and retrieved one for himself, then found a jerky treat for Luke.

Luke's coat glistened with rain. His ears were still pricked and his nose active. I was glad all the running and work we'd been doing had kept him from getting soft.

We worked our way back to the gully, and I let him off-leash. I motioned down to the bottom. "Seek!"

Luke started down. He slipped but caught himself. I followed him, holding onto roots to keep from sliding on the slick clay. Once a root gave way, and I started falling. Nate grabbed my shoulder, supporting me as I scrambled to find secure footing. By the time we got to the bottom, we were both a mess, covered in mud, wet and cold.

Luke was out of sight. "The dog went that way," Nate said, gesturing down the ravine. He looked up at the pouring rain. "We got us a frog-strangler."

Great. A hick Tim Tebow.

We picked our way down that ditch. It was slow going, past rocks and tree debris that interrupted the flow of the stream running down to the river, making waterfalls and pools we had to skirt around. "This'd be hard in the daytime," I called out to Nate, who had taken the lead. I had to trust Luke was ahead. I couldn't see or hear him. "How far to the river?"

"Three-quarters of a mile," Nate said over the drumming of the rain. "Twenty minutes, I reckon, in these conditions."

That's when I heard Luke bark. My heart jumped. "Did you hear him?"

The dog came racing back. He dodged Nate, got to me, and grabbed the tug on my belt. I could hardly believe it. "He tugged!"

"Let's go!" Nate moved faster.

"Good boy, good boy. Seek!"

Luke raced on ahead.

For fifteen more minutes we worked past shrubs and boulders, tree roots and slippery mud. I fell and Nate helped me up, then he fell and cracked his kneecap, hard, on a rock. "No matter," he said, "just keep moving."

All the while, Luke dashed back and forth, barking. Finally, he stood still and barked and there, partway up the wall of the ravine, was an indentation made by the root ball of a huge, fallen oak. And a little blonde-haired boy lay curled up in the mud.

"We got him!"

Words can't describe the way I felt. It was like fireworks and Christmas morning all wrapped up in one. Like a perfect score in agility. Like seeing your dad for the first time in forever.

Nate felt the boy's pulse while I praised Luke. "He's alive! Thank God! You take care of him while I call it in."

Take care of him? How?

"Joey?" I said, approaching the boy as Nate got on the radio. The toddler's eyes opened a little, but he didn't cry. When I touched him, he was freezing cold.

Nate returned. "We got no cell signal, and we lost radio contact."

"I don't know what to do."

"Warm him up. Here, I'll do it."

Nate jerked off his pack and pulled out a Mylar emergency blanket and a small, chemical hot-pack. He stripped off the little boy's wet clothes, dried him with a small towel, and covered him with a spare T-shirt.

"C'mon, little guy, wake up," he said. The rain was coming hard again, and Nate had to work fast.

Unzipping his own jacket, Nate pressed the boy close to his chest and covered him with the Mylar. "Here, break this." Nate handed me the hot-pack and I bent it, releasing the chemicals that would create heat.

"Hypothermia?"

"Yes. But he's breathing, and his pulse is steady. Soon as he warms up, I'll go back for help."

"Wait," I said, unzipping my jacket. "Give him to me."

Nate hesitated, then complied. "Keep him horizontal if you can, and don't apply the heat to his arms or legs. Keep it near his chest but not directly on his skin."

Cradling the boy against my body, I stroked his wet hair and called his name. "Come on, Joey. Wake up. Wake up now." I pulled the Mylar close around him and my jacket over that. Fatigue mixed with fear and elation created a storm of emotions in me. *Don't die on me, kid! Don't you dare die.*

"Come on, little guy. You can wake up now. Look, see the big dog. He found you!"

Luke had discovered a place to lie down, finally tired after all of his searching. He turned and looked at me when I said the word "dog," and thumped his tail. "Yes, you are a good boy."

When I looked up, Nate was climbing the side of the ravine. It took a minute to realize what he was doing—heading for high ground to get a signal back to the base camp.

I leaned over and kissed the little boy on the top of his head and instantly remembered doing that to Brooke when she was little. Where had those tender moments gone?

"They're comin'." Nate's eyes were shining when he returned. "How's he doing?"

Just then, little Joey Washburn opened his eyes and began to cry.

9

It doesn't get much better than finding a lost kid two days before Christmas. The elation of the parents, the relief of the law enforcement officers, the press swarm (which I managed to mostly avoid), and the happy newscasts that followed created a bubble of goodwill. It also made Christmas Day at my mom's house easier. For once I didn't feel like an outcast. They had something safe to talk to me about.

Only once during that time did the dream edge into my sleeping mind, like a mockingbird harassing me. I woke but reoriented myself quickly and managed to fall back to sleep.

Two weeks after Christmas I found myself sitting across the table from Nate at his favorite steak place.

"Feels good, don't it?" he said, grinning at me.

I had to agree with him. It did feel good, good enough to make me reconsider quitting SAR. Maybe if I stuck to the live-search team, I'd be okay. That thought had obsessed me over the last couple of weeks.

Dinner was courtesy of the sheriff's office in Westmoreland. When Nate called to tell me about the gift, he'd suggested this place. Its location on the outskirts of a strip mall parking lot was nothing to brag about, but Beef 'n Brew knew how to cook steak.

With its nouveau log cabin décor and noisy bar, B&B (as the regulars called it) had created a guy-friendly, meaty enclave in a country increasingly full of small plates and pretty vegetables. In the parking lot I'd seen a bumper sticker: EAT BEEF THE WEST WASN'T WON ON SALAD.

I ordered a T-bone and Nate had sirloin. The smell wafting up from the plates as the server set them down predicted a terrific meal.

We talked about the search and the reactions to it while we ate. About halfway through my meal, my curiosity shoved my reserve out of the way. "Nate, I realized I don't know the first thing about you. Are you married?"

"No. You?"

I shook my head. "Where do you work?"

"At the community college."

"Really? What do you teach?"

He took a big drink of water and chewed on the ice, but he kept his eyes on me. He was up to something. "I cut the grass."

I gave him a twisted smile. "Not much grass cutting going on in January."

"You are right about that."

"So...?"

"I fix things."

"Besides dogs?"

He laughed. "It's the dogs fixin' me mostly." He took a drink of water. "Time was I thought I'd use the GI bill to go to school. I enrolled in classes, but I saw they were advertising for a maintenance worker. Figured I could use the money. After a while, I just dropped the classes." He fingered the knife next to his plate. "Thing is, I found out I could bring my dog."

"Sprite?"

"The dog before her. Springer named Maggie. I was spending

six hours or so on the riding mower, and she would ride with me. Jump off once in a while. They got so used to seeing me with that dog, they didn't blink an eye when I started bringing her with me on inside jobs. Fixing plumbing. Painting. Laying carpet. You name it, Maggie and me would do it. I got to be known as the dog man." He grinned. "Which was fine by me."

"I love having Luke with me."

"I got hurt over there in Afghanistan. I came back messed up. Real messed up." Nate's eyes caught the candlelight. "A dog was one of the things saved me."

One of the things. I didn't want to pursue that.

"Dogs are funny, picking up on stress, trying to make us right. Balance out our emotions." He let that hang in the air between us. When he looked up again, I felt his eyes piercing me like a scalpel dividing bone and marrow. "I've noticed Luke doin' that with you."

I blew that statement off with a shrug and a redirection. "Why were you so negative at first about Luke and me doing SAR?"

"I weren't."

"Yes, you were." I wasn't going to let him dodge that.

He laughed softly and shook his head. "Okay, I was. I guess I was afraid."

"Afraid of what?"

Serious hesitation followed. Nate stared at his fork as if he were willing it to move. I knew he was buying time.

Finally, he lifted his gaze. "Afraid of getting involved, of having to walk someone down the same mean road I been on. Afraid of stirring up my own past."

"What are you talking about?" As soon as that question was out of my mouth, I regretted it. I should have just laughed it off, sidetracked the conversation, changed the subject. But the rocket had been launched, and there was no calling it back.

"Like I said, I saw the way Luke was acting toward you. I thought, this girl's been through something."

My breathing became shallow. What did he know?

"I saw him nudging you when you got stressed, protecting you, trying to balance you out. Trying to take on your negative energy is the way some put it. I saw him doing a version of what my dog did in Afghanistan when the rockets were whistling overhead, and I was shaking under all that body armor. I didn't know what your story was, but I was afraid of getting involved with it. And that's nothing but selfishness and unbelief. And I'm sorry."

My mind raced. There was this weird buzzing in my head. I felt exposed, like someone had just opened a window into my messy soul. Heat flushed my face.

Quickly, I seized an escape route. "My dad," I said, averting my eyes, "was an NYPD officer. He died on 9/11, running into the South Tower." I put down my fork. "It's been a hard loss to get over."

Nate squinted. "How old were you?"

"Twelve."

"Tough age for a girl to lose a dad."

"Very hard." I continued on with the story, about how I was at school and how my mother came and got me and how we sat on the couch, clutching each other while we watched the news on TV, and how we knew, in our hearts, that my dad was dead.

It was a good story and it was true, every word of it. But I knew it was not *the* story. It was not the root of my anxiety. Not the source of my nightmares. Not the reason for the iron-fisted fear that gripped my heart and sent me retching on the side of the road.

If the partial truth was actually a lie, then I was guilty as sin.

Swiftly, though, I diverted the conversation. "What happened to you? How'd you get your scar?" I nodded toward his left arm. I willed my eyes to relax. I even smiled.

I had gotten good at deception.

"In Afghanistan, I had a Belgian Malinois named Rock. He was young, restless, and the most courageous dog I ever worked with. Beautiful dog. Our job was hunting IEDs buried in the road, weapons caches, anything we could find.

"One day we were driving down a road another unit had cleared. We were two weeks from going home, and we thought we were in safe territory. All of a sudden, an RPG came out of nowhere and landed right on the vehicle we were in.

"I remember the explosion. I remember the smell of fire, of burning flesh. I remember my leg being trapped, not being able to get away from the flames.

"When they got to me, Rock was lying on top of me, dead. Still trying to protect me."

My throat slammed shut.

"Everybody died but me," Nate said. "Every person in that vehicle, including Rock. They shipped me home to the burn unit at Brooke. Wanted to do skin grafts. I told 'em not to bother. I wanted to die.

"I was one angry SOB. I swore, I cursed. I jerked IVs out faster'n they could plug 'em in. One day this guy came in, a double amp. Rode that wheelchair like it was a racehorse. Smooth as silk.

"His name was Peter Turner, and that dude would not leave me alone. He came every day, rolling into that room like he was the sun risin'. Talkin' to me. Tellin' me how I could make it, how I needed to make it, and how there was a reason I made it through.

"I hated that guy. But after a while, I got used to him. And then I missed him if he was late. 'Got hung up in PT,' he told me one day. 'Had a kid who didn't think he could walk again.'

"'What happened?' I asked him. 'Oh, he walked all right. I wouldn't let him quit.'

"I knew then I didn't have a chance with Peter. He wouldn't let me die. What's more, he wouldn't stop talkin' about Jesus. Jesus this, Jesus that. I hated that too. Over time, he made Jesus real to me. He got me reading the Bible. He gave me hope, he did. Hope anchored in heaven."

Nate's tattoo?

"By the time I left that burn unit, Peter had planted faith in me." Nate pulled up his sleeve. "I got this tat the day he died," he said, revealing a large anchor with words I couldn't quite read.

I took a sharp breath. "Peter died? How?"

"Got hit crossing the street in a crosswalk right off base. Killed him instantly." Nate shook his head. "Survived two tours and two amputations, only to be taken out by a distracted driver." He looked at me with those blue eyes. "God's ways are mysterious indeed."

Mysterious? I sat frozen, stunned by what Nate told me. The music from the bar behind me suddenly seemed jarring. Nate's story didn't match. Peter was all, "Jesus this and Jesus that" and then gets killed crossing the street? C'mon!

I couldn't imagine a god who would operate that way.

Nate changed the subject. Maybe he sensed my discomfort.

"So what about coming back to SAR?" he said.

I felt my face flush. "I never actually quit."

He let me have that half-truth.

"But here's the thing—I don't want to do human remains. I just don't want to."

Nate nodded. "Okay."

"Live searches—fine. I'm in. But not HRD."

He leaned forward. "What threw you? Finding that girl?"

I was not going there. "Look, I've seen bodies before. I just don't want to spend my time hunting for them."

He twisted his mouth like he was chewing on that statement. But he swallowed it. "So we keep you on the live team. We can do that." Nate put his napkin on the table. "I'm glad you'll be back. Emily will send you the schedule, or you can get it off the website."

I nodded, knowing neither one of us said the obvious. Sometimes a live search has a body at the end of it.

10

I HAVE to admit I was relieved to be back doing SAR. I loved working with Luke, loved being out in the fields and woods, and loved watching the other dogs. The team included shepherds, two Malinois, a few border collies, a couple of Labs, and Nate's little springer.

Luke was okay with all of them, except the Malinois. They'd mouth off at each other once in a while, and I was careful to maintain some distance.

Together, Emily and I mapped out a training plan for Luke, one that could potentially get us operational by spring. It was ambitious, but as I said, once I set my mind on something, I'm all in.

Nate raised his eyebrows when he saw the plan, but he didn't try to stop us. I guess Luke had won him over.

I started with the agility component. Luke could already jump up on the tailgate of a car. I made a quick trip to Home Depot and snagged a long, twelve-inch wide board and some cinderblocks, then set up the board-walk task in Bruce's backyard. I also found a collapsible tunnel online. Soon we were practicing for fifteen minutes several times a day.

I started taking the required online courses, things like "Introduction to the Incident Command System" and "National Park Service Basic Search and Rescue," and a course in "Blood-borne Pathogens." I signed up for a CPR refresher course at our local hospital and a four-week, first-aid class.

Meanwhile, I was becoming more popular as a private investigator. My Richmond and Charlottesville caseload had grown as my reputation spread. That was fine by me. The more time I spent away from Northern Virginia, the better. Still, the increase in paying jobs and my attention to those courses were keeping me up late at night.

To qualify for SAR, I also had to participate in two searches as a walker, plus spend a night out in an emergency shelter. My first callout came on an icy-cold February day at 2 p.m. A dementia patient had wandered away from a home in an area just outside of Charlottesville. Mrs. Sullivan, 87, used a cane and had heart disease and diabetes along with the dementia. It was just the kind of case I wanted to help with.

When Luke saw me drag out my pack, he went ballistic, jumping around and barking. I shushed him three or four times, then sat him down and told him this search wasn't for him, and when I got back, I'd take him for a long run.

As I walked out to my car alone, I could hear his loud protest barks. I glanced up and saw the upstairs lights were on—Bruce was home. I could only hope Luke would settle down soon.

Twenty minutes later, I arrived at the search site. The incident commander, a guy named Jim, had assigned me to be Emily's walker. I was thrilled. I'd get to see Flash work. Nate was there, too, just watching the process. And maybe judging me. I didn't know.

Within ten minutes, I had my maps, GPS, radio, and a small notebook all set, and we had been briefed on the parameters of the search. I slipped on fingerless gloves, then leather gloves over them. I wouldn't be much use if I had frostbitten fingers. After adding a hat and checking for my water bottle, I shrugged on my pack and was ready to go.

The search area consisted of rolling hills with modest houses set on an acre or two. Mrs. Sullivan's house backed up to the woods. To the east was a series of fenced yards and pastures. Family members and neighbors had checked the woods and the road. I wondered about neighbors' sheds. Had anyone looked in them?

I asked about that and was told all had been cleared.

Emily and I set out following Flash, beginning at Mrs. Sullivan's back door. At first, he headed into the woods, the logical route for a dementia patient. But then, he took a hard turn to the east. Emily and I looked at each other. Had he picked up the scent of a searcher? No way could an 87-year-old woman clear all the fences Flash was leading us toward.

"I trust my dog," Emily shouted, answering my unspoken question. All I could do was follow, marking the turns on my GPS, and taking notes.

We crossed three fences and entered a field where a brown-and-white pony stood munching a mound of hay. Flash raced by the pony. I heard him bark, then he came racing back, skidded to a halt in front of Emily, and barked three times.

Exactly three times.

Emily looked back and me and grinned. "Come on!"

We ran over rock-hard ground, down into a gully, and there lay Grandma Sullivan.

At first, I thought she was dead. She wore an oversized man's coat. She looked pale. But Flash's barking roused her, and as Emily and I got close, she lifted a hand and touched him.

A miracle in my mind. That is, if I believed in them.

Quickly I called it in. Within five minutes, EMTs were on the scene. Nate came, too, beaming at our success. "You done good," he told me, grinning.

"She went totally opposite from the way anyone expected!"

"That happens."

Still pumped from our success, I arrived home an hour and a half later, just as the sun set. I strode into the house, thinking about the run I'd promised Luke. As I opened the door, shock buffeted me.

Luke lay on my bed, right on the sheets, having pawed away the comforter and blanket. He looked up at me, without raising his head, a guilty look on his face.

The guilt was well deserved. He'd ripped up the rug near the door and shredded it. He had chewed doorjamb and pieces of wood lay scattered on the floor. He'd scratched the door. And a book I'd left on the couch had its cover torn off. Half the pages lay on the rug.

"Oh, Luke!"

He thumped his tail. I imagined that was as close to begging for forgiveness as he'd get.

I took pictures on my iPhone. Then I began cleaning up the mess. I wasn't yet finished when Bruce, my landlord, called to me. "Okay to come down?" he asked.

"Sure." As soon as he came into view, I began my apologies. "I am so sorry. I'll replace or repair everything, Bruce. I promise."

"He was howling and barking for most of the time you were gone."

"He saw me take my SAR pack. He must have wanted to come with me."

"I don't mind the occasional barking, but he can't eat my house."

"I know, Bruce, I'm sorry. I'm really sorry."

In the end, my landlord established some boundaries. Luke had to stay in a crate when I wasn't there. And I'd fix everything within thirty days.

Fair enough.

I continued cleaning up for the next half hour, then took Luke on his run and fed him. He, of course, acted like nothing had happened. I was still stunned.

When we got back, I sent the pictures to Emily and Nate, showered, and dropped into bed. I was exhausted and knew I had a big mess to fix. Still, all I could see in my mind's eye was the old woman reaching up to pet Flash and the smiles on the faces of her family members when we brought her back alive.

The next day Nate texted me, volunteering to help me fix the damage. I didn't know what to think at first. I was so used to doing everything by myself.

But I didn't know a thing about fixing doorjambs or laying carpet. I figured the least I could do was have Nate over so he could tell me what needed to be done. As he stood in my apartment, explaining in his soft voice what he'd do, I decided to accept his help.

Over the next week, Nate sanded the door, replaced the doorjamb, and painted them both. Together we replaced the carpet. I grew used to listening to his stories as we worked, even if I did have to ignore all the Jesus talk. I figured it was part of being who he was, a southerner.

Of course, he brought Sprite with him, and soon the two dogs were buddies. When we were done, I invited Bruce down to inspect the repairs. He was super pleased. He and Nate got to talking, and before I knew it, Bruce had told him about the running trails and invited him to use them.

"Thank you, kindly," Nate said. "I'll take you up on that."

Great. Now Jesus will be running in the woods with me. But really, I was pleased. Nate was good company.

ON APRIL 15, two weeks later than I'd planned, Luke and I were certified operational. I was ecstatic. Nate created a little ceremony, and afterward, when he asked me if he could take me to dinner to celebrate, I readily agreed.

I enjoyed our friendship. Not a hint of romance. Just two people who loved dogs and had begun to trust one another.

Perfect, in other words.

To no one's surprise, for our celebratory dinner, we ended up back at Beef 'n Brew. It was Nate's go-to place for eating out, and it was quickly becoming mine.

While waiting for our steaks, I asked him questions about searches he'd been on. Nate reminded me of my Uncle Bobby, my father's brother, the one who gave me Finn. He knew how to tell a good story.

At one point, Nate pulled out his wallet. He wanted to show me a picture of his dog, Maggie. As he pulled the picture out of its plastic sleeve, I saw another picture behind it—a young woman, pretty, with brown-braided hair. "Wait, Nate, who's that?"

He turned beet red.

I grinned. "Come on, who is it?"

"Somebody I knew once."

"And her name is ..."

His eyes narrowed, like he was trying to figure out the distance to a cliff he was about to step off. "That there," he said finally, "is Laura O'Brien."

"And she is..."

"The only woman I ever loved." Nate slapped his wallet shut and put it back in his pocket. Clearly, he hoped that would end it, but I wasn't done.

"Where did you know her? What happened to her?"

Nate hesitated. I could see he was trying to get out of telling the story. I wasn't about to let him. "Come on, Nate!"

He took a deep breath. "She was my high-school sweetheart, the one who liked the pipe."

"And ..."

"And that's it."

"No it's not. You're still carrying her picture."

"I musta forgot it was in there."

"Ha! No way! I'm not buying it. What happened to her? To your relationship?"

"You are a nosy rascal!" He blew out a breath and then fixed his eyes on me. "When Momma died and Daddy got mean, I took off. Joined the Marines. My plan was to send for Laura once-t she graduated." Nate bit his lip. "It weren't a good plan. I realized once I was in, she deserved better than I could give her. Then I got hurt, and I wasn't fit for nobody."

"So did you go back to see her later when you got out?"

"Heard she was married. And I...I couldn't face that, her being with another man. I guess I'm a coward for that."

"No, I get it." I felt a sudden surge of empathy. "I'm sorry, Nate."

His mouth twisted into a wry smile. "It's okay. I'm used to my own company now. And I got my dog. And once in a while, I find someone I don't mind spending time with."

Of course, he meant me.

"'Cept when they ask too many questions."

Our steaks came, and we switched topics. He told me about Iraq and Afghanistan, the way they trained their dogs, and how he learned to do dog massage to help relieve his dog's stress. I told him about ... well, I stuck to my dad, my dog Finn, and mountain trail races.

The food was so good I barely noticed the bar behind me was getting noisier. But as dinner went on, I noticed Nate's eyes flick back there several times.

We had just declined the server's offer of dessert when Nate looked back toward the bar again. This time, his eyes stayed fixed there.

Suddenly, he reached for his wallet. Withdrawing a hundred-dollar bill, he put it on the table. "Pay the bill, will you? And meet me outside?"

What? Before I could respond, he got up, moving purposefully. I turned to see where he was going, and my heart sank. That FBI agent, Scott Cooper, stood toe-to-toe with another bar patron. His red face told the story. He'd been drinking, and he was angry.

11

—————

THE SERVER RETURNED with the check, and I handed him the hundred bucks. "Bring me two cups of black coffee to go as well. Quickly."

I watched Nate walk up to Scott like he was an old friend. He got between him and the other guy, put his arm around Scott, and started ushering him out of the bar. Scott resisted, yelling at the other man behind Nate's back. In the process, his coat flopped open, revealing his gun. A huge bouncer, probably twice Nate's weight, appeared. Nate held up his hand as if to say he had the situation under control.

I could hardly stand still, but I had to wait for the change and the coffee. Little jolts of adrenaline sparked through me. I tried to anticipate how the scene would play out. Would the other guy attack from behind? Did he have friends in the bar? My body felt like coiled wire. I was ready to spring.

The bouncer moved in the other guy's way, blocking him from Scott. I saw Nate muscle the much-larger agent toward the door.

The server came back. I took the change, quickly figured a tip, dropped it on the table, picked up the coffee, and hurried outside.

The spring chill hit me like a slap. Across the parking lot, I saw Nate trying to push Scott Cooper into the front seat of his Tahoe.

I jogged over to them, spilling a little coffee, and slipped into the back seat. Nate glanced over his shoulder at me. I'm not even sure Cooper knew I was there. I handed one cup of coffee to Nate, and for the next fifteen minutes, I sat listening to him as he tried to calm Scott down.

"You get arrested for fightin', you could lose your job. You know that, man."

Yes, Cooper did know that, but the SOB he'd been arguing with had made insulting remarks about a woman who was there. On and on Scott raged, slurring his words, until at last the second cup of coffee began to take effect and the real story emerged.

Scott leaned his head back against the headrest. "That girl the dog found—Faith. Back in November."

"Yeah?"

"There's another one, found in a wooded area west of there. 'Bout a year ago."

"On federal property?"

Scott shook his head. "No. But it seems like there's a connection. My boss says move on, let it go. But I can't. It seems like they're linked somehow."

Nate rubbed his jaw. "What makes you think they're linked?"

"Blonde. Same build. Lying on their backs, posed in the same way, in a little clearing in the woods. About the same age." Scott closed his left hand into a fist and pounded it once into his thigh. He cursed and ranted about men who abused women.

I was with him on that.

Then he made his story personal. "I got a daughter, thirteen. Her mother took her to live in California after our divorce to punish me."

"What'd you do?"

Scott remained silent for a minute. "Worked too much. Drank too much. And I, uh, messed up."

"With another woman?"

I saw Scott give him the slightest nod possible. "Somebody at work."

"Grace can be hard to come by when that happens."

Nate, the philosopher. I guessed Scott had no idea what Nate meant. Neither did I. Grace was something church people said before meals.

"So, you got this young 'un out in California and you're not there, so you cain't protect her."

"Drives me crazy."

"Cain't get a transfer?"

"I hate California. But I may have to."

Nate continued. "So you got these cases, but you don't have any physical evidence linking the two bodies ... no DNA, nothing?"

Cooper exploded. "How can he get away clean like that? No hairs, no semen, blood ... what's he doing, wearing a HazMat suit?" He rubbed his hand over his head.

My mind automatically formed other questions. Tire tracks? Shoe prints? Were either or both victims sexually assaulted? Were they strangled the same way? From where did they disappear? How were they found? How long had they been dead? Were they killed where they were found, or transported after death?

Old habits die hard. I forced myself to stop trying to help solve both cases.

Scott turned to Nate. "Hey, the first girl was found a year ago. Could a dog find a scent this long after?"

"What are you thinking?" Nate asked. "They took the body, right?"

"Yeah. I don't know. Maybe anything connected to her that the other guys missed. Evidence. A necklace, or a piece of clothing ...

anything that might carry DNA. Would the scent still be out there a year later?"

Nate shifted in his seat. "Cadaver scent can last for years. My guess is, they cleaned the place good. But I got a little dog I don't mind trying on it."

A little dog. Sprite. Thank goodness he wasn't talking about Luke. Because I wanted nothing to do with it.

Still, in my mind I was already deciding how I would investigate that year-old crime scene.

"Tell you what," Nate said. "Let's revisit this in the light of day. I think I can help you, at least to clear your mind about whether evidence got missed."

"Thanks, man." Scott started to get out of the Tahoe, but it was clear he was still unsteady on his feet.

Nate turned around and looked at me. I knew what he wanted. I held out my hand for his keys. "I'll follow."

I watched as Nate guided Cooper over to a black Nissan Rogue. I saw Cooper turn toward Nate, even push him a little, as if he were protesting Nate driving his car. But when he pushed PANIC instead of UNLOCK on his key fob and then couldn't stop the horn, he gave in.

Nate helped him into the passenger seat, waited until he had his seatbelt buckled, and then walked around the car to the driver's door and started the engine. As I tracked along behind them, I kept wondering why he had gotten involved. What was Cooper to him? The guy had been aloof at best from the get-go. He was a sloppy drunk. And Nate could have gotten into a mess if he hadn't been able to stop that fight.

Was the Rogue I followed Cooper's personal car? Nate could get in trouble for driving a government vehicle.

I couldn't stand obnoxious drunks. In fact, Cooper fell into most of my can't-stand categories. Arrogant. Egotistical. Dismissive. Even if he did love his daughter.

Cooper's townhouse was about thirty minutes away. It had a

first-floor garage, but Nate parked out front. So maybe the Bureau car was locked up in the garage. Which would make sense with all the firepower they carry in those things.

I debated whether I should follow them inside but decided to wait and enjoy the quiet night. Listening to Scott Cooper had triggered something in me. My mind would not settle down.

"You sure went out of your way with him," I said when Nate emerged and climbed into his car. I had vacated the driver's seat when I saw him come out. "What made you do that?"

Nate didn't answer until he'd started the car. Then he turned and looked at me, the streetlight catching in his blue eyes. "I been there, where he is now. Got help when I didn't want it. Got put on the right path and found a life I didn't know existed. Least I can do is pass that on." He pulled away from the curb.

"You didn't jump at the chance to help me." I meant it as a tease but there was truth in that statement, and he answered it seriously.

"You being a woman complicates things."

Oh, really? I wanted to say, but for once, I kept my mouth shut.

When I got home that night, I couldn't relax. Couldn't let go of Cooper's story. Couldn't let go of Nate's answer to my questions.

I had no idea what to do with Nate and his crazy ideas.

I knew how to tackle Cooper's worries though.

With my stomach tied in knots, I pulled out my old whiteboard and markers. I drew a vertical line down the middle and began listing the facts of the two cases. When I had exhausted what I knew, I went online to discover what I could about the first case, the young woman found near Warrenton, from news reports and public records. I tried matching it up with what I knew about the young woman Luke had found.

Then I took it a step further, printing out pictures and portions of maps, taping them up, each on its own side, one under Victim A, the other, Victim B.

In other words, I created a murder board. Two hours into my analysis, I could understand Scott's concern. Could a serial killer be working the area?

12

———

SCOTT COOPER SWIGGED DOWN two more Advil. Then he rested both hands on the edges of the water cooler and dropped his head, staring at the stainless steel as if it held the answers to his questions.

"Tough night, Scott?"

He turned and faced his coworker. "A little rough." No point in denying it. He'd seen his face in the mirror that morning. Scott nodded toward the papers in D'Sean Phillips's hand. "What are you working on?"

Phillips slapped the papers against his left hand. "The Good Ol' Boy bank robber. Plaid flannel shirt. John Deere hat. Mud on his boots. He's hit four banks in three jurisdictions in three months."

"Anyone hurt?"

"Nope. But he showed a gun on the last job."

Scott nodded. Part of him wished he had bank-robbery cases. Property crimes, essentially. Maybe then he could sleep at night. "Go get 'em."

Truth was, he wouldn't be happy chasing robbers. He'd specifically asked for violent crimes. He was on a mission, a mission he'd chosen when he was seventeen.

Scott walked back to his desk tucked away in a corner of the bullpen of the FBI's Northern Virginia Resident Agency. Out of the window he could see the Blue Ridge Mountains to the west, their soft folds and rounded tops a sharp contrast to the Rockies. He'd grown up in Denver hiking, fishing, and skiing in those rugged mountains with his Dad. All that had come to a sudden, screeching halt.

Scott closed his eyes, willing the pounding in his head to go away. He'd let his coffee get cold. Somehow, he didn't think it would go down well this morning.

Forcing himself to focus, he opened the computer file tracking his caseload. He had thirty active cases, everything from a cold-case murder to a couple of trafficking cases to child porn and assault on a federal officer. The latter involved a guy who'd coldcocked a park ranger when she tried to give him a ticket.

He could hear his boss's raised voice across the room. Couldn't quite see who was in his office. The pressure had ratcheted up and Supervisory Special Agent Tony Alenzo's temper was short. If people only knew.

Scott wrote notes on three of his cases, identifying some leads to check out and questions to ask. It'd be a good day to make the rounds, get out of the office. Before that, though, he couldn't resist checking on something.

Glancing up, he saw his boss was still occupied. He refocused on his computer. He had several databases available to him, including ViCAP, the Violent Criminal Apprehension Program. He entered a search for missing small, blonde women in a four-state area: DC, Maryland, Virginia, and West Virginia. He saved the results as a pdf and sent it to his cell phone.

Across the room, he saw another agent leave Alenzo's office. He logged out of the secure database, locked the computer, and moved quickly toward the elevators.

"Back in a couple of hours, boss," he said as he passed Alenzo's office door. He didn't wait for a response.

He'd mentally created a circuit to follow this morning, working on all three cases. The first was the cold case. Loudoun County police had requested FBI assistance on the twenty-year-old murder of a young man.

The day had started out sunny, the temperature a perfect seventy degrees. The drive through rolling hills and farmland was easy enough that Scott could let his mind drift. He was trying to remember what he'd told the dog guy last night—Nate. It wasn't like him to confide in people. The alcohol had loosened his tongue. Plus there was something about the guy that made Scott feel like talking.

He seemed to remember asking if the dog could help with that case near Warrenton. Why in the world had he asked that? He had access to the best databases in the world and the finest lab. How could a dog help?

The murdered girl near Warrenton wasn't his case. Wasn't even an FBI case. The only reason he was interested in it was because it was similar, a bit similar to the Prince William Forest Park case.

And a little bit like his sister's.

Scott shook his head to dislodge his thoughts. His boss had told him to leave it alone. He had a boatload of cases to work. His sister's abduction and murder had taken place two-thousand miles away.

In the words of his daughter's favorite movie, he told himself, "Let it go, let it go..."

If only he could.

The Loudoun County detective working the cold case was retiring in a year or so, and the case of the murdered young man bugged him. The boy was seventeen, a star athlete, and a straight-A student at a local high school, not known to use drugs or drink excessively. He'd taken his date home, dropping her off at midnight. A newspaper deliveryman found the boy's body in his car behind a shopping center at four in the morning. He'd been shot once in the head.

Scott listened to the detective and looked over the case file. He outlined what the Bureau could do, made some suggestions on lines of investigation he'd pursue, and promised to follow up in a month. When he walked out, he carried the weight of the frustration he knew the detective felt.

He saved the park ranger for last. Brenda Langley worked for the National Park Service. He'd arranged to meet her at an office in McLean. He was a little surprised that both Brenda's supervisor and a Park Police investigator chose to sit in on the meeting.

"I was making my rounds, you know, driving through the park, and I saw this guy walking into the woods," Brenda said, tucking her short gray hair behind her ear. "I stopped, got out, and walked over to him. He had his back to me, but I could see he was dumping something. I said, 'Hey, what are you doing?' and he turned around and hit me. Laid me right out."

Didn't she know enough to stay out of reach? He cleared his throat. "Do you have a description of this guy?"

"Nope. Never saw anything but the back of his head."

"Height? Weight?"

"Average height, average weight. He had on a green Army-type jacket. Brown hair."

"How about his vehicle?"

"There wasn't any. Not that I saw."

"You think he walked into the park?"

"No idea."

Scott made a couple of notes. "So what happened then?"

"I woke up. Called for help on my radio."

"And ..."

"And help came. Transported me to the hospital. I had a concussion."

Scott nodded. Something about this woman annoyed him. "Could the other rangers tell what the guy had been doing?"

"They didn't find a thing." Brenda pressed her lips into a straight line. "I insisted the FBI be brought in. I want this guy arrested."

"I'll write it up," Scott said. "This happened where, on the Parkway?"

"Prince William Forest Park," Brenda said.

That piqued his interest.

"I immediately asked for a transfer."

"Can you show me where, exactly, this happened?" Scott asked.

The Park Police investigator produced a map, and she pointed out where the assault had taken place. It was nowhere near where Faith had been found.

Scott took the map, noted the date and time of the assault, and promised he'd look into it. The Park Police investigator offered to walk him to his car.

"I wouldn't invest a lot in this," he said.

Scott turned, raising his eyebrows.

"It's the third incident she's reported in six months. We think she's bucking for early retirement."

Scott nodded. "Okay, then. Thanks."

As he drove back to the office, frustration gripped him. So his boss thought it was perfectly fine to spend time on the phantom assault of Brenda Langley, but not follow up on a possible link between two murders? Whatever happened to agents using their own brains to follow leads?

Impulsively, he pulled off of Interstate 66 and into a gas station. He pulled out his phone and scrolled through his contacts. He kept the dog man's contact info, didn't he? Nate something? He searched for "Nate," found the entry, and punched the number.

13

"WHAT WAS I THINKING?" I said to myself the next morning.

Luke looked at me. His ears twitched.

Thanks to my decision to create a murder board, I'd gotten a lousy night's sleep. And now every time I sat down to work on my cases—the cases that were putting a roof over my head—all I could think about was two murdered girls.

Maybe I should take my laptop and go work somewhere else. But no—I'd have to put Luke in his crate and, well, I didn't want to.

So when Nate called late that afternoon and asked me if I wanted to come with him and Cooper to check out the site where Victim A had been found, I knew the answer. No, absolutely not.

What came out of my mouth was, "Sure. Where and when?"

I wanted to see Sprite work, I told myself as I drove to the site on Saturday morning. After all, the body was long gone.

Luke lay in the crate in the back of my Jeep. I wasn't going to use him. I just didn't want him stuck at home. He'd be fine on this cool spring day, especially if I left the lift gate open.

Victim A was found on private property off a two-lane road near Warrenton in the foothills of the Blue Ridge. The local detective working the case met us there. He'd gotten permission from the landowner for us to go on the property.

When Nate saw I'd brought Luke, he said, "We gotta walk in a good ways. Better bring him with us."

I didn't want my dog getting another snootful of cadaver scent, even if it was a year old. I also didn't want to leave him well out of my sight in an unlocked car for an extended period of time. So I let him out and leashed him up.

I hung back a bit from the three men, feeling like an intruder. I noticed we were following the same kind of red paint marks on the trees that I'd seen when we'd gone back to the Victim B site. I also noticed it was easier for me to think of them as Victim A and Victim B rather than Julie and Faith. We walked fifteen minutes into the woods. I actually timed it.

When we stopped, I saw immediately why Scott Cooper had been nagged by the similarities in the cases. Although some of the underbrush had grown up, this site was in a little clearing in the woods, just as with Faith. Deep in the woods, just as with Faith.

I could see Scott showing Nate some eight-by-ten glossies— crime-scene photos. I told Luke to stay. I quietly walked up behind them and looked over Nate's shoulder. The young woman lay on her back, her sightless eyes staring upward, her arms stretched out, as if she were making a snow angel.

I turned away from the death stare.

"Y'all back up and let Sprite here have some room to work," Nate said.

I was happy to oblige. We moved about fifty feet from the body site.

"Nice dog," the detective said, nodding toward Luke. He was smart enough not to try to pet him. "Does he do this too?"

"Just live searches," I replied.

Scott looked at me, frowning slightly, before saying, "But he's the one that found the other body, right?"

"That was a fluke," I said quickly.

Beyond us, little Sprite worked hard, her stub tail going a mile a minute. Nate kept her in close, leashed up, asking her to "search it out" while pointing to the ground near his feet. This was a different kind of working than what I did with Luke, who ranged freely, often out of sight, while he was seeking human scent. I watched, fascinated by what they were doing, wanting to observe, but not see.

The body had been intact when they removed her, right? No chance of a body part emerging from the leaves?

Luke sat at my side, his eyes fixed on Sprite. I could feel him brimming with energy. His tail swept the ground. He wanted to work. It had been a mistake to bring him. What was I thinking?

Sprite slowed down, her nose plastered to the ground. Luke stood up. We both knew what Sprite was doing. She'd found the exact place the body had been laid, and she was sniffing every piece of that scent, her little nose twitching. Luke whined.

Suddenly, Sprite gave her indication. She sat and looked up at Nate. "Good girl, good girl!" he said, turning her away from that spot. He pulled a tug out of his pocket and wrestled with her for a minute. Then he moved further away, to the very edge of the clearing. "Search, search it out!" Search for more.

Luke nudged my hand, as if to say, "When do I get to play?" He could be quite insistent. To my right, Scott was asking the detective about Victim A—did she have a boyfriend, what about her relationship with her parents, any history of drug or alcohol abuse, depression, or suicidal thinking?

Quietly, I turned and moved away from them. When I glanced back, Cooper was watching me leave.

I focused on the towering oaks, poplars, and maples around me to settle my stomach. So much beauty. I gave Luke a little leash. We were well away from the crime scene. No harm in letting him sniff.

Behind me, I could hear Nate's soft voice, "Search it out!" He was so patient with his dog and with the search itself. He'd told me once that searching for human remains was different, slower and more delicate, than live searches. "But the older I get," he'd said, grinning, "the more I like a search objective that don't run away."

I guess that was supposed to make me feel better about the idea of finding dead bodies.

Ahead of me was a big, fallen tree. Maybe if I sat down for a bit, my head would clear. I checked the log for bugs, then sat. Luke kept sniffing around in the leaves, moving to the end of his six-foot leash. Back at the crime scene, I saw Sprite stop again, this time at the base of a large tree. Nate looked up at Scott. Sprite sat.

"Good dog, good dog!" I saw Nate reward her. Then he pulled a small can of spray paint out of his pack and marked the tree with a small blue dot.

What did that mean? The dog had smelled cadaver scent, obviously, but I was trying to imagine what would have happened to create that. Did the killer prop the body there before laying her on the ground?

Then I saw Sprite alert near a fallen log. I stood up so I could see better. She pawed at the ground, at a little pile of leaves, then sat and looked at Nate.

Curious, I moved closer.

Nate moved one leaf, then turned away and rewarded Sprite. He gestured toward Scott, and both he and the detective moved quickly. I couldn't help but follow.

"Somebody's been sitting on that log, whittling wood," Nate said, gesturing toward the little pile of wood shavings on the ground.

"Why would they do that?"

Nate shook his head. "To make a fire?"

"Do you have an evidence bag?" Scott said to the detective. His voice sounded sharp.

The detective checked his pockets. Clearly, he didn't think this morning's expedition would amount to anything and he wasn't prepared. And I knew Scott had brought his personal vehicle, not the Bucar.

But Scott apparently had had high hopes. He pulled a plastic evidence bag out of the pocket of his 5.11 khakis. "I'll take pictures," he said, "then you collect it. It's your case."

Once Nate was convinced Sprite had found everything she was going to find, we left, walking out of the woods under a bright blue sky. "Be good to let the dogs run a bit," Nate said. "Let 'em relax."

I waited, though, for five more minutes, until we were well out of the cadaver zone. I didn't want Luke running back there. Thankfully, he only had eyes for Sprite. I let him loose and the two of them raced around, chasing each other, while we four humans walked out silently, our minds fixed on the terrible fate of the young woman whose death had brought us to this place.

Questions whirled in my head. One prompted me to move ahead, next to Nate. "I don't understand," I said to him. "Sprite's an HRD dog. Why'd she alert on those wood shavings?"

"I don't rightly know," Nate said.

I dropped back again. We made it to the cars. I saw Scott hand the detective a business card and then he took off. I got Luke's water bowl out of my Jeep and poured water in it. Sprite trotted over, and the two of them lapped it up noisily. I could hear Nate and Scott talking about ten feet away next to Nate's Tahoe.

"Why'd the dog alert on the shavings?" Scott asked, echoing my question.

Nate took out a toothpick and started chewing on it. "Not sure."

I looked over at them. "What if the guy was handling the body with gloves on, and he didn't take them off before picking up wood and whittling it?"

Both men looked at me.

"Wouldn't the smell transfer?"

Nate nodded. "That's a possibility."

I continued. "No fingerprints were found on the body, right? So that implies he was wearing gloves."

"Be odd to whittle with gloves on," Nate said.

I frowned. "Why else would you cut wood shavings like that? Start a fire?"

"Clean the knife?" Scott said. "There weren't any knife wounds."

I wished I could shut up. But I kept going, like an overanxious first-grader. "Maybe he'd tied her with ropes. Maybe he had to cut the ropes to pose her. Maybe he wanted all the fibers of the ropes off the knife." My heart pounded.

"Maybe he just wanted to sit with her a while," Nate said softly, "and whittlin's what he did." He looked at me. "Like pullin' out my pipe. A nervous habit."

Luke came over and nudged me. He sat next to me and leaned on my leg. I rubbed his head, aware that Nate was observing the dog's reaction to my own display of nerves.

Nate whistled for Sprite, put her in her crate, and shook hands with Scott. "Let us know if you find something."

Scott said he would. He looked like he would like to stay and talk longer. I wondered what he had ahead of him this Saturday with no family around. Would he go into work? To the gym? Or would he end up in some bar?

Nate looked at me. "See you tonight?"

"Yes. Eight o'clock." Battlefield SAR had a night training exercise scheduled. It would be a long day.

14

I WENT home to get some rest, but I couldn't resist updating my murder board with the wood shavings Sprite had found. While I wrote, though, I debated erasing the whole thing. Why was I feeding my obsession?

In the end, I left it. I tucked the board behind the couch. Maybe I'd just forget about it. Out of sight, out of mind.

Luke crashed on the floor in the sun, stretching out in his favorite spot. Soon I could hear him snoring. I laid down and covered myself with a quilt, but my mind would not let me rest.

Instead, I got up, stepped over Luke, and opened my laptop. Maybe I could get some work done before tonight.

Four divorces and one child-custody case later, I had done all the stuff online that I could. I'd have to burn some shoe leather to develop more information, but that could wait 'til next week.

Just as I was getting up from my desk, my phone rang. My sister Brooke. *What now?* "Hey, what's up?" I answered and paced over to my only window.

"Well," Brooke said, "I was just thinking about you and your cool dog, and I was wondering if I could come out with you on a search? Or watch you practice?"

"What? What brought this up?" I crossed my right arm across my chest and pressed the phone against my left ear.

"Well, you know, seeing you, and then hearing about you guys finding that boy, I don't know, it just got me interested."

"In what? Search and rescue?"

"In all the things dogs can do, you know, like guiding the blind, sniffing out drugs, and finding bedbugs. I've got a term paper due soon, and I've been having trouble finding a subject."

"And you thought dogs would be a good subject."

"Well, yes, and then I thought of you, and so, can I come?"

"When's your paper due?"

"Monday."

"Monday?" I admit I exploded.

"You guys have a practice tonight, right? I could be there about the time you start."

"How do you know that?"

"It's on the website." She could have added, "you dummy" and it would have been appropriate. "So can I meet you there?"

"I ... I'm not going," I lied. "So, no. You'll have to do your research some other way."

There was a pause as Brooke regrouped. "Well, could I go anyway? Could you call somebody, like that Nate guy, and ask him if I can come?"

"Brooke, no!"

"My paper's due on Monday!"

"Well, that's your problem, isn't it? You shouldn't wait 'til the last minute. You should know that by now." The edge in my voice sounded like condemnation. It wasn't. It was fear. The last thing I needed was my family intruding in my life.

"I know, I know." Brooke sighed. "Okay, I'll figure something else out."

I clicked off her call, a heavy wave of guilt washing over me. She was my sister. I could help her. But that would mean her being closer than arm's length. I just couldn't do that.

I moped around my apartment after Brooke's call, mindlessly straightening things and putting laundry away. At six-thirty, I got my SAR pack out. Luke opened one eye, then raised his head. "Yes, you're going too," I told him, and he jumped up and started his happy dance. I checked that I had everything—emergency blanket, first-aid kit, maps, GPS, rain gear, food for him, food for me, water, a long leash, multi-tool ...

The location of the training was half an hour away in an industrial park off a main road. We loaded up at quarter 'til seven and drove off. Clouds overhead had thickened, and the forecast predicted rain, but not until ten or so. I did my best to forget Brooke and get excited about this training.

The location turned out to be more urban than I expected. There was a lot of traffic on that four-lane road, even at eight o'clock on a Saturday night, and the front part of the industrial park was an unfenced parking lot. I pulled up next to Emily's SUV. She had Flash on a leash. I wanted to scope out the place before I let Luke out.

"Hey, Em!"

"Jess! Glad you could make it."

I looked around. "So what's the deal? Have you worked here before?"

"No. First time. There are some specific challenges Nate wanted to address."

"Like ..."

"There's an array of culvert pipes behind the building and a rubble pile. There's also a shed with a ladder. Behind the property is a wooded area with a dense bramble patch, a stream, and a small bridge."

"Okay." Around me, I could see four other trainers preparing their dogs. "We're doing live finds, right?"

"Yes, trailing and air scent. We'll work in teams, one dog plus handler, one walker, and a victim. It'll be hard in the dark." Emily smiled at me. "But then, you've proven yourself there!"

"Luke did, anyway."

"Oh, Nate was very complimentary of you. He said you showed true grit, searching for that little boy."

A warm feeling spread through me. But why did I care what Nate thought? Maybe I was still looking for my father's approval. My mother had accused me of that once.

Emily looked at her watch. "I'll get things started. Nate said he'd be about fifteen minutes late."

I raised my eyebrows. Nate was never late.

"He's with Beth."

Beth? "Who's Beth?"

Emily hesitated. "Oh, that's right, you joined last fall, right? I'm surprised he hasn't told you about her."

I shook my head. What else didn't I know about Nate? "A date?"

"Oh, no!" Emily glanced down and patted Flash, who wagged his tail. She took a deep breath and looked at me. "Beth is a long-time member of Battlefield. She's in her late fifties. Last summer, she was diagnosed with cancer, colon cancer. Stage IV.

"About two months into her treatments, her husband left her. Twenty-four years of marriage. He said he found her cancer depressing. Just walked out." Emily paused. Her words sunk into me like weights. "Some of us tried to pick up the slack, Nate most of all. He's taken her to appointments, brought her meals, sat with her when she's gotten scared." Emily had tears in her eyes. "He's been amazing."

"I had no idea." I frowned. "But there's no ... relationship?"

Emily smiled. "He's just a good guy." She checked her watch again. "He asked me to get things started. So, five minutes 'til kickoff, okay?"

"Sure." I turned toward my car and let Luke out of his crate. Everyone seemed to be keeping their dogs on leash, so I did, too, walking him over to some bushes and letting him make his mark. All the while, I was thinking about Nate knowingly walking into that cancer situation. It occurred to me he was a glutton for punishment.

"All right, let's meet up, people!" Emily called. While Emily explained the format for the evening, my mind mulled over my conversation with Brooke. I found myself looking for her. As impulsive as she was, I half expected her to show up, unannounced and uninvited. Was I going to be angry when she did!

I'd be paired up with Micah, a handler with another German shepherd, for the first exercise. Luke was disappointed when I put him back in the crate. He laid down with a thump. "Deal with it," I said to him, "and don't chew anything."

"Anybody watching the cars?" I asked Emily, who affirmed that was the case. Good, I could leave the liftgate up. The temperature was seventy-two and falling. Luke would get a nice breeze the way I was parked.

Micah's dog, a small female named Gem, worked differently than Luke. Whereas Luke was all flash and flair, Gem was quiet and methodical.

Our first challenge required navigating through a series of culvert pipes to find a search subject hidden behind a brick pile. The dog had to navigate through the pipes on her own; they were too small for the handler to follow. I found out later the "victim" had to work hard to get to her hiding place.

Luke would have screamed through those pipes like a subway train, leaving me scrambling to keep up. But Gem went through carefully, sniffing the seams and noting who knows what as she went. Still, she kept at it, and ten minutes later had found her victim.

Next, we worked the shed with a ladder and then the rubble pile. But she must have caught a sharp object on the rubble pile because she came out limping and began licking the pad of her left forefoot. Micah pulled her then before we got to the woods and took her to a grassy area to clean and dress her foot.

Nate had joined us by the time it was Luke's turn. "Everything okay?" I asked him.

"Yeah," he said, then turned to direct a team to another challenge.

Luke handled the challenges as I expected, with energy and strength, even if he did tend to overrun his victim. I was off my game though. Was it because of Brooke? Nate? I stumbled, literally, when we searched the rubble pile and fell flat on my face, bruising my arms and one knee. I hesitated in front of the pipes. Luke stopped and looked at me, confused. He refused to climb the ladder, something he'd never done before. Was he sensing something in me?

Coming back from the exercise in the woods at about ten o'clock, a hard rain began to fall. My knee hurt, and I felt defeated and almost teary. Even I recognized that was an overreaction. But I cared about SAR, and here I was messing things up for my awesome dog. The thing I had worried about, my sister showing up, hadn't even happened. I shook my head at my own paranoia.

Despite the rain, Nate wanted to hold a quick debriefing. A few handlers popped open umbrellas, but most of us just put our dogs up and stood there in our rain gear, letting the water run off us onto the asphalt parking lot.

I had my back to the road. Nate was facing me, and the other handlers were spread around in a crescent. Suddenly, I heard a horrible noise, brakes screeching and tires screaming. I instantly tensed. I saw Nate's eyes widen. A lightning bolt of fear flashed through me. I turned, my heart in my throat, just in time to see a huge tractor-trailer truck and several cars sliding off the road and toward us in an avalanche of metal, glass, and rubber, with sparks flying.

"Look out!" I screamed. I grabbed Emily and pulled her out of the way.

The screeching seemed to go on forever. When it stopped, the vehicles had plowed into three of our cars.

Handlers scrambled to check on their dogs. I saw Nate, moving toward the truck. "Call 911," I yelled, turning to grab my first-aid kit. I knew it was easy to miss the obvious in the aftermath of an accident.

Dazed drivers and passengers slowly climbed out of smashed cars. I headed for a family in a crushed SUV. I was moving as if in a dream, hardly aware of my actions, strictly on autopilot. "Who's hurt?" I asked.

A man collapsed onto the ground holding his head. A woman screamed, "My babies, my babies!"

I looked in the SUV, which had rolled but landed back on its tires. Two little kids were belted securely in their car seats. The baby was crying; the older one looked stunned. But as far as I could tell, they weren't hurt.

I had never extricated a little kid from a modern car seat before, especially in the dark. All those straps! But I used my lighted visor, and after a few choice words, I got the toddler out, then the baby.

"Ma'am, ma'am," I said to the hysterical mother. "Look, they're all right." She was bleeding, so I said, "Come, sit here, and let me help you."

By this time, the scream of sirens filled the air. I had just managed to get the woman seated near her kids and was applying pressure to the cut on her head when the EMTs came and took over.

I stood and looked around. I picked up my first-aid kit and walked slowly back toward my Jeep, the lights of the emergency vehicles and the sounds of their radios playing with my mind. I had trouble breathing. It felt like I was sucking air through a straw. Then suddenly, I was in another place, another time.

What would have happened if I'd pulled further off the road? If I'd reacted more quickly to the odd sound I'd heard?

I felt for my gun on my hip. Of course, it wasn't there. My head began to spin.

I needed Luke. I needed my dog.

The emergency lights bounced off the metal of Luke's crate and reflected in his eyes, which were fixed on mine. He whined. I tried to make out voices, tried to understand what was happening. I looked down at my wrist, expecting to see a splintered bone protruding from it, but it was whole, healed.

Numb, I opened Luke's crate. He jumped down, and I leashed him up. I had to get away from those lights and the harsh radio squawks. I needed to run.

I heard a voice calling me as I walked behind the building, but I kept going. I heard my feet crunching on gravel, heard my own breath coming hard, felt my heart pounding, throbbing like a bass drummer beating inside my chest. I felt the adrenaline screaming through me like a banshee.

Just beyond the culvert pipes, I collapsed to the ground and curled up, sobbing and shaking. I felt like a train was bearing down on me, or a truck. I was going to die! My mouth felt dry.

Luke pressed himself against me, his hot breath in my ear. I wrapped my arms around him, burying my face in his wet coat, hanging on to him like the lifesaver he was.

I don't know how long I was there—fifteen minutes, maybe? Twenty?—before Nate found me.

"Hey, hey, girl, you all right?" he said.

I looked at him through eyes full of tears and rain, sorrow and pain, and I shook my head.

15

NATE HELPED me to my Jeep, loaded up Luke, and drove me home. He got me inside and pushed me toward the shower, where my tears mixed with the hot water.

By the time I stepped out and dressed, he had towel-dried Luke and Sprite, and had a cup of hot tea waiting for me. I sat on the couch and tried to calm down.

Once he saw I was taken care of, he showered, dressing himself in the spare clothes he always had with him. Such a Boy Scout.

"You did good with that family. Thank you," he said, finally sitting on the floor across from the couch.

I just shook my head. I couldn't look him in the eye.

"All our people are okay. Dogs and all. The trucker, he didn't make it."

I squeezed my eyes shut, imagining the scene inside the cab, so thankful I had gone toward the car. "That's sad," I managed to say, but I felt guilty for my selfish attitude, my cowardice. Then I opened my eyes. "Did you see my sister? Brooke? Was she there? Did she see me? Behind the culvert pipes?"

Nate frowned, puzzled by my question. "No one was there. Just you and me."

I hoped he was right.

"Did you expect your sister to be there?"

Logically, the answer was no. But logic seemed to be taking a back seat in my head. "She wants to watch sometime. I don't know why I thought she might be there."

"You looked ... you looked like you were having an anxiety attack," he said softly.

Luke came and laid down near my feet. I teared up.

"It's okay," Nate said. "I been through those many times. Look." He pulled up his sleeve. Thick burn scars covered his arm.

I tried to keep the shock off my face. I know I failed. Those scars represented weeks and weeks of pain. Tears ran down my face, tears for my friend's anguish, tears for sorrow and fear and suffering.

Nate slipped his sleeve back down. "You don't go through that without aftereffects. I been through many panic attacks." Then he looked deeply into my eyes. "And I'm thinking you've had your own trauma."

It was an open invitation for me to share, but my throat closed up. I groped for words and found a half-answer. "I had a bad accident once."

That was like calling the soup course a full banquet. Why was I so reluctant to tell the truth? I automatically touched my own, scarred arm.

Nate waited a moment to see if I'd go further. I didn't, and he accepted my response. "The brain retains a memory of those things," he said. "Brings 'em up at odd times. Feels like it's happening all over again, right now. Feels like you're about to die."

I felt my head nod, just a little. And I don't know if I was curious, or if I was trying to redirect Nate, but I asked him, "Do you still have those? Panic attacks?"

"No. Used to get triggered a lot. I'd hear a loud boom—even smell smoke—and afore I knew it, I'd be shaking, scared to death. Then I'd get angry. Coped with it by drinking, I did. Didn't want anyone to get inside my head, didn't want nobody close."

"But you got over them, right?"

He nodded.

"How?"

"Peter came along. Things changed."

I sighed. "I know...God." I rolled my eyes.

"What Peter said gave me hope. Once I had a little bit of hope, I had the strength to ... to let go of my pride and get some help. I entered counseling, kicked the booze, started reading the Bible, found more hope."

Sprite had been sleeping next to the wall. As Nate talked, she woke and curled up next to him, lying half on him. He began stroking her coat.

He looked straight at me. At first, I met his gaze, but I couldn't hold it. "I wish," he said softly, "I could give you that hope, that anchor. I wish I could make you see, and feel, how much God loves you."

I started shaking again, trembling at first, then shivering. It was like his God talk was making me *more* anxious.

I stood to my feet. "I'm glad it works for you, but I don't get it." I crossed my arms, trying to stop the trembling.

Nate stood. "I know." His eyes shone like two mountain pools in sunlight. "And I'm praying for you."

A lightning-like heat flashed through me. My hands balled into fists and dropped to my side. "Don't bother. It won't work." I turned on my heels and went to my bedroom.

I knew he wouldn't follow. He was too much of a gentleman.

I crawled into bed and pulled the covers up. Luke came in and flopped down next to me. After a while, I heard Nate leave and a car start up. I realized he must have had somebody drop off his Tahoe.

There were good people in that SAR group. I didn't think I was one of them.

16

I'D BE LYING if I said I didn't feel regret the next day. Nate was unfailingly kind. I could have been more polite.

Oh, stress. What you do to me.

There wasn't much I could do on a Sunday to advance my cases, so I decided to escape to the mountains. I packed water for Luke and me and set off for the Shenandoah National Park, about a half-hour drive. I parked at my favorite trailhead, and we ran for an hour.

Spring came a little later in the park because of the elevation. The trees were shorter too. But the dogwoods still laced the woods, and the birds still sang. The rain had ended, the sky was clear, and the run was therapeutic for both of us.

Still, while driving home, I had to work to keep the sound of screeching tires and the images of those vehicles tumbling toward us out of my mind. When I walked into my apartment, I discovered Nate had left me two things the night before—a small, pocket New Testament that looked like it had been to war and back, and the business card of a female psychologist.

Irritation rose in me. I opened the drawer of the end table and threw them in.

On Monday I launched into my cases, traveling to Richmond and poking into the corners of my subjects' worlds. There were always secrets to discover, and once in a while a juicy crime to report. But mostly, I followed two things—money and sex. Greed and lust provided me with a solid living.

As I was about to leave Richmond, I got a text; Battlefield had called a special meeting for Thursday night. Curious.

That day, I made it a point to exercise Luke well. By the time I put Luke in his crate so I could go to the meeting, he was tired.

I drove to the bank building where the meeting would be held. On the way my mother called me. I was just finishing up with her when I parked and got out of the car. Emily stepped out of her car next to me. I waved and continued my conversation with my mother.

"Sure, sure. I know. It just wasn't convenient, Mom. It's not a tourist attraction. I know. I'm sorry it came across that way. Right. Right." Then I ended the call.

Emily smiled at me.

"My mother. Complaining about how I treated my nineteen-year-old half sister," I explained, irritation prickling like cactus.

"Nineteen? She's a lot younger," Emily said.

"Yes. And she's their baby, and I'd better never forget it." I relished my sarcasm.

Thankfully, Emily changed the subject. "How'd Luke do the other night?"

"We had an off night. Totally my fault. I was preoccupied." Had Emily heard about my meltdown?

"We all have off nights." Her words carried little comfort.

The location was in the bank's meeting room, so I had assumed, correctly, that dogs weren't part of it. We ended up sitting far away from Nate. I was glad of that.

A representative from the Virginia Department of Emergency Management was the presenter. He talked about how important volunteers were to VDEM, and how much our contributions were valued by the citizens of the commonwealth, yada, yada, yada. He mentioned several recent productive searches, including the one for Joey Washburn. A streak of pride ran through me.

Then he brought up the accident on Saturday. He talked about post-traumatic stress and some signs to watch for. I glanced at Nate, since he'd been the one to deal with the deceased trucker. His face looked impassive. Then I saw Kevin, another handler, looking straight at me, his eyes practically burning into me. Suddenly, I felt undressed. I looked away, hoping he hadn't noticed my face redden.

The VDEM guy sat down, and Susan, the leader of our group, brought up a few more issues, most of which were encouraging. Then Nate took the podium. He thanked everyone for their support for Beth over the last year. He gave an update on her cancer, then said, "Her time is coming to an end. If you want to see her, you can come by for a short visit. I'm headed there now. Probably will be there all night."

As I said, Nate was a glutton for punishment.

I opted out of the visit to Beth, since I didn't know her. I'd seen enough death.

Back at home, while I changed my clothes, I fumed. From some of the things Emily said, I thought Nate must have shared about my anxiety attack. Plus that guy, Kevin, stared at me all night. I'd seen Nate talking to him before the meeting started. Had he told him too? I thought personal stuff like that should be confidential.

I woke up several times that night, anxious and afraid. I tried to figure out how to confront Nate, rehearsing what I would say to him. Predictably, the next day I felt like I'd been battling for my life all night. Completely exhausted.

But I had work to do. And so I soldiered on. I'd call Nate that afternoon.

17

SCOTT COOPER SHUFFLED PAPERS, trying to work up some interest in the cases he had on his desk. Mondays at the office were a drag.

His thoughts ran back to Sunday. There'd been a hellacious storm the night before, but he'd carried out his plan anyway, going back to the woods where Faith's body had been found.

Officially, that case was low priority. Unofficially, it was the first thing he thought about in the morning and the last thing he thought about at night. There was more to it than one young woman being snatched from a coffee shop. He was sure of that.

So he'd returned to the now-cleared crime scene. He was looking for wood shavings, something that would link Faith's murder to Julie's. But after scuffing around in the leaves for an hour, searching the little clearing where Faith's body had been found, checking every fallen log within fifty feet, he'd come up with nothing.

Maybe he should have asked the dog man to come with him.

He sighed. Maybe he was getting a little obsessive.

His conversation Sunday afternoon with his daughter hadn't helped. Mandy was developing that know-it-all teenager attitude.

He hardly knew how to talk to her anymore. Staring at the calendar on his desk, he realized in less than two months she'd be coming for a week-long visit. Part of his visitation rights.

What in the world was he going to do with her?

He made a note to put in for leave. It bugged him that his ex-wife had already given Mandy a cell phone. "All her friends have them!" That was Suzanne's justification.

Did she have any idea what kids were doing with phones these days? The apps that led them straight into the dens of predators? Sexting? Nude pictures that would live on the web forever and get sold to whatever basement-dwellers wanted to leer at their young bodies?

Scott's stomach roiled.

One thing for sure, if there was some pervert targeting young blonde women in Virginia, he sure couldn't give Mandy the kind of freedom he knew she'd demand. He could see endless rounds of arguments in his future. Maybe he should cancel her visit. Maybe he should fly out there instead. Maybe—

His boss interrupted his thoughts, shouting from across the room. "Cooper! Brian's got a tip on his Good Ol' Boy bank robber. Can you help?"

"Yep!" Scott jumped up and grabbed his raid jacket. Great! A knucklehead to pound on. Just what he needed.

NATE TANNER SHIFTED his weight in his chair in the coffee shop just off the community college campus where he worked. Across from him, Battlefield SAR Director Susan Lewis sat, her head turned to her left where Kevin Holder outlined his case.

Nate had told them he'd give them twenty minutes. Sprite was outside on the dog tether. Right now she was in the shade, but the sun would soon shine directly on her, and he wasn't about to leave her there for long.

He didn't want to be part of this meeting anyway. When he heard what Kevin Holder wanted, his anger had surged.

Why'd they have to address this now anyway? Why after what happened last night? Beth was dead. The group was grieving. And Kevin was focused on this? His petty jealousy?

"Look, the rules say you have to be comfortable finding people dead or alive. I say, if Jessica can't handle HRD, if she's that unstable, she shouldn't be operational, even if she is on the live-search team." Kevin sat back and crossed his arms.

"The rules don't say that. Just the introduction to SAR on the website. Look, give her a break," Nate said, fighting to stay calm. "None of us expected to find a body on that first practice run. It was a shock."

"And she almost quit over it, right? Didn't come to practices for a month or more."

"How do you know that was why?"

"Carol saw her reaction. She told me. And then last Saturday night? What happened? Why was Jessica hiding behind the culverts? I saw her there. She was shaking like a leaf. Crying."

"And did you see her before that?" Nate tapped his finger on the table. "Did you see her taking those babies out of the car? Did you see her calming that mother down? Did you see her taking action while others stood around?"

Kevin didn't budge.

Nate pressed him. "Or maybe, maybe you were there when Jess went on a three-hour night search in the pouring rain two days before Christmas. Did you see her save a little boy's life?" Nate leaned forward. "Did you see any of that, Kevin? Or do you just have eyes for puttin' folks down who are doin' better'n you?" His face felt hot. He turned to Susan, who looked flustered. "That girl," he hesitated, groping for words, "she's got grit, she does. Her dog is superb. And we'd be fools to discourage her."

Susan swallowed, then looked back at Kevin. "I, uh ... I see your point, Kevin, but really, isn't this a little premature? I mean, she's just barely gotten started with us."

"You've got to take command, Susan. Deal with it now. Or no one will respect your leadership." His words were like a whipcrack.

Nate's eyes flared. He bit the inside of his lip to force himself to calm down. When he thought he could control his temper, he spoke. "Kevin," he said in a voice that was almost friendly, "Jess is new, and she needs a little grace from us. You want to know what grace is? Grace is overlooking an error. It's what Max gives you when you mess up as a handler and he still wags his tail when he sees you." Max was Kevin's Malinois, and his success rate was one of the lowest in the group.

Nate didn't wait for Kevin to respond. "You want to know why Max doesn't work as well as Sprite, or Luke? It's because he doesn't trust you." He paused to let that sink in. "I've seen you using an ear pinch on go-outs when he was slow to respond. I've seen you bully him when you're frustrated, pushing him with your knee and chucking him under his chin. Max will never work for you like Luke works for Jess. You're a force trainer. And that dog, he gives you grace and loves you anyway. I say Jess deserves that same grace."

Nate stood up. "One more thing, Kevin. You will never, ever head up any SAR organization I'm a part of." With that, he turned and left.

18

PAVEMENT POUNDING on my cases in Richmond and Charlottesville kept me busy most of the day. My methodology was simple. I interviewed former boyfriends, girlfriends, employers, coworkers ... anybody, really, who knew my subject and would talk to me.

Most people move through life leaving a trail of little grudges, petty jealousies, and small hurts behind, like the scent cone left by the skin cells we humans shed whenever we move. I saw myself as the search dog moving back and forth through my subject's past until the scent intensified, and I found someone who would give up the information I needed to nail down something my lawyer could use.

It was a lot like being a cop, only usually the offense I was investigating wasn't criminal, it was personal. Today, by the time I was ready to head home, I had a notebook full of new information and a ton of guilt for leaving Luke in his crate all day. In the winter I could bring him with me, but summers were too hot for him to wait in the car while I interviewed people.

As I left Charlottesville, I worked on a script for my unfinished business—confronting Nate. If I hit a clean stretch of road,

I could call him while I drove. I had to make sure he knew my boundaries. I had allowed him to see my anxiety. I didn't want him talking about it.

An accident on Rt. 29 made me divert onto smaller roads. I was surprised when I came upon a sign for the college where Nate worked. Curious, I took a detour and had circled halfway around the campus when I saw a familiar figure, sitting on a freshly mown hill next to a large lake, a springer next to him. Nate.

I pulled over and up onto the lawn, hoping I'd finish this before a campus cop came along to ticket me. Striding toward him, I inhaled the scent of the cut grass. He had his back to me and didn't move, even when Sprite turned toward me.

I moved around so I could face him. "Nate?"

He looked up, and I saw the fatigue in his face. A sweat stain darkened his shirt from his neck halfway down to his waist. He'd probably been cutting grass all day. "Hey," he said.

I was surprised he didn't stand. "Nate who did you tell about ... about Saturday night?" My voice had a serrated edge.

His face fell into a frown. I could tell he was searching his memory.

"About, you know, after the accident, when you drove me home?" I could not bring myself to use the terms "panic attack" or "anxiety attack." I also was totally deviating from my script.

Still, I pressed him. "I don't like people talking behind my back. I don't like you breaking confidentiality..."

"No." His voice was soft.

"... even with Emily. Last night I spoke with her and from what she said, I believe you talked to her. About me."

He frowned.

"My issues are mine to deal with! Got it? They're private!"

He took a deep breath and averted his eyes, staring out over the lake until I turned to see what he was looking at.

There was nothing there, nothing.

"Do you understand?" I felt like I was talking to a five-year-old.

"Sure."

"All right. Thank you." Then, as a gesture, I bent down and patted Sprite. "I'll see you sometime." But Nate just sat there.

I didn't get an apology, I thought as I strode back to my car, but I did get my point across. That was clear.

I was feeling pretty good about confronting Nate until I got home. I let Luke out and while he was relieving himself, I checked my email. There was a message from the Battlefield director saying Beth had died last night, and arrangements would be forthcoming. Nate, she wrote, had stayed with her all night and was with her when she died.

No wonder he'd looked so tired.

Confronting him was bad timing on my part. I started to send a text to Nate. But I was never sure what to say in a message like that. What exactly are "condolences"? "Sorry for your loss" was so ... generic. Even worse was "sending positive thoughts your way."

I had no words of comfort for people who'd lost a friend or family member. Not even myself.

I changed my clothes and took Luke for a run. He deserved a good one after being cooped up all day, so we ran for five miles. I was sitting on the grass outside my apartment, stretching, when my phone rang. I looked, and it was Susan Lewis, director of Battlefield. I assumed she was calling to give me information about Beth's funeral. I figured I hadn't known Beth well enough to attend, so I let the call go to voicemail.

After my shower, I returned her call.

"I wanted to share with you," she began, "that I've received a complaint, a question, really, about your fitness for SAR."

A hot flash ran through me. "What? Who complained?" I began pacing in my apartment, my anger at full throttle.

"I'm not at liberty to say."

I closed my eyes. I could picture her with her little, shy border collie. Soft dog, soft handler. I ramped up my argumentation. "What exactly am I being accused of?"

"It appears there's been some concern about your reticence to deal with HRD."

"Was it Nate? Is he the one ... because I shared some things in confidence—"

Susan cut me off. "Oh, no! Not Nate. Certainly not Nate."

What? I stopped pacing.

"In fact, he defended you strongly. He's a big fan, let me tell you!"

A flood of guilt washed through me. It was like standing on the beach as the sea washed away the sand beneath my feet.

Susan continued. She used words like "grit" and "superb" and they swam around in my head, little yellow ducks bobbing on my ocean of despair. All the supposed truth I had conjured in my mind was wrong. I could feel myself sinking, sinking, helpless and weak. I sat down hard on my couch.

"Bottom line is, Jessica, based on what Nate said, I think you'll be fine. But if you ever do feel like the stress is getting to you, please let me know sooner than later. We can always arrange a break."

By the time she finished and we hung up, I was in tears. I'd been such a jerk. To Nate of all people.

I curled into a fetal position on my couch and wept. Luke came and laid his head next to me. I patted him and he lay down with a sigh, right next to the couch.

Over the next hour or so, out of the swirl of emotions inside, came clarity. For years I'd been searching for some kind of star to steer by, something outside my own head, that I could use as a guide.

Maybe I was searching for an authority figure. Maybe I was searching for my dad. My former partner had come close, but then he was gone. Dogs provided some of what I was looking for, at least in terms of love. Then Nate came along.

Nate's steadiness, his soft speech, his country manners, his gentleness and kindness, combined with his knowledge, had become a safe spot for me, a rock on which to crawl when the slime became too hard to deal with.

And now I had shattered that rock with my own hand, just as I had smashed other rocks before.

I wanted to call him. I could not move. I was frozen, paralyzed, heartsick.

After a while, I fell asleep and slept until just before six. Luke nudged me when I stirred. I sat up and realized I'd slept for ten hours.

Luke was developing an elephant's bladder by necessity.

I grabbed a quilt and took him outside. I sat down in one of the Adirondack chairs Nate had made for me and watched the sun slowly rise over the trees to the east, a "fine stand of mixed oaks and poplars," Nate had said. Red oak. White oak. Post oak. Chinkapin oak. I heard a pileated woodpecker and a Carolina wren and an Eastern bluebird. These were all things I'd learned from Nate. He knew more about nature than anyone I'd ever met.

He knew more about life. And he was helping me see the world in layers, dimensions I had never noticed before.

Suddenly, I knew what I had to do. I got up, called Luke, and went inside. I didn't have Nate's address, but hey, I knew how to find people. It's what I did.

I pinpointed his location in fifteen minutes. I fed my dog, showered, got dressed, and left.

His house was only twenty minutes away. I found his mailbox and turned down through the woods, down a long, rutted gravel driveway, across a small creek, and up again until I came upon a clearing. There, perched on the side of a hill, sat a small log home. I could tell it was kit-built, and I could imagine Nate constructing it himself, piece by piece over time. It was that kind of home.

I saw his Tahoe parked off to the side and an old pickup in the back near a shed next to cords and cords of stacked firewood. The house faced south. In front and to the left was a huge garden with row upon row of vegetables emerging from the soil. He had edged the garden with bright yellow and orange flowers and fenced it to keep the deer out.

I rolled down all the windows and heard Sprite barking. Not until I got out of the car did I see Nate, standing on the front porch, his pipe in his hand.

I raced toward him, tears blurring my vision. At first, he stood still, but then I saw him move quickly down the six porch steps. We met at the bottom and melted into each other's arms.

"I'm so sorry, I'm so sorry!" I whispered.

He squeezed me and kissed the top of my head, just as my father had done when I was six and chucked a rock at a boy and broke my dad's car window. Was the universe sending me a sign?

He kissed my head again.

My tears flowed freely. He released me and pulled an old-fashioned handkerchief out of his back pocket and handed it to me. I wiped my eyes and blew my nose. "I accused you of something you didn't do. I am so sorry. Please forgive me! Please!"

"It's all right," he said.

Sprite's barking drew our attention. We both turned. She was at my car jumping as high as she could, trying to see Luke.

Comic relief.

"Go let him out. They can play and we can have some coffee," Nate said.

I let Luke out of the car, and he and Sprite took turns chasing each other. She was little, but like most females, she didn't hesitate to put him in his place if he got too rough. When it was clear they weren't going anywhere, I climbed the steps to Nate's porch, opened his front door, and yelled, "Can I come in?"

"Sure!"

I stepped into a great room with glistening, honey-colored logs stretching up to a cathedral ceiling. Shiny wood floors repeated that color. Two guitars and a banjo hung on one wall. A massive, river-stone fireplace and chimney flanked by tall, amply filled bookshelves dominated the end of the room to my right. I had no idea Nate was such a reader.

I walked past a brown-leather couch and matching recliner and across a stunning oriental rug, woven in deep red and beige with black accents. I touched the cool, smooth stone of the fireplace and wondered if Nate had built it himself. My eyes turned to the bookshelves, and I began reading the titles. I found books on dog training, dog first aid, dog breeds, dog food, and dogs in war.

No surprise there.

The next shelves included Bibles (four of them) and what must have been study books— concordances, commentaries, a Bible dictionary. *Why would he need a separate dictionary?* Next to them were books on Christian history and a whole string of books by C.S. Lewis. Then there were what I would call self-help books, with titles like, *Desiring God, Where is God When it Hurts,* and *Suffering and the Sovereignty of God.*

Nate must have spent a lot of time trying to come to terms with his injuries and losses.

I ran my hand over the titles as if I could glean some wisdom by just touching them. I went on to find books on science, nature, construction, philosophy, psychology, health, and then, to my shock, poetry and novels.

As I said, I had no idea Nate was such a reader.

"You hungry?"

His voice, coming from the kitchen area, surprised me. I turned. "Sure."

I walked over to him, and he handed me a plate full of eggs, bacon, and toast.

"Let's eat on the front porch," he said. "It's a fine morning."

He brought out orange juice and coffee and napkins and set them on the rustic table I suspected he built. I waited while he retrieved his own plate. The dogs lay on the grass, chewing sticks in the sun. A hawk circled overhead, the only feature in the cloudless sky.

I sat quietly as Nate said grace, then I said, "I'm sorry about your friend."

He nodded and began talking as we ate. He told me all about Beth's death, about the music and the prayers and the Scripture verses, and about what he called a "great peace." There was something about the telling of it that comforted him, I knew, and so I sat quietly, not commenting, not asking questions, not even rolling my eyes or gritting my teeth when he said things I didn't buy.

His view of death was a lot different than mine.

I couldn't deny, however, that sitting on that front porch with Nate settled my soul like nothing else had, not even running, for a long, long time. His home was a place of peace; *he* was a place of peace.

An hour later, as we carried our plates back to the kitchen, I heard his cell phone go off.

"Excuse me." He answered the call.

I continued cleaning up, marveling at the small, but well-equipped kitchen, the open shelves, the gingham dishtowels. The window over the sink looked out into the forest behind the house. A hummingbird feeder hung just outside it. His house was much homier than mine, or even my mother's.

I could hear Nate talking. When he came back into the kitchen, his face looked serious. "That was Scott Cooper."

My heart thudded.

"Another young woman is missing up in the mountains."

MY PEACE SHATTERED like a dropped plate. "Have we been called out?" Already I had pulled my phone from my pocket to check.

Nate shook his head. "No. Somebody from the Blue Ridge Trafficking Task Force contacted Scott. It's not our case, not yet."

"What are the details? Is she like ... like the others?" Part of me wanted to know, part didn't.

"Very similar. Small, blonde. This one's got a little kid at home. Community college student. Never came home from her part-time job at Walmart."

"Is Cooper going up there?"

"Not yet, though from the way he talked my guess is he'll wrangle a way to get there." Nate stretched his shoulders. "Speaking of community colleges, I'd better get to work."

"Thanks, Nate. Thanks for everything. Breakfast ... everything."

"You're welcome." He gave me a quick hug. "Be easy on yourself, okay? Give yourself a little grace."

I looked at him. There was that word again. I had no idea what he meant.

I drove home pondering the contrasts of the morning—the

peace at breakfast, the jarring report soon after. Life, I thought, was surely crazy.

I had no idea just how crazy it was about to become.

Luke was tired out from playing with Sprite, so when I got home, I changed into work clothes, put him in his crate, and left for Richmond. A lawyer I'd never worked for before had given me a case. A woman wanted to know what her husband was really doing when he was supposedly working late at the office.

Sounded like my typical case. Except the husband was the lieutenant governor. And the wife was the daughter of a former governor.

Oh, boy.

I'd taken a lot of government classes in college, and I knew that in Virginia, lieutenant governor was a largely ceremonial position, almost a part-time job. Still, it was an important post. Politicians viewed it as a stepping-stone to the Executive Mansion, since Virginia is the only state that won't allow governors to serve more than one term for four years in a row. A messy divorce would certainly derail Joshua Porter's political ambitions.

Porter had a big car dealership in Albemarle County, near Charlottesville, and two houses, one in Charlottesville and one in the trendy Fan District of Richmond. I headed there now to start with his wife.

Eleanor Porter was an auburn-haired former Miss Virginia, a graduate of Sweet Briar, a private women's college. Dressed in a light-blue silk suit, perfectly coiffed and manicured, she sat properly perched on a beige wingback chair while we spoke.

I felt absolutely shabby, sitting across from her. Still, I managed to ask my questions and walk away with four leads and a hinky feeling ol' Joshua wasn't the real politician in the family.

How much weight did Eleanor carry with Daddy's old political cronies? And had I just unwittingly enlisted in a coup attempt?

Focus on the question, I told myself. Was Joshua having an affair?

I knocked around Richmond for a couple of hours, hitting a coffee shop I knew catered to politicians, and later, a bar where they hung out. I ginned up an excuse to visit the office of a state senator who I knew was a crony of Porter's, and I chatted up his secretary. The place was pretty empty—the General Assembly was only in session a few months a year—so I had a lot of freedom and the secretaries had a lot of time.

Gosh, people will talk. I was a stranger, yet soon I knew about a senator's bourbon problem, another one's lobbyist connections, and a kinky little affair a delegate had literally under the table.

By the time I left Richmond, I either had enough leads to sink Joshua Porter, or the script for a tacky, made-for-TV movie. I wasn't sure which. One lead led me to a restaurant not far from Porter's auto dealership in Charlottesville where I had arranged to meet Eleanor's college roommate, Judith Randolph.

I should have recognized Randolph as an Old Virginia name, but I didn't. Between the accent, the stylish blonde hair, and the pale-beige silk suit, I felt like I was in a scene from *Gone with the Wind*. Mrs. Randolph sat down, took off her gloves, ordered tea, and began talking.

She'd apparently seen Joshua Porter in various restaurants around Charlottesville with a woman "way too pretty" to be an associate. She'd followed them in her car on one occasion to the famous Boar's Head Inn, a favorite of the Old Dominion's elite. Once, she'd caught them in an embrace that was "more than friendly."

Then Mrs. Randolph leaned forward. She looked like she was about to reveal her juiciest tidbit. I leaned forward to catch it. Then the door opened up behind her. And in walked Joshua Porter.

"Hold on," I whispered urgently, but Mrs. Randolph continued.

"I saw them," she said, "embracing ..."

"Judith!" Joshua Porter not only saw us, he recognized his wife's friend by the back of her head. "How are you, darling?"

Mrs. Randolph turned sixteen shades of red. "I ... uh ... I'm well, Josh." She extended her hand.

He took it and kissed it. I sat frozen in my seat. "And you are ..." he said, looking straight at me.

"A friend," I said, "Alice Longworth." Seriously? I had to choose the name of Theodore Roosevelt's daughter?

Porter's eyes told me he was on to me.

Note to self: Decide on an alias before you need it.

I turned to Mrs. Randolph. "I'll be in touch about that library project. Thank you for considering it. Good day."

Then I left the restaurant, my cover blown, the case against Porter in tatters.

I called Eleanor's lawyer, told him what happened, and apologized. My most potentially lucrative case yet had slipped from my grasp.

I went to bed discouraged. Fortunately, I was distracted by a search-and-rescue callout at 2:00 a.m. A high school couple had not returned from a date. The boy's car had been found at the end of a dead-end dirt road in the foothills near Sperryville. Searchers had fanned out in the woods, but there was no sign of them. Both were sixteen. Both should have been home by eleven.

I admit, I was still a bit shaky from the accident we'd all experienced just a week before. But I also knew I needed the distraction and so I agreed to respond. As I was getting ready, Nate texted me. He'd be my walker.

When we arrived at the incident command post and received the details about our subjects, I had to catch my breath. The missing girl was small, but she had dark hair. Thank goodness.

I was happy to be working with Nate. I knew automatically if the couple was dead, he'd do the body work, and I'd be able to back off and focus on the dog.

We got our assignment—a rough, ten-acre area extending up the mountain. Kevin and his Malinois had also responded, but there'd be another dog team between us and him, and I was glad of that. Kevin had taken the downhill search area, the more likely way for humans on foot to travel. The other dog team was following an old path that ran parallel to the ridge. Nate and I headed uphill, following a fire trail.

The temperature was in the 60s, perfect for a strenuous climb. Overhead, the clear night sky sparkled with a thousand stars. The fire trail was well-maintained, and I was thankful we didn't have to crawl across the boulders I saw littering the forest floor.

But I should have known Luke wasn't going to follow a straight path, and soon we were snaking through the woods. Nate had an easier time than I did crossing the boulder fields, so he took the lead and gave me a hand up at times. Wiry and tough, his strength amazed me.

We'd been hiking for about an hour and a half when the base commander radioed us. The couple had been found. Kevin's Malinois had discovered them resting under a tree, two miles from the command post. They were fine, just lost.

That was good news. Nate and I began making our way down. At Nate's suggestion, he went ahead and hid and I told Luke to "Seek!" and he "found" Nate and got rewarded. The idea was to give Luke a payoff, to keep him ready to play the game.

We got back to the base and checked in at the desk. I was glad the kids had been found, but irritated it was Kevin who'd found them. Still, I was too tired to think of much besides getting home and going back to sleep.

A few minutes later, I stood at the rear of my car with the liftgate up, giving Luke a drink before I crated him. Nate stood to my right, talking with me. His Tahoe was parked to the left of the Jeep. He was saying something about the dogs when I saw movement between the two vehicles and heard a noise. Then my heart jumped, and my eyes widened. Max, the Malinois, had seen Luke's rear end and was charging him.

All I could do was jerk Luke out of the way, get between him and Max, and brace myself. Nate must have heard the dog because the next thing I knew, he was yelling. I looked and saw him grab the Malinois by the ruff, hands on either side of his neck.

Max twisted his head, and I saw blood fly. Nate wrestled him down to the ground and held him there, the dog's body writhing, his jaws latched on to Nate's arm. Meanwhile, I clung to Luke's leash. He was lunging, barking, ready to get in the brawl.

"Kevin!" I screamed. "Kevin, your dog!"

Finally he came running. "What happened? What'd you do to him?" he yelled at Nate. I swear his snarl was worse than his dog's. He reached down and grabbed his dog's collar, and Nate let go and moved away. I saw Kevin twist the collar as he lifted the Malinois to his feet, choking him. He glared at Nate. "You do that to my dog again and I'll—"

Nate's chest heaved with exertion. "You're done, Kevin. I'm writin' this up. No more." His fists clenched and unclenched.

Kevin cursed him up one side and down the other. I turned away, shaken by the conflict. Heart pounding, I motioned to Luke to kennel up. I wanted him secure. As I latched his crate, I heard Kevin say, "What happened to that grace you were talking about, huh, Tanner?"

I heard Nate say something about blood. I turned and saw red dripping off his arm.

"Nate!" Alarmed, I yelled for a medic. "Enough of this!" I took Nate's arm. "Come on, Nate. Come sit down before you pass out."

Kevin left, dragging his dog with him. I was never so happy to see anyone walk away. I guided Nate back to my car. I needed to stop the bleeding, quickly. I searched for a clean towel in the back of the Jeep. Luke moved in his crate, still agitated. While I was looking for a towel, Nate pulled his shirt off. What I saw took my breath away. Scars—thick, ropey scars—covered the entire left side of his body from his chest to his waist and maybe beyond. They were an echo and an amplification of the scars I'd seen on his arm.

Shock twisted my stomach. Tears sprang to my eyes. He looked away. I grabbed his shirt and pressed it against the worst of his wounds, biting my lip.

Seconds later, an EMT showed up. I was glad to step back and let him take over. There was too much to process, too much for me. I wanted to cry.

"Jess."

Nate's voice brought me up short.

"Let Luke out. Keep him on leash but let him walk around. Help him relax."

Always thinking of the dog. That was Nate.

Fifteen minutes later, the medic had cleaned Nate's wounds and stopped the bleeding. They wanted to transport him to the hospital, but he refused. I promised the EMT I'd make sure he got a prescription for antibiotics as soon as the urgent-care places opened up in a couple of hours.

Later I asked Nate, "Why did Max do that?"

"Sometimes the devil gets into 'em," he replied.

I doubted that.

SCOTT COOPER LOOKED AGAIN at the entry in the NCIS database.

Sandy Smith, 19, 5'2", 110 lbs., Caucasian, blonde hair, blue eyes
Last seen leaving Green City Walmart at 10:05 p.m., Monday,
driving a dark-red 1999 Toyota Camry.

What the entry didn't say was that Sandy was a single mom, living with her parents, trying to make a go of it after messing up in high school. Her little boy, age three, was missing his mommy.

Scott's friend Tom McElroy, an investigator with the Virginia State Police, had filled him in on those details. Now Scott was trying to figure out how he could justify getting involved. Agents were supposed to initiate investigations—that was part of the job. But they had to account for their hours, too, logging everything on an infamous time-management system. No one wanted to get gigged for having too many dead-end investigations or unproductive hours. Plus, most missing persons cases were handled by local law enforcement, at least initially.

That's when Scott thought of human trafficking, an FBI priority. The Interstate 81 corridor, a major thoroughfare for trucks, was known for trafficking. The north-south route ran through the Shenandoah Valley, not far from Sandy Smith's home. Truck stops dotted the corridor.

Had anyone checked security and highway cameras for pictures of Sandy? Could Sandy Smith have been lured away by someone who could trap her into prostitution? Doubtful but feasible. Just feasible enough to justify action.

Energized, Scott left the office and headed west. He called Tom on the way; once he got to the mountains, cell phone coverage could be iffy. An hour and twenty minutes later, Tom met him at the Warren County Sheriff's Office near Front Royal.

"She was reported missing about 6:00 a.m. by her parents," Sheriff Brett Walters told him. "That's when they realized she hadn't come in from the night before."

"Was it typical for her to stay out after work?" Scott asked.

"Not often, and she always texted them. They babysat her kid, a three-year-old boy. Her usual routine on nights she worked was to get off at ten o'clock and then drive home. Took about forty minutes."

"So she should have been home by eleven."

"Right."

"Who's been interviewed?"

"Coworkers. Boyfriend. Old boyfriend. The boy's father. Her parents. Neighbors. Daycare workers. People at the college."

"And you have nothing."

Tom spoke. "No one's seen her. No one knew of any plans she'd made. Old boyfriend has a valid alibi."

"Drug use?"

"Not that we can find." The sheriff checked his notes. "We have her on a security camera at Walmart leaving the parking lot at 10:15. We've got nothing after that."

Walters threw the paper he was holding back down on his desk. He looked at Scott. "Why's the FBI interested?"

Scott shifted his weight. He paused. "Trafficking in the I-81 corridor."

"Drug trafficking?"

"Human."

Walters shook his head. "These young people go missing all the time. Get tired of being responsible. Want a new start. Don't know how to leave home, so they just disappear."

"She had a little boy."

"Even more reason to leave if you're tired of responsibility."

Scott weighed his next move. He pointed to a map. "You have truck stops here, here, and here." He looked at Tom. "Have they been checked?"

Tom shifted his jaw. "We looked at the one." He gestured toward the stop closest to them. "Talked to the people there. They didn't see her."

Scott turned his attention back to the sheriff. "I'd like to reinterview some of these local people. Would you mind?" It was a courtesy question. He was going to do it anyway.

Walters hesitated before responding. "No." He stood. "I have a meeting, but I'll have someone make copies of the contact information."

"Perfect. Thanks."

Ten minutes later he was on his way. Scott thought out his approach to the interviews the way he always did. Who had the most to gain, and who had the most to lose if Sandy disappeared?

He decided to start with her parents.

Horace "Hap" Smith and his wife Alice lived off a barely paved road in a one-story house that looked like it was sinking into the ground. Green mold grew on the dirty white siding. Several little riding toys lay scattered in the yard.

Scott knocked on the door, and dogs began barking. After a while, a woman he figured to be about fifty years old opened the inner door just a crack. He showed his creds, and she unhooked the screen. Three yappy little dogs rushed out.

Alice showed him in to the dark living room where a small, towheaded boy sat on the floor playing with Matchbox cars. Behind every crime catalogued in the databases lay a bunch of broken hearts. Scott knew that well.

Sandy's mother motioned for him to sit on the couch. Did she expect him to interview her in front of the boy? Scott glanced around quickly for an alternative. "How about the kitchen table?" At least there he could keep his voice down and have a chance the kid wouldn't hear.

"All right." Her voice dripped with fatigue.

They sat down and Scott went over the facts—the last time she saw Sandy, Sandy's relationship with the boy, with his father, with the old boyfriend ... and with her father.

With that question, Alice hesitated. "I told him she was too old for him to whip her. I did that. But would the tomfool man listen?"

Scott forced himself to show no reaction. "When was the last time he disciplined her like that?"

Alice looked at the ceiling. "Had to be she was fifteen, I reckon. 'Cause a year later, that 'un was born." She gestured toward the boy.

"And where does your husband work?"

"Down't ga-rage in town."

"You have other kids?"

"Nope. She's it. Pretty little thing too. Too pretty for her own good if you ask me." She said that with kind of a huff, as if she was as jealous as she was concerned about her daughter.

Out of the blue, anger swept over Scott. His parents had loved his sister. So had he. They'd cried buckets over her death. He couldn't fathom his father "whippin'" his sister at age fifteen. He couldn't imagine his mother being jealous of her.

Why was life so unfair?

Just then the little boy came walking into the kitchen and

handed his grandmother a car. The wheels had come off. She fumbled with trying to fix it.

"Can I try?" Scott said, holding out his hand. Alice Smith muttered something and gave him the car. He looked at it and saw the problem—something was blocking the slot where the axle went. He removed it, pressed the axle on, and handed it back to the boy. "There you go." The boy took the car and ran back to the living room.

"If that girl thinks we're gonna take care of her kid full time, she's got mush for a brain," Alice Smith said, watching him go.

Scott masked his reaction. "So, if you had to guess, where do you think your daughter is, Mrs. Smith?"

Alice Smith eyed him like a wary cat. "I think she run off with some guy."

"Her boyfriend?"

"No, not him. Any fool can see it weren't that boy. Some man."

Walking out of the Smiths' house ten minutes later, Scott felt like one of those yappy dogs. Annoyed.

He drove down "into town," to the "ga-rage" on Oak Street where Hap Smith worked. Two men looked up, staring, as he parked. In this town of pickups and old cars, they could tell by his Bucar exactly what he was—"govmint."

Hap Smith had his head in the engine of a Ford pickup. He barely acknowledged Scott when he identified himself.

"Is there someplace we could talk?" Scott asked.

"Right here's fine. I got a job to do."

Me too. He asked Hap a few questions, got a feel for his personality, and then asked, "Where do you think she is, Mr. Smith?"

Hap Smith's head came up. He turned toward Scott, his eyes flashing. "If I knew, I wouldn't have called you folks now, would I?" He threw a rag he was holding down on the engine block.

"Your wife thinks she ran off with a man." Scott watched for a reaction.

"There ain't no way."

"Why do you say that?"

"One word—Timmy. She loved that little boy with everything in her. He's what got her up in the morning and kept her going all day."

His passion surprised Scott.

"There ain't no man gonna keep Sandy from her boy." Hap pointed his finger at Scott. "You find my girl and don't quit 'til you do."

SCOTT RETURNED TO HIS CAR, started his engine, and set out for Rocky Ridge Community College.

Three hours later, Scott made his way back down from the mountains.

He'd talked to folks at the college where Sandy Smith was enrolled, at the Walmart, and at a coffee shop. Then he'd gone to see the old boyfriend. Ex-boyfriends are always a possibility when a girl disappears. But within five minutes, he'd become convinced the kid had nothing to do with it.

Then the kid gave him a tip. Sandy might have stopped for gas on the way home at a small convenience store where she'd worked as a high-school student.

So Scott made one more stop. The small convenience store, simply called Bobby's, sat at the intersection of two country roads. When he walked in, his senses recoiled at the smell of stale smoke and spilled beer.

One customer stood at the counter, which was being manned by an unshaven guy about fifty. A stream of smoke rose from the stub of a cigar clenched between two of his fingers.

Scott browsed around the shelves, picking up a small bag of chips and pulling a bottle of water out of the refrigerated case. The customer left, and Scott went to pay.

Normally, he would have identified himself and asked the

clerk about Sandy, gathering as much information from his words and nonverbals as he could. But something made him hold back. Instead, he made some small talk about the weather and commented about needing a break from driving.

He left, but instead of going to his car, he casually walked in the parking lot, drinking his water, pretending to look at the scenery. All the while, he was making mental notes.

There were no security cameras. Because of the junk piled high in the windows of the tiny store, the clerk could not see much of the parking lot—just the pumps, really. The area behind the store and off to the right provided plenty of opportunity for suspicious behavior.

So, had someone waited for Sandy in this place? Happened upon her? Had she been followed?

Scott walked behind the building and looked down into the woods. No houses or other businesses were nearby. No one to observe a kidnapping or even a suspicious car. He looked down at the ground. In a couple of places, he saw tire tracks, but anybody could have driven a wheel off the gravel.

Satisfied he'd learned everything he could for now, Scott got in his car and threaded his way down out of the mountains. The setting sun cast a golden glow over the rich farms of the foothills ahead of him. The corn, almost six feet high, looked thick and green, the soybean fields lush. He liked the east—the hardwood forests and rolling farmland, the fruitful agricultural land. Just not the skiing.

He didn't have much to show for his afternoon. Why did he torture himself? He didn't have to pursue his gut feeling. This missing woman wasn't his case. He could walk away, and no one would say a word. In fact, his boss would be thrilled.

Fact is, he hated what some men did to women. Fact is, he couldn't shake what happened to his sister, what could happen to his daughter. It felt like ground glass in his soul, cutting and shaping him in ways he barely recognized.

An hour later, Scott drove on the road that led to his neighborhood. But when he came to his street and mentally pictured himself pulling into his driveway and walking into an empty house, he couldn't do it. He drove straight past it.

WHEN NATE WALKED into Beef 'n Brew, he spotted a familiar figure at the bar. He walked over and slid onto the bar stool next to Scott Cooper. "How's it goin'?" Scott turned toward him. From the look in his eyes, Nate figured he was about three beers into it.

"It's going," Scott responded, taking a deep breath.

The bartender spotted Nate. "The usual?"

Nate nodded. A minute later, the bartender put a tall glass full of a dark soda with cherries and lime.

Scott eyed it. "Rum and Coke?"

"Dr. Pepper," said Nate, taking a drink, "with cherries and lime. No rum."

Scott grinned. "What are you? Fourteen?"

"You should try it," Nate said. "Clears the mind."

"Already I can't sleep. Why would I want my mind clear?" Scott took a long drink. "What happened to you?" He gestured toward the thick white bandage on Nate's arm.

"This was from an RPG attack in Afghanistan," Nate said, pointing to the burn scar on his arm, "and this was from a dog bite. This here," he said, shoving his sleeve up to reveal his anchor tattoo, "this was from finding hope. Which one do you want to know about?"

Scott blew out a breath and shook his head.

"What's got you going?" Nate paused. "That situation up yonder?"

"Spent the afternoon up there."

Nate could feel the weight of that statement. "Have you eaten?"

Scott shook his head.

"Why don't we get some dinner?"

So they moved over to a table in the dining room and ordered steaks. "And black coffee for both of us," Nate added, ignoring the surprise on Scott's face.

After the server left, Nate looked at Scott. "So, what's going on?"

Scott recounted his day, the trip to the mountains, the interviews, the convenience store, the people he met. Their steaks came and they ate and talked, batting around ideas. The dining room was nearly empty, and they could talk freely as long as they kept their voices down. Nate asked him a few pointed questions about the girl and her family.

"Seemed weird to me that he would physically discipline her at age fifteen," Scott said. "I can't imagine spanking my daughter. But then ..."

"But then they're ignorant hill folks, right?" Nate finished Scott's thought. "Oh, I don't mind." He grinned. "I will say this, we're rougher up in the mountains."

"Her mother thinks she ran off with some man."

Nate pursed his lips. "My daddy used to say, 'When a boy goes wrong it's one thing, but when a girl goes bad there's no touching her.' Girls can bring a heap of trouble, they can."

"Her father doesn't think she'd leave her son."

Nate nodded. "Somebody drive the route?"

"I'm sure they did."

"Did you look at the topographic maps?"

Scott shook his head.

"You want to come to my place and see what we can figure out?"

Scott checked his watch. "It's 9:30. You got to be at work in the morning?"

"At seven. But I can leave at three."

"Let's do it then."

21

NATE HAD PROMISED to teach me dog massage after work the next day. He'd told me to come by anytime, so I planned to be at his house at four. I also wanted to check his arm and make sure he'd filled the prescription for antibiotics after he left the urgent care. Why I thought he needed me to take care of him when he'd been alone all these years was beyond me.

I was surprised to see another car parked in his driveway when I pulled up. I instantly recognized it as a Bureau car. Scott. I debated whether to leave, but Luke knew where we were. He was looking for Sprite, his tail banging against his crate. I had no choice but to get out.

As I walked toward the house, Luke raced before me. I had to laugh. I could see Sprite jumping up and down in the living room, trying to see Luke through the front window, her ears flying. She looked like she was bouncing on a trampoline.

Before I got to the steps, Nate opened the door, and Sprite came racing out. "Come on in!"

"I don't want to interrupt—"

"No, you're fine. Come in." Nate held the door open for me.

As my eyes adjusted, I saw Scott standing over a bunch of

topographic maps spread out on Nate's table. He looked up and nodded. "Hi, Jess."

"Scott."

"Nate was telling me about your search the other night. Glad you found those kids."

"Me too." I nodded toward the maps. "What are you two doing?"

"Got another young woman missing up west of Warrenton."

"I heard." A little tremor ran through me. "It's your case?"

Scott screwed his mouth into a wry twist. "Not quite."

Nate stood watching the dogs through the front door. He turned toward me. "I'm sorry, Jess. I forgot about our massage date."

Scott raised his eyebrows.

"Dog massage," Nate said, clarifying. "Do you mind waiting a few minutes? It'll give the dogs a chance to tire themselves out."

"No problem," I said.

Nate walked over to the bookshelves to the right of the fireplace. He pulled a book off the shelf. "Here. Start with this."

It was a book on natural remedies for dogs, and it included a chapter on massage. I began reading it, but I couldn't help but overhear the guys' conversation. The young woman's name was Sandy. She had a little boy. She was going to school and worked at Walmart. She lived with her parents.

I heard them talk about possibilities, about personalities, about how and why people just disappear. I heard them enter one investigative cul-de-sac after another.

Tension built in me like ozone before a summer storm. Finally, I opened my mouth. "They haven't found her car?" The two men stopped and turned toward me.

"No."

"What was the weather like the night she went missing?" I got up from the couch. "Was it raining? Dry? Foggy?"

They didn't know. I pulled out my phone and searched a

weather app. "Rainy. Thunderstorms beginning about nine, ending around midnight. When was she last seen?"

"Ten-fifteen," Scott said.

"Did someone walk the route she normally drove home?"

"There's two routes," Scott said, "one if she had to get gas, and a shorter one if she didn't. The sheriff's office drove both multiple times."

"But no one walked it."

"It's a long way."

I looked at the map. "Show me the Walmart." Scott pointed to it. "And her home?"

Scott put his finger on that, then traced the two routes with his finger. "She either went this way, or this way. These would have been her normal pattern."

I studied the routes closely. On a topographic map, the closer the lines are together, the steeper the terrain. It's easy to see hills, plains, mountain peaks, and drop-offs. I looked at Nate. "Can I make a couple of pencil marks?"

"Sure."

I placed five marks on one route, three on the other. "Look here," I said to Scott. "The road curves, and the lines show a steep drop-off. Even if they don't walk the whole route, these places should be walked."

"Because her car might not be visible from the road. Thanks, Jess!"

Worry stabbed me. Had I said too much? I shifted his attention back to the map. "If she went off the road in a storm, she could be well out of sight."

"Thank you." Scott turned to Nate. "Can I borrow these?"

"Sure."

Scott rolled them up. "I'll bring them back."

As I watched Scott leave, I felt a shimmer of fear, like a ripple on a pond, move through me. Why did I speak up? I wasn't involved in this case, not at all! Did I show my hand?

What could I say? I'm an investigator. It's what I do. It's who I am. And the idea that an important angle might have been missed compelled me to speak.

"Let's get the dogs." Nate's voice jarred me out of my thoughts.

"Okay."

He walked to the front door and whistled. Both dogs came running. "How is it that my dog responds to your whistle now?" I asked, teasing.

Nate looked at me, those blue eyes sparkling. "Charm. Works on women too."

I grinned at him. "Yeah," I said, looking around. "I see so many swarming you."

The dogs settled down quickly, tired from playing outside. It was cooler in the house, and they were ready to relax.

We sat down on the floor in the great room. I was surprised when Nate put on some relaxing instrumental music. "For the dogs?" I asked.

He shrugged. "For me anyway."

Sprite lay on her side on the floor in front of him. He began with her head, slowly moving his hand, massaging behind her ears, then stroking the space between her eyes with his thumb.

I followed suit with Luke. I had him lie on the floor in front of me. He was three times as big as Sprite, but I imitated Nate, gently rubbing my big dog while Nate quietly instructed me. It wasn't long before both dogs were relaxed.

We worked our way down the dogs' bodies, massaging each leg, being careful around their paws, then rubbing circles down the sides of their spines. I found myself mesmerized by the music, the gentle touching, and Nate's soft voice.

By the time we were finished, the two dogs were totally chill. Nate motioned for me to follow him. We went to the kitchen, washed our hands, and he made tea. It was late in the day for coffee.

"You ever get relaxed like that?" he asked me as we sat down at his table.

I laughed. "Nope."

"Ever had a massage?"

"Nope."

He told me about a place he went to in Charlottesville. "'Bout once a month. It helps with muscle tension and anxiety as well. It's totally legitimate."

I listened but I knew I wouldn't follow through. "Not to change the subject, but how's your arm?"

"It's fine."

"Did you get the antibiotics?"

"Yes, ma'am." He grinned at me.

"All right then." I called Luke, preparing to leave.

"See you Saturday?" Nate asked. Battlefield would be training at an area on the grounds of Montpelier, James Monroe's estate.

"For sure."

"Thanks for helping Scott today. Smart idea, walking the route." Nate stuck his hands in the back pockets of his jeans. "You know a lot."

I turned away as I felt my face color. Yes, I know a lot. Too much of it from experience.

22

WE NEVER MADE it to Saturday. The next day I got a text from Nate asking me if it was okay for him to give Scott my phone number. I agreed, then instantly regretted it, so when he called, I let it go to voicemail. I sat there staring at my phone until I got the beep, indicating he'd left a message.

Why was Scott calling me? What did he want? Why didn't he just tell Nate?

Had I said too much when I suggested they look for a car off the road? Had he figured me out?

Should I add paranoia to my list of psychological problems?

I decided to ignore the message. Let it age. But it followed me around the apartment like Poe's raven.

Finally, I listened to it. *Hey, this is Scott. Thanks for the suggestion yesterday. It was spot on. I faxed that topo map up to the investigators, and they found Sandy Smith's car. Right at one of your marks! So thanks. That was a very smart idea.*

I sat down hard on the couch, tears streaking my face, visions swarming my brain like bats. It was like the dream, only I was awake.

Luke came over and nudged me with his big nose. "Oh, Luke!" I ran my hand over him, rubbing him behind his ears, and he licked my tears. I buried my face in his fur and thanked whatever power in the universe sent him to me. "Am I ever going to get past this?"

Then a realization struck. They'd found the car. But not Sandy.

I sat straight up. What about the woman?

I worried about that over the next couple of hours, but I didn't want to call Scott. Or Nate. Then, at about two that afternoon, I got a text. Battlefield had been called out. From the location, I guessed it was the same case.

Within seconds I had a call from Nate. "You goin'?"

I hesitated.

"We can work together."

I swallowed. "Then yes. I'm going."

I called the incident commander, told her I would respond, and got instructions.

As soon as I pulled my SAR pack out of the closet, Luke went crazy, barking and turning in circles. "Yes, you, goofy dog. You're coming. I know better than to leave you home."

I reported to the search command site at 3:58 p.m. Nate was already there and talking to Scott and a trooper from the Virginia State Police. I walked over to them, leaving my Jeep running to keep Luke cool. It was 92 degrees and humid, even all the way up in the mountains.

Scott introduced me to the trooper, Tom something, and told him it had been my idea to check the places where the road fell off precipitously. I felt myself redden, and I'm sure he thought it was from modesty.

It wasn't.

"We think the car left the road up there," the trooper said, pointing to a place on the curve. "It ended up a good twenty feet down." He pointed to a place where a battered Toyota lay crushed against a tree. Crime-scene tape surrounded it now.

"No sign of her?" I asked.

"Just a bunch of junk from her car—textbooks, old McDonald's wrappers, that kind of thing—scattered between the road and there."

"Could she have survived that crash?" Scott asked. "That car obviously rolled."

Clearly, he didn't know much about car crashes. Without thinking twice, I said, "Yes."

The trooper glanced at me, and once again, my face reddened.

He continued the conversation. "She could have crawled out of that. Might have a head injury. Could be disoriented, down in the woods somewhere. That's why we need them." He gestured toward me and Nate.

"Well, then. Let's get going," Nate said. He was looking straight at me. Watching and judging, I thought.

I raised my chin, trying to appear confident. "What's the plan?"

"Let's go talk to Susan."

Susan Lewis was in her fifties. I got the impression she was happier working the command post than actually searching. I guess when you get older, searching, especially in the mountains, gets harder. Gray-haired and plump, she readily accepted Nate's suggestions on how to proceed.

We had two live-search teams—Luke and me, and Emily (who was just arriving) and Flash. Since Emily was more experienced, and probably had the steadier dog, she would take the road in case Sandy had survived the crash and walked back up the hill.

Meanwhile, Luke and I would search the woods. A deputy would be Emily's walker, Nate would be mine.

"Sprite's in her crate, next to my car. She's in the shade and there's water in her crate. But if we get delayed and she gets too hot, put her back in the car and run the AC." He plopped his keys on Susan's clipboard.

"I will," she responded.

Nate looked at me. "Ready?"

"I'll get my dog."

Luke was thrilled when I let him out of his crate. I kept him on leash at first, letting him sniff and relieve himself. Out of the corner of my eye, I saw the LEOs looking at him. I felt proud. Luke is one good-looking dog.

When I was ready, I joined Nate near the rolled-over car. I decided not to look at it. The last thing I needed right now was a flashback.

Instead, I concentrated on Luke and his joy, and on the possibility that we could save the life of Sandy Smith. After going over a tentative search plan with Nate, I turned my back on the car and sent Luke off into the woods. "Seek, seek!" I told him.

I was ten paces into it before I remembered I hadn't checked the wind or marked the start location on my GPS. I shot a panicked glance back at Nate.

"It's all right. I got it." He held up his GPS.

The going was rough, all downhill, with sharp rock outcroppings interrupting the forest floor. The trees, mostly oaks and poplars, soared sixty feet high. Underneath grew dogwoods, hollies, and wild mountain laurel. I knew I had to watch for snakes, especially timber rattlers and copperheads. Bears, too, and I wasn't even keen on running across a buck in these woods.

I slipped a few times. Thin tree branches whipped my pack as I went by. I was thankful for my good boots and the fact it hadn't rained in several days, but I could have done without the heat and humidity. Sweat ran down my back in a salty stream.

Nate and I didn't talk. There was too much to do just concentrating on keeping our footing, but I could hear him behind me, steady and sure, and it gave me comfort.

About forty-five minutes into it, Luke, who was out of sight, barked. He barked but did not run back and tug.

Not a good sign. I stopped and looked at Nate.

He must have read my face. "I'll take the lead," he said, willing to shield me from another unexpected cadaver.

We found Luke lying on a huge outcropping of bare-faced granite, jutting out over a small valley. No body in sight. Nate held up his hand. "Wait here."

I noticed that he approached the cliff carefully, and I realized he was looking for footprints or evidence. He moved onto the granite. Luke wagged his tail and barked, but he kept focused on me, the source of his toy.

Nate peered over the edge of the cliff, then turned back to me. "Call him over there and reward him. I don't see anything, but my guess is he can smell it.

There is a line from somewhere that goes, "O Death, where is thy sting?" I can answer that question. The sting is in the smell, rancid and bitter. The sting is in the decay, the sightless eyes, the swarming flies. The sting is in the flesh, melting away like butter in the heat. The sting is in the pain felt by the people left behind.

There is nothing but sting in death. Nothing.

I moved diagonally away and called Luke to me. I played with him, throwing his ball, limiting him to three or four times because I didn't want him to get overheated. Then I poured water into his portable bowl and focused on him slurping it up. Anything to keep from seeing what I didn't want to see.

Seconds later, Nate appeared at my side. "I've radioed Susan. The LEOs are coming in. Emily is bringing my gear and Sprite."

"Your gear?" I looked at him, alarmed. "What are you going to do?"

"I'm goin' down that cliff and see if I can find that girl."

"You're climbing down?"

"Rappelling. With Sprite." Nate looked me in the eyes. "Jess, you don't have to stay here. You can go back if you want. I'd understand if you do."

I hesitated. I felt like such a chicken.

"Or you can wait, and I'll ask one of the officers to walk you out. Or you can walk out with Emily."

I rubbed my neck, my fingers slipping on sweat. I didn't want to leave Nate alone in the woods. I didn't want to walk back with only my fear for company. I didn't want to admit I needed a babysitter. I didn't know what to do.

"'Course, I could use your help," Nate said.

"I'll stay." I straightened my shoulders.

Nate nodded. "Let's relax, then, 'til they get here."

We set our packs down on a flat rock. Nate's shirt was plastered to his back. He pulled it off and poured water over his head and chest.

I stared at his scars. "That must have been terrible," I said, lifting my eyes to meet his gaze. "I can't imagine the pain."

He smiled softly. "It was the broken road that led me to a better place, the place I am now."

I didn't know how to respond to that.

Nate gestured toward Luke. "Best leash him up so he doesn't disturb too much ground. This may be a crime scene."

I clipped the leash on my dog and moved away from the area. I walked around, letting Luke sniff, thinking about my own broken road. My father's death was bad enough, but I was young, and with the help of Finn, I bounced back. I went to college, established a career, and earned some recognition I think Dad would have been proud of. And then came that night, that dreadful night that changed everything.

Luke tugged me over to a log, following some scent. What was it? A squirrel? A chipmunk? I walked with him, content with letting him be the boss, watching him sniff, thinking of what a screwup I really was. If Nate knew the truth, he'd hate me.

"Hey, Jess?"

I heard Nate's voice and started to turn, but then my eyes spotted something. Luke was nudging something next to a log. He looked back at me, panting, then started to paw whatever it was. Instinctively, I pulled him away, and then I froze. My throat closed up, my heart beating hard. I blinked to be sure of what I saw. A small pile of wood shavings.

23

NATE'S FACE turned fierce when he saw what Luke had found. "Cooper was right." He glanced around. "It's possible the dude's watching us. Not likely, all the way out here, but possible." He looked at me. "You stay close. And keep your eye out."

He pulled his radio off his belt. "This is supposed to be a secure channel, but I don't trust it. So I'm not going to mention what we found."

I nodded.

He clicked the transmit button. "Susan, Romeo Alpha."

"Roger that," she radioed back after a hesitation.

"Romeo Alpha" meant "request assistance" from law enforcement. It was used in a variety of situations. In this case, Nate was signaling the possibility of a crime. And who knew? The perpetrator could be nearby, watching.

For the first time in two years, I wished I was carrying.

Nate clicked the radio again. "And Susan, tell Cooper he was right."

"That's all?"

"Yes. He was right."

We had a good half hour to wait before the others showed up.

"Luke will alert if someone's around." I forced confidence into my voice.

Nate didn't answer at first, and I realized it was because he was thinking some idiot with a sniper rifle could pick us off from three-hundred yards. Then he spoke. "I doubt anyone but us is out in these woods today."

Still, he seemed unusually watchful as we waited.

Finally, Luke raised his head, and moments later, I heard the sound of our reinforcements approaching. Cooper was first on the scene. He was carrying a large duffel bag, which I instantly realized was Nate's. Emily followed Cooper, with Sprite on a leash.

Nate greeted Sprite first and then pointed to where Luke had indicated he smelled human remains. "Could be she was layin' there," he said, "or could be the smell is comin' up from down below."

"Or both," Cooper responded.

"Yep." Nate led him and the deputy sheriff over to the pile of wood shavings. "The dog found this too."

"Just like the other case."

I was standing a way off. Emily came up to me. "Are you okay? What happened? Why'd we go on alert?"

I told her there was an indication this could be part of a string of similar murders.

Her eyes widened. "I thought she just ran off the road!"

I saw the men circling up. "Let's go listen to the plan."

When we got there, Nate was explaining how he could rappel down the cliff, with Sprite, and search down there. "If Luke was smelling the updraft, she might could still be there."

Dead, I thought. She could be there dead.

"What do you need from us?" Scott asked.

"Help with the gear is all."

"There's no easier way to get down there?" Tom, the state trooper, said.

"I checked the map. I don't see a way any quicker," Nate responded.

But how do you get back up? And how do you keep Sprite safe? I'd never seen anyone rappel with a SAR K-9 before.

I was about to get an education.

Nate chose a good oak tree for his anchor, throwing his weight against it and kicking the trunk to make sure it was solid. He ran a rope around it and rigged some locking carabiners. The men all clustered around him, drawn by the clinking of the hardware, the myriad of ropes, and Nate's knot-tying skills. They were fascinated—so was I.

Then Nate stepped into his climbing harness, which included a utility belt with all kinds of equipment hanging off of it. He rigged his rappelling gear, tugging on it to double-check his knots.

Sprite seemed nervous as we watched, or maybe restless. Emily stood next to me, holding Sprite's leash. She leaned over and said, "He's the only one in Battlefield who can do this."

"From his military service?" I asked, and she nodded.

I watched him check and double-check his equipment. Then he turned to me. "Jess, my pack."

"Got it." I told Luke to stay, handed the leash to Emily, and walked over to where Nate had left his pack. It must have weighed fifty pounds. Quickly, in my head I added it up. Nate weighed like one-hundred sixty, and between his pack and Sprite, he would be carrying ninety pounds down that rope.

Okay, I could see him sliding down with that much, but how could he climb back up?

But I was wrong. I set the pack down. Nate looked at me and said, "When I get down there and send the rope back up, I want you to clip my pack onto this." He pointed to a carabiner. "Then lock it." He thumbed the screw part of it. "Send it down slowly. Got it?"

"Yeah. For sure."

"Get one of these guys to help so you don't lose control. I don't want fifty pounds coming down on my head."

"I'll help her," Cooper said.

"Bring Sprite over." He gestured to Emily.

I took Luke, and she walked Sprite to him. That little springer knew exactly what to do. She put her four feet into the four holes of her harness that Nate had laid on the ground. He pulled the harness up and buckled it around her.

They were now ready to go, to step off that cliff into oblivion, trusting rope and hardware, knots and prayer to keep them safe. I knew prayer was part of it. It had to be. Because it was Nate.

"My biggest concern is keeping Sprite from crashing into the cliff when she's hanging below me," Nate said. "I need you all to spot me. Just stay back from the edge."

"I'll watch from the side," Cooper said.

Nate nodded. "Okay, now Emily, you come here. I want you to lift Sprite to me. Got it?"

"Okay." Emily didn't sound very sure of herself, but as Nate dropped back, Emily handed him Sprite.

Nate looked at me and smiled. "Now you know why I like little dogs."

Emily moved back from the edge. She glanced at me, and I saw the same fear on her face that was probably on mine.

Holding onto his rope, Nate edged down until he was hanging in open air, his feet braced against the face of the cliff. Then he carefully lowered Sprite between his legs until she was hanging by her harness about six feet below him. I could hear his soft voice speaking to her. She remained motionless, except for her little tail.

They were one carabiner failure, one frayed rope away from death. They were fifty feet off the ground, swinging in midair. Yet that little dog trusted Nate, trusted him when all of her instincts must have been telling her to scramble, fight, find solid ground. She trusted him, because ... because of love.

I rubbed Luke's ear. Did he trust me that much?

More to the point, did I trust him that way? Anyone? Had I ever?

Nate let his legs drop.

I moved next to Cooper, hardly able to watch my friend.

"And he descended into hell," Cooper muttered.

Nate slowly moved down the cliff. Foot by foot, a little at a time. I held my breath.

"Slow down," Cooper yelled as Sprite swung a little too close.

"Okay."

He started again, then finally, after what seemed like forever, I heard him yell, "Sprite's down!"

Thank goodness. That put Nate just six feet up. He'd survive that.

Then we heard Nate on the radio. "On the ground. Sending up the rope."

Cooper looked at me. "The pack?"

"Right." I put Luke on a down-stay, walked over to the rigging, clipped the carabiner on the top of Nate's pack, and locked it.

"I'll drop it down," Cooper said. "You play out the rope, slowly."

I was glad I had gloves on.

"What will he do now?" Tom asked me when we knew the pack was down.

I closed my eyes momentarily. "He'll take a water break, let the dog settle, and then he'll ask his dog to search. She's trained to find human remains."

"Whew, wow," he responded.

"To the dogs, it's just a scent. It means they get their reward. It's all a game to them." I sounded so confident. Inside I wasn't at all. It was never a game to me.

That's all the conversation we got in before Nate radioed up. "Found her."

I felt a stab of something. Fear, actually. Dread. I knew about this. I knew about death.

Nate texted a picture to Scott, who tried to show it to me.

I pretended to look but refused to let my eyes focus. He showed it to the others, and they began hustling. Now there was a homicide investigation to organize.

I walked away, far enough to convey disinterest, close enough to hear what was going on. I was surprised when Scott yielded to the state trooper, and then Tom yielded to the deputy sheriff, saying it was his county, his case. They were just there to assist.

That's the way it should have gone down, but with a bunch of alpha males, you never know.

I checked my watch. The sun had set twenty minutes ago. Night was falling. I wanted to get out of the woods, but I didn't want to leave Nate.

I turned to Cooper. "Can we help Nate get out of there?"

He radioed down to him. I heard Nate's voice. "I'm stayin'."

A deep chill went through me.

Now and then we have to spend the night out in the woods, by ourselves, in makeshift shelters, sittin' over a dead body.

Cooper looked at me. "He says he's staying. It could be all night."

"He's equipped to do that. We all are," I told him. I sounded so sure of myself. I was such a liar.

"Why? She's not going anywhere."

I took a deep breath. "Predators, vultures ... or the perpetrator could come back."

Emily heard us. "Nate says 'Every person is an image-bearer of God, deserving of respect and honor.' That's why he stays."

Scott raised his eyebrows.

Emily shrugged.

Something in me wanted to rise up and defend Nate, but I had no words to use. My phone rang. Nate. "Hey," I said.

"Go home, Jess."

I turned away from the others. "I don't want to leave. You might need me, for Sprite or something." I'd left my other partner, not by choice, but because that's what happens when you go unconscious. I'm not the type to leave.

"Ain't nothing you can do here, Jess." His voice was soft.

There was a pause, which I did not fill with an answer.

"At least go get a motel room." Another pause. "I done this before, many times. I'll be fine …"

Just at that moment, a shot rang out.

My heart slammed into my chest. All six of us on the top of the cliff dropped to the ground. My phone clattered against the rock, eight feet away.

I gripped the ground with my fists. The wet smell of the forest filled my nose.

Luke lay down next to me and pressed his body against me. He licked my ear. He probably thought this was a game. I knew it wasn't.

To my left, I could hear Cooper calling for help on his radio. Actually all the LEOs were. Then Cooper touched my arm. "Belly crawl back farther into the woods." He motioned with his hand. "Go on now. You too," he said to Emily.

"My phone!" I whispered.

"You go now!"

What right had he …? I glared at Cooper and started to crawl toward my phone. He put his hand on my shoulder and shoved me down. Dirt filled my mouth. Fury flashed through me. When I raised my head, I saw him scrambling to get the phone himself. He threw it at me. "Go!"

That jerk!

It was no time to argue. I belly-crawled into the woods to where Emily crouched behind a tree. Luke crawled with me. On the way, I felt my phone vibrate.

Safely in the woods, I sat up and looked at it. Nate sent me a text: *Don't worry. Found a cleft in the Rock of Ages. I'm safe.*

How odd. What in the world did that mean?

At least I knew he was alive.

Within fifteen minutes, darkness had fallen. I knew we were nearly invisible now unless our hunter had night-vision glasses. I heard the sound of a chopper. It was either the FBI or state police —either one would be able to search the woods using infrared. I could barely stand still; my flight-or-fight system was in full flight mode. I felt like a thousand birds were in my gut trying to take off.

"What should we do?" Emily whispered. We sat low, hiding behind a tree.

"Just be quiet. Don't open your phone. Wait until the officers tell us what to do."

Cooper crawled over to where we were. I was still spitting mad at him. "The chopper has someone in the woods, west of here."

"The shooter?" Emily asked.

"We'll know soon enough." He turned to me. "Nate's okay. I spoke with him. He's behind a rock with the dog."

That irritated me. All I got was a quote I barely understood.

I was even more irritated when two deputies came over a few minutes later and said they were ordered to escort us out of the woods and back to our cars.

Of course I protested. "I don't want to leave. My partner's still down there."

"Sorry," the taller deputy said. "You have to."

"Says who?" What was I, ten?

"The sheriff, for one."

Emily was getting nervous, I could tell. She plucked at my shirt. "Come on, Jess."

But I was used to guys trying to tell me what to do. And I wasn't about to—

"Leave, Jess. Now." Cooper's voice told me he was in command-and-control mode.

"But ..." I turned, and he stuck his phone in my face.

Frowning, I took it from him.

"Hey, girl." Nate's voice made my heart settle down a little. "I need you to do something for me. Take Emily and Susan and go to a motel. Settle in. Get some rest. Let the dogs relax. And we'll debrief in the morning. Okay?"

"What about you?"

"Cooper and I have it worked out. He's pretty strong. He thinks he can safely come down on the rope. When it's light, the evidence techs will relieve us." Nate hesitated. "Do it, Jess. Please."

My spirit sagged. Unacknowledged fatigue spread over me like sludge. Suddenly, my arms and legs felt heavy, my chest burdened. "All right," I said softly. "I will."

For Nate, I would. Not for Cooper. Not for the sheriff. For Nate.

24

I DIDN'T SLEEP much that night. Even Luke was restless. I heard
him get up, pace around the motel room, and lie down with a
huff over and over. It was like we needed closure, needed to see
Nate and Sprite come back up that cliff, needed to tie up the ends
on that search, making it right.

I'll be honest. I was glad I hadn't seen the young woman,
happy I didn't have to add another body melting into the ground
to the scrapbook in my head. I might not be religious, but even I
knew that we weren't just talking about a jumble of flesh and
bones. A soul had been snuffed out, the intangible substance of
a life.

I remembered as a twelve-year-old watching the news on 9/11.
Seeing the fear on peoples' faces, the horror, hearing those awful
phone calls from people trapped in the towers saying goodbye to
their loved ones.

I remember being told my Dad had died, trying to wrap my
head around the fact he was dead, and wondering, as I lay in my
bed, just where he was at that moment. It was inconceivable to
me that he would just cease to exist.

Flesh and bones and blood—mere matter—cannot account

for love. Or loyalty. Or sacrifice. There had to be something more, but I couldn't put it all together.

EMILY, Susan, and I were eating breakfast the next morning when Susan got a text from Nate. "He wants to debrief at ten o'clock, which is good because I have to write the report today."

"Where?" I asked.

"The motel has a small meeting room we can use. Checkout time is at eleven, so why don't we pack up and check out before that."

Fine with me. I was ready to go as soon as I saw Nate was okay.

I checked out and had everything in my Jeep except Luke. I thought it was too warm for him to be in there, even with the liftgate up. So, I took him into the motel conference room with me and found Emily and Susan clustered around the coffeepot.

Nate walked in at about 9:50 a.m. with Sprite, who wagged her tail like crazy. He looked exhausted, but he made it a point to ask about each of us—were we able to get some rest, how were the dogs, and stuff like that. It was like we were the ones who'd spent a hard night alone in the forest.

Scott Cooper entered after Nate. I shot him a look, still angry with him. Tom arrived and then some of the deputies. Apparently, we were all debriefing together.

The lead sheriff's deputy, Roger something or other, took control of the briefing. He asked Nate to start.

I had tensed up as soon as the guys walked in. Even though I was "just a dog handler," I decided to ask questions. To this day, I'm not sure why.

Nate reported that it had taken Sprite less than ten minutes to find Sandy's body. It looked like she'd been tossed off the cliff he'd rappelled down.

"So, she wasn't posed?" I asked.

He frowned a little when he answered, "No."

Another deputy said they were still questioning the man they'd picked up the night before. He'd admitted to shooting his rifle, but said he thought he was shooting at a bird. As far as they could tell, he wasn't connected to the dead woman, and his intent was not to shoot Nate or any of the rest of us. But their investigation would continue.

"Have you retrieved the slug shot toward Nate?" I asked. I peppered them with more questions. Were they doing ballistics testing? Was there any connection between him and Sandy Smith at all? What kind of rifle did he have? What kind of scope?

I could feel people staring at me. Like a reactive dog, I was on my toes.

I glanced toward Cooper to gauge his response.

Roger said the body was in the process of recovery even as we talked. Doc, the medical examiner, and his crew and the evidence techs had been able to get to the site by four-wheelers.

As for the SAR team, Nate said, "I think our mission is about wrapped up."

That was our cue to exit. Susan and Emily were all too happy to leave. I followed behind them but stopped as Nate called out to me.

"Hey, Jess, you doin' all right?" he asked.

I looked over my shoulder in the hallway and stopped. "I'm fine. I was worried about you."

"Once that shootin' stopped, me and Sprite found a good place to set up. Lit a fire. Made dinner." He smiled. "It was good. Peaceful."

Peaceful. Seriously?

"Then Cooper joined us." Nate nodded behind me. "Speaking of which ..."

I turned. Cooper walked toward us. Immediately, the muscles in my jaw tightened. I wondered why he hadn't stayed in the room with the other officers.

"You asked some good questions, Jess," he said.

I didn't like the way he was looking at me. I shrugged. "I'm an investigator." Then I turned to Nate. "How'd Sprite do?"

While he told the story about his dog and their night together, I could still feel Cooper's eyes on me. Pressure built in my back muscles, like a big lizard was climbing up my spine. I knew any minute my body would start trembling.

"What made you think about what kind of scope was used?" Cooper said, interrupting Nate.

My heart thumped in my ears. Luke must have sensed my stress, because he shoved his muzzle in my hand. "I thought it was important to know. He could have been lying. I mean, if he had a good scope, he would have seen what he was shooting at." I jutted out my chin to convey confidence. "I'm surprised you didn't think of that."

I turned back to Nate, hoping he'd pick up the conversation again, but he was staring at Cooper. The pause in the conversation seemed like a yawning black hole. I felt myself slipping in.

I had to get out of there. "Well, I'll see you later," I said, gathering Luke's leash. I turned to leave.

"Jessica!" Cooper said.

I turned. His face was flush.

"Jessica Chamberlain! I remember now. I know who you are. You're that cop—the Fairfax County detective. The one who let the suspect slip his cuffs and kill your partner. How in the *world* did that happen?"

A bomb went off inside me, blowing out my guts and scrambling my brain. I looked at him, horrified, and then at Nate. I turned and ran. I heard angry voices behind me. I could barely breathe.

My feet hardly touched the ground. Luke scrambled to keep up. I opened the back of the Jeep, ordered him into his crate, and slammed the liftgate. Then I jumped in the driver's seat and cranked over the engine.

Nate emerged from the building, running toward me. "Jess! Jess!" I heard him call. I jerked my Jeep into gear and pulled away, burning rubber. He pursued me, but I kept driving. Anger raged in me.

Anger and panic are a volatile mix.

I hit the state road at about sixty-five, well above the posted speed limit, and careened down the mountain blindly. All that I feared had come upon me. I was exposed. I trembled so hard I could almost hear my bones rattling.

I went too fast around a curve, crossed the centerline, and nearly hit an oncoming SUV. I overcorrected and felt my tires slip off the road's edge. I gripped the wheel with both hands, pulled back onto the road, and felt the Jeep fishtail. Somehow, I got it under control again.

The vehicle was under control. Not me.

Shame poured through me, sizzling like lava as it hit my blood. The voices of accusers screamed in my head. Lee Park had died because of me. Me! It was my fault. My incompetence. I'd never live that down.

Cooper knew. Nate knew. Now everybody knew.

My tires screeched around another curve. I was still headed down, down, down toward the foothills. I felt the car rock, nearly breaking its grip on the road. Another curve lay ahead of me. Straight ahead stood a gigantic, solid tree. A thought flashed in my mind. *Why not drive straight into it and stop the pain?*

Yes!

Then Luke banged in his crate, and I knew that, although I could kill myself, I could not kill my dog.

I let up on the gas. My Jeep settled.

Tears gushed down my face. I sobbed. I groped for a napkin.

How I managed to see well enough to drive, I'll never know. I steered toward home, missed my exit, and kept going for an hour more, only half paying attention to the highway, my thoughts coming in short bursts, my tears still streaming down my face. The whip of shame drove me relentlessly.

When I realized I had driven in a large circle, when fatigue blurred my vision, I gave up. I had to go home. There was nowhere else to go.

I found my way down familiar backcountry roads and pulled into my driveway. I released Luke from his crate. I didn't bother to go inside. Instead, I curled up in one of the Adirondack chairs in the yard. Luke sniffed around for a while as I stared blankly ahead. He found a ball somewhere and brought it to me, but I didn't feel like playing. I wrapped my arms around my legs and rested my head on my knees. I wished I could just go away.

My mother's words rang in my head. *Why in the world did you want to be a cop anyway? Didn't you know things like that could happen? Look what happened to your father!*

Visions of that dreadful night played over and over in my head—the darkness, the rain, the suspect, the fatigue, the pain, and my partner's dead eyes. I put my hands over my ears to block out the screams. My screams.

A car drove into the driveway. Nate got out along with Sprite. I buried my face in my knees. By the time he got to me, I was sobbing again and shaking.

He didn't say anything. He just sat down in the chair next to me. I could smell his Old Spice cologne and see the mud on his boots, and in one single unselfish moment, I wondered if he'd gotten any rest at all.

"Go away," I said. I knew he wouldn't. Instead, he reached over and took my hand.

We must have sat there for twenty minutes before I finally stopped shaking and I finally spoke. My voice broke. "He was right."

"Tell me about it." Nate gently squeezed my hand.

"My partner ..." I hesitated and shook my head, unable to finish my sentence.

"Let's go inside."

I followed him into my apartment and curled up on the couch. He made tea. He was good at making tea.

The dogs flopped down near each other. Nate put a steaming mug on the end table next to me, then sat on the floor with his back leaning against the couch. It was like he knew the telling would come easier if we weren't face-to-face.

He was right. The story spilled out. "We were both detectives. Lee was the old pro; I was the young hotshot." My mind went back to that time, to Lee Park's kindness, his humor, and my enthusiasm. I loved going to work every day.

"So we go out one night to interview a witness on a homicide case. We're talking to this woman when her live-in boyfriend shows up unexpectedly. He's immediately hostile. He asks us to leave. So we do, but we hesitate on the front porch, because we can tell this guy is really angry.

"Next thing you know, we hear her screaming. So we go back in, and he's choking her. She's blue, her eyes rolling back, and we intervene to stop him. Once he's facedown on the floor, I cuff him. We decide not to wait for the uniforms and take him in ourselves.

"The guy was maybe five feet ten and strong. We put him in the back of our unmarked car. No cage. We're on a four-lane road in a wooded area, and I'm driving in the pouring-down rain. Suddenly, I see motion out of the corner of my eye. I hear a gasp and turn. The suspect is choking Lee! Somehow, he had gotten his cuffs out in front. He's killing my partner!

"I pull to the right shoulder, throw the car in park, and reach for my gun. Then I hear brakes screeching and a crash and ... and we roll over and over. When I wake up, I'm all bloody. My arm is broken, and my partner Lee is staring at me with these ... lifeless eyes." I started shaking again, weeping softly.

"It took them fifteen hours to find us. Fifteen hours of drifting in and out of consciousness, aware of two things—my pain and Lee's lifeless eyes."

"What happened to the suspect?"

"He got away. He's still on the run. He had lied to that woman about his name, where he worked, everything. She'd met him in a bar and invited him home. I've spent the last two years wondering—did I secure the cuffs correctly? Did I pull off the road all the way? What happened? Why didn't the truck that hit us stop?

"My partner died, and I hate myself for that. He had a wife and an eight-year-old boy. And a dog."

"Luke?"

I burst into tears again. "Yes!" It took me a bit to get control. "Luke flunked out of tactical training. He wouldn't bite. Lee found out about him and wanted to try him on search and rescue. He loved that dog! Talked about him all the time. But Luke was too much dog for Lee's widow. When I went to visit her, Luke was confined in a small backyard run. She didn't know what to do with him. When I saw that, I volunteered to take him. It was the least I could do."

"You eventually went back to work?"

"Yes and ... it was bad."

"The other cops?"

I nodded. "Lee was popular. But the guys, they resented me. Like I had jumped the line. Gotten promoted unfairly."

"They blamed you for Lee's death."

I nodded.

"But the internal review didn't."

"No, it cleared me. But I couldn't get away from the notes in my locker, the talk, the rude comments. And if things weren't bad enough, somebody posted the part of the report that said my blouse was ripped open, as if the suspect ..." I couldn't finish. It was too obscene. Too humiliating. I shivered and sat up straight, horrified by my own recollections. I had never, ever told anyone else about that. Not even my mother.

I blew my nose. "Six months later, I left. I'd wanted to be a cop since I was twelve, and I failed."

"It wasn't your fault, Jess. Suspects get loose. It happens."

"It was my fault! It was. What's more, I'm not tough enough. I couldn't cut it." I started sobbing. "I couldn't handle the harassment."

I braced myself for more comforting words, words I would fight. But that's not what happened.

Through my tears, I saw Nate drop his head. Then he rose to his knees and turned toward me. I shut my eyes. My heart trembled like an aspen leaf.

"Breathe deeply, Jess. In through your nose for four, hold it for seven, blow it out for eight."

I followed his instructions.

"In for four, hold for seven, out for eight," he repeated.

I felt him put his gentle hand on my head, felt its warmth, like a helmet protecting me. I heard his voice and realized he was not talking to me, he was praying. Too upset to follow what he was saying, I concentrated on the breathing. In for four, hold for seven, out for eight.

He put his thumb right between my eyes in the spot where I'd seen him rub Sprite and Luke. His hand on my head, his thumb between my eyes, his voice—they were conduits of peace. I could almost feel it flowing into me like warm syrup. My heart beat slower.

In for four, hold for seven, out for eight. I leaned into Nate's compassion, wrapping it around myself like a quilt. As my tears subsided, he took his hand off my head and rocked back on his heels. But he didn't quit praying. I was amazed he could find so much to say.

But then, I was a mess.

25

NATE SLEPT on my couch that night. I offered him the bed and said I'd take the couch, but he would have none of it. The next morning over breakfast I thanked him for helping me.

"When you bring something like that into the light, it diffuses the power of it," he said.

I cocked my head.

"I told you. I've been through it. I tried keeping it all in, hidin' how much I was hurtin'. I wore an angry mask until I couldn't anymore." Nate shifted his jaw, measuring his next words. "Then when I started speaking what was in here..." he placed his fist on his chest, "it helped the healin' start."

I quickly rejected his analogy. "But Nate, you didn't *do* anything! You got hit with an RPG, that's all." I reddened immediately. "I didn't mean that the way it sounded. What I meant was you weren't guilty, not like me. I as much as killed my partner."

"Did you intentionally fail to cuff your suspect properly? Did you intentionally wreck your car? Hurt your partner?"

"No, of course not."

"Then that's false guilt, same as I was carryin'. False guilt and shame." He rose to his feet. "We all got plenty to feel guilty about, but what happened with Lee, that ain't part of it for you."

Plenty to feel guilty about?

He didn't explain further, and I didn't ask. Instead, he made it very clear to me that if I thought about hurting myself, I was to call him at once. I rolled my eyes as if he were being dramatic.

I didn't tell him about the tree.

He stopped me with a look. "I been there, Jess. I know. Sometimes the devil puts it in your mind your life ain't worth livin'. That's a lie. A damnable lie."

I watched as Nate cleaned my little kitchen area, washing dishes, putting food away. Sometimes he was a puzzle. He simultaneously drew me to himself and scared me.

Nate stayed pretty close over the following few days. I didn't want to leave the house, and he seemed to know that. He ran the dogs and brought me groceries. Best of all, he let me take the lead on initiating conversations, some of which were deep.

"Do you still have them, the dreams?" I asked him one day.

"Once in a while, when somethin' reminds me," he responded.

"Like what?"

"Fire."

"But you burn wood."

"I mean fire out of control—a house fire, a car fire, a forest fire." He took a deep breath. "Once we responded to a search for human remains in a fire. That set me back weeks. Couldn't sleep, couldn't eat." He shook his head. "You never forget the smell of burning flesh. Especially, when it's your own."

I shivered thinking about that.

"I b'lieve it was the sound of those cars crashing that set you back that night we did the training."

I nodded. "Yes." I stared off to the side of the room, seeing that night, envisioning my panic. "I was okay as long as I had something to do. When I stopped, that's when it hit." I looked at him. "How do I get past that? Or will I?"

He eyed me as if considering what to say. "For me it was Peter's friendship, counseling, and finding God."

"I had counseling."

"We can always use more. Plus, you didn't have a friend you could open up to. Now you do."

He left out the God part. I decided to add it for him. "And the whole God-thing, I know." I ran my hands down my jeans. "I need practical help, not some pie-in-the-sky talk about an invisible being."

Nate's jaw tightened. My glib comments had offended him. I looked away, unable to face him. When I looked back, instead of anger, his eyes brimmed with compassion.

He stood up and gestured. "It's time you get out of this house. Let's go for a run."

At the word "run," both dogs jumped up, and Luke barked twice. I didn't move.

"Come on," Nate said. "Get your shoes on. You can't stay inside forever." He grinned. "You said you wanted practical help. This is it. Get up! Let's go."

Luke came over and nudged me. I muttered a protest, but I launched myself to my feet.

That was the first of what would be many runs. Nate would come before work, after work, whenever he could get away and drag me out in the woods to run. And we'd talk. He'd share some country story or a bit of wisdom, tell a joke or make some crazy comment that was sure to get me riled up.

He was slowly drawing me out of my shell ... until something made me clam right up.

We were sitting in my Adirondack chairs on a beautiful evening after a five-mile run. The dogs lay sprawled out on the grass, happily panting. Now and again, one would lumber over to the water bucket I had set out for them and slurp noisily.

The sky at dusk was a beautiful, deep blue, and stars were popping out here and there. A gentle evening breeze caressed my skin. I was actually feeling relaxed when I heard a car pull into the driveway. I assumed it was my landlord Bruce. It was dark enough I couldn't see past the headlights, even shading my eyes, but when the car pulled toward us and not around to the front, I knew it was not him.

Nervous, I glanced at Nate, but he appeared calm. The door opened and the dome light came on. Scott Cooper.

I started to get up, but Nate put his hand on my arm. "Just wait," he said gently. He stood up. "Scott," he said, shaking Cooper's hand. "Have a seat." He offered his own chair.

I did *not* want to be alone with that man! I stood to my feet, then Cooper gestured. "Both of you ... sit," he said. "I won't be here long."

Luke sensed my stress. He got up from where he'd been sleeping, came over, and lay down at my feet. The warmth of his body was a comfort to me. I crossed my arms, hoping to stop the trembling before it started.

Thump, thump, thump. My heart beat like a bass drum, sounding out my fear, my shame, my anger.

Cooper cleared his throat. "Just a couple of things." He squatted down so he was more on eye level with us. "Jessica," he said, shaking his head, "I've been accused of having no filter. I say things I shouldn't. I was blunt and rude to you. I assumed what I heard was true and that wasn't fair. I'm sure I hurt you, and I am sorry."

His words hit my ears like horseflies buzzing and bouncing off. I wanted to swat them away. Why did he think my wounds could be healed with cheap words?

Scott reached down and plucked up some grass, fingering it. "I was wrong. This friend of yours," he said, gesturing toward Nate, "nearly decked me for talking to you that way."

"That I did," Nate said.

"He was right, and I am truly sorry. Second," Cooper said, "I wanted to thank you both for your help in this case. Because of what you found, we've been able to open an FBI investigation. It was the evidence you uncovered that established the link between these deaths and allowed me to do that. Having an official case opens up a lot of resources—profilers, fast-track forensics, extra personnel. So thank you."

Nate waited for me to respond, and when I didn't, he said, "Glad to help you, Scott. Hope you find this dude quickly." He rubbed his beard. "You figure out why this one's different? Why he didn't pose her, if it's the same guy?"

"I think so."

My ears perked up. I just could not turn off the investigator in me.

Scott picked up some grass and started drawing it out of his hand, blade by blade, and throwing it on the ground. "I interviewed the guy who took that potshot at you. We had cleared him for the murders, but when I pushed him, he remembered something interesting. He'd been in the woods the day after Sandy disappeared when he came across this guy on top of the cliff. He seemed out of place. Nervous. Said he was looking for his dog but Jackson—the shooter—saw the guy didn't have a leash or anything. Just a knife on his belt."

I was in such a dark mood I was only half-listening, but Scott's words triggered a memory. When I'd searched the suspect that dreadful night, after I'd cuffed him, I found a knife on his belt, an unusual one. Distracted by that, had I missed something else, a handcuff key, maybe? Hidden in a pocket?

I shook my head to dislodge the fresh shame and forced myself to listen to Scott.

"So the guy seemed off, and Jackson got concerned, and left quickly. He'd forgotten about it, though, until I talked to him again."

"So maybe Jackson interrupted the murderer and that's why he threw the body off the cliff?"

"That's what we're thinking." Scott rose. "Jess, again, I'm really sorry."

I nodded and hoped he didn't see it in the dark.

Nate stood. "Let us know if we can help."

"I sure will." Cooper turned and walked to his car. When he started the ignition, his headlights were so bright I felt as though they were searching every inch of me. I got up abruptly and walked into my apartment.

Nate followed me. I heard the door close behind him. "It took a lot for him to do that. He's a proud man."

I turned to him. "Don't even think about lecturing me on forgiveness. Don't even go there."

Nate raised his eyebrows.

Something flashed in my mind—the feeling of his hand on my head, his thumb between my eyes, his voice softly praying. My face grew hot, and I turned away.

"I 'spect I should be goin'. Thanks for the run." He hesitated. "You going to be okay?"

I took a deep breath, trying to get hold of my emotions. I faced him. "Yeah, thanks."

He nodded and started to leave. At the door, he turned and looked at me. "You want practical? Just so you know, forgiveness is one of the most practical things a body can do." And then he left.

26

As SCOTT COOPER walked into the Behavioral Analysis Unit, his mind flashed back to his new-agent training at the FBI Academy eleven years before. He and Suzanne had been married for two years. Amanda was just eighteen months old.

Maybe it had been selfish of him to pursue his dream of becoming an agent. Maybe he was single-minded and obsessed as his wife had claimed.

Still, he had loved every minute of his training. The classes, the camaraderie, the physical challenges ... even the pepper-spray test, in which he'd had to defend himself and protect his gun after being sprayed in the face with capsaicin. It had been brutal, but he survived. In fact, he thrived at the Academy. In the end, he was elected class spokesman.

At the time, he'd hoped his wife would be proud. She wasn't. She'd sat with his parents at graduation and smiled and nodded at the reception, but when they were alone, she'd complained. A lot.

The fact that his first office assignment was New York didn't help. She was a California girl born and bred and living in a big East Coast city so far from her family seemed to keep her perpetually angry. Five years later, their marriage blew up altogether, forcing him to become a long-distance dad.

All those thoughts streamed across his mind like a tickertape. Up and down, good news and bad, day after day.

He shook his head to dislodge those thoughts, walked up to a receptionist, and identified himself. Gary Taylor, she said, was waiting.

Taylor was an old-school profiler, or behavioral analyst as they preferred to be known. Tall, gray-haired, and angular, he sat at the walnut conference table next to Scott going over the evidence from the file—the crime scene and autopsy reports, photos, police reports.

"Tell me again how you got involved in this?" Taylor asked.

Scott told him about victim number two, the body the dog found, and then noticing the similarities with the older case from near Warrenton. He didn't tell Taylor about how his gut twisted at the thought of these murders, about the similarity of the victims to his sister.

Another agent entered the room. "Colleen Baker," she said, introducing herself. She looked over Taylor's shoulder at the pictures spread out over the table. "A serial murderer?"

"We think so," Scott said.

"Is there a signature?"

"Two of the three were posed, lying on their backs in clearings deep in the woods. They looked almost peaceful," Scott said.

"How about this third one?" Baker pointed to the body of Sandy Smith.

"Her neck was broken like the other two."

"But she was, what? Thrown off a cliff?"

"It's possible the guy was interrupted and had to get rid of her quickly," Taylor said.

Scott nodded. "Thing is, near victims two and three, we found a little pile of wood shavings. It was weird."

"But not victim one," Baker said.

"Right."

"And none of them were sexually assaulted."

"Correct." Scott looked at the two profilers and took a deep breath. "So what's your process? Where do we go from here?"

Taylor and Baker looked at each other. "We'll take a few days to analyze what's here. You'll want to do victimology on all three victims. We'll help you set up a couple of questionnaires for investigators to use for that," Taylor said. "Then we'll sit in on any meetings you have and help you analyze what you've discovered."

Scott nodded. "This could take weeks." He was thinking about his daughter's upcoming visit.

"At least."

Scott drew in a deep breath. "In the meantime, would you say we're looking at an organized or disorganized killer?" He knew a little.

Taylor pursed his lips. "Based on the posing? And the fact their bodies were transported to a specific place? Possibly organized, but I'll reserve judgment on that."

"So if he's organized, we're talking what? An educated person? Average or above-average intelligence? What?"

The two profilers looked at each other. "It's too soon to be definitive," Baker said, "but organized killers are the ones who plan attacks, who use ruses or ambush strategies to snare their victims. They're street-smart but may or may not be intelligent." She folded her hands. "Tell you what. Give us some time to look over this, and then we'll be ready to meet with your team. Sound good?"

What choice did he have?

Scott walked out of the building feeling weighed down. "Weeks" seemed like a long time. But he knew it could actually be years, or never.

He got in his vehicle and checked his watch. Five o'clock. When he pulled out of the parking lot, his thoughts nagged at him. Then, on impulse, instead of heading toward home, he headed southwest.

An hour later, his tires crunched over gravel as he drove down the tree-lined driveway toward Nate Tanner's house. He'd stopped on the way and picked up barbeque at a place Nate said he liked when he called him to see if it was okay to stop by.

As Scott pulled up, the dog came barking at his car. He saw Nate on the south side of the house. He was splitting wood, lifting a log, placing it on a thick stump, then driving his axe down through it. A pile of firewood lay to his right. He had his shirt off, and even from the car Scott could see the sweat glistening on his back.

It wasn't until Scott walked closer that he saw the scars. He took a deep breath, absorbing his shock, before saying, "Hey."

Nate drove the axe through the oak log and threw the pieces on the woodpile. "How's it going?" He squinted in the bright light.

"It's going." Scott held up the bag of food. "Ready to eat?"

"Sure. Meet you on the front porch."

Scott walked up the six steps at the front of Nate's cabin. The honey-colored wood seemed so natural. He wondered what it took to keep the bugs out of it. He set the food down on the small table and sat down.

"Hey, dog," he said, holding out his hand to Nate's springer. She had followed him onto the porch, but Scott couldn't remember her name.

The dog sniffed his hand, her tail wagging, then turned as the door opened and Nate emerged from the house, wearing an army-green shirt and carrying two glasses in his hands. "Lemonade okay?" he asked, setting them on the table.

Scott grinned. "You trying to turn me into a teetotaler?"

"Wouldn't hurt."

Nate sat down and said grace before they began working on the pulled-pork sandwiches Scott had brought. The sun had dropped behind the house, casting a long shadow on the front lawn. He soaked in the peacefulness of Nate's place, the black-and-white dog lying on the porch, her ball at her nose; the rich, green garden; the woodpile promising heat in the winter.

But he couldn't get his mind off the scars on Nate's body. "What happened to you?"

Nate raised his eyebrows.

"Those burn scars."

"RPG. Afghanistan."

"Wow." He shook his head. "That must have been hell to get over."

"Changed my life, it did. And not all in bad ways." Nate took a big drink of lemonade. "So what's up with you, Scott? Why the visit?"

Nate's question pulled Scott out of his own murky thoughts about pain and suffering and the purpose of it all. He put down his sandwich, wiping the grease off his fingers on a napkin, and began telling Nate about BAU and profiling and organized versus disorganized killers. He talked about signatures and forensics and patterns of behavior. He talked about the time it would take to identify a suspect.

Talking about that stuff put him back in his wheelhouse, in control, and he liked that. "So, they said the posing—that and some other stuff—trends toward an organized killer, someone who uses ruses, who plans his attacks, someone with street smarts. So my question is, how does that fit with someone who sits on a log cutting wood with a knife?"

Nate rubbed his beard and stared out across the field in front of his house as if the answer would emerge from the grass like a butterfly taking flight. "Most folks who like to whittle come from the country. It's a nervous habit, or they're getting ready to make a fire, or they just like cutting wood." He looked straight at Scott. "Maybe that fact is an outlier—or the rest of it is."

"You mean their assumptions?" He picked up his sandwich.

Nate shrugged. "I haven't studied murderers. I'm looking at it in a different way. These girls were carried deep in the woods. Who does that? Someone who's familiar with the woods, knows how not to get lost, and isn't afraid of what's back there. So I'd be looking for a hunter. A woodchuck—"

"Woodchuck?" Scott took the last bite of his sandwich and wiped his mouth.

"Someone who cuts and sells firewood by the truckload, usually in the suburbs. I'd be looking for someone like that, or maybe even a hiker. Park ranger." Nate shifted his jaw. "The guy's strong too. Think about it. Carrying even a hundred-pound body deep in the woods—that's not easy."

"So what's with the wood chips?"

Nate shrugged. "Maybe he needs to think a while. Maybe he's not ready to leave her. Maybe he's recovering from his hike." He reached in his pocket and pulled out his pipe. "I sit and stick this in my mouth a lot. Don't even smoke it. Just like the comfort of it. Maybe he's that way with a knife and whittlin'." He put the pipe back in his pocket.

Scott thought about Nate's theory, trying to fit what he knew about serial killers with what the dog man said.

"God knows who this guy is," Nate said after a pause. "I'll pray he'll let you know too."

A flash of anger pushed Scott to his feet. He walked over to the porch railing and leaned against a post while he stared out into the yard. The dog nudged her ball. He picked it up and threw it, launching it across the front field. Sprite went racing after it.

Nate whistled. "You play baseball?"

"Pitcher," Scott said, turning to Nate, "in high school and college."

"You try out for the majors?"

Scott shook his head. "I got scouted, but I knew what I wanted —the Bureau." He took a deep breath. "Can I try my hand at your axe?"

"Sure!" Nate rose. "Let me put this stuff in the trash, and I'll meet you out back." He picked up the remains of their meal.

Scott walked around to the side of the house. He'd swung an axe before, in Scouts, but it had been a long time. He lifted the axe, felt the blade, and jiggled the head to make sure it was secure. Then he picked up an oak log and set it on the stump. As Nate walked out of the house, he swung the axe over his head and planted it in the log. It split with a loud *crack!*

"Not bad," Nate said, grinning. He picked up the two pieces and threw them on the woodpile. "I'll set 'em up for you."

They worked together for the next half hour, Nate lifting logs onto the stump, Scott splitting them. Some of them were big enough he needed to make multiple cuts. But the feel of the axe in his hand, the sound of it hitting the wood, and the smell of freshly cut oak affected him right down to the core.

With every new log, Scott felt the challenge; with every *crack,* he felt his strength. Helplessness and frustration flowed out of him in his sweat. Finally, chest heaving, he held the axe and looked at Nate. "We never found the guy who killed my sister." Scott wiped his brow with his arm, glancing at Nate as he did.

Nate's eyes widened. "Your sister?"

He fought the inevitable nausea, closed his eyes, and nodded. Then he gestured toward the stump, and Nate put another log on it.

"When was this?" Nate asked.

Crack!

"I was seventeen. So, nineteen years ago."

The oak made a solid *thud* as Nate pitched the pieces on the pile, picked up a new log, and set it in place.

Crack!

"Snuck out one night to see a boy and never came home. We found her body the next day in a park. She'd been raped and strangled." Even now he could feel the weight in his chest and the stinging in his eyes.

"That's terrible."

Crack!

His breath was coming hard now. "So, all I'm saying is, God may know who this killer is, but he may just keep that to himself. Like he did ..."

Crack!

"... like he did my sister's."

Nate didn't argue with him. "You joined the Bureau to try to find that guy?"

"No, to put as many of those guys away as I could. But no matter how hard I work," Scott said, "the murders just keep coming." Sweat rolled down between his shoulder blades.

"And the pain doesn't go away," Nate added for him.

Scott didn't answer. He couldn't. A snake had wrapped itself around his voice.

Nate put the last log on the stump. Scott hit it hard. Three times. Then he drove the axe into the stump itself, deep enough for it to stick. He wiped his hands on his khakis. "Thanks, Nate."

"Yeah, man." Nate cocked his head, looking at him with those bright blue eyes. Scott looked away, unable to hold his gaze. The snake squeezed again. The dog man clapped him on the shoulder and kept his hand there for a minute. "You want to talk about it?"

He shook his head. "Nah."

"Now, or any time," Nate said. "I'm available."

"I gotta get home." Scott turned toward his car, then stopped. "I don't get it. She was just a normal girl. Why her?"

"That's the question. It's hard, Scott, what you been through."

Scott took two more strides toward his car, then turned. "How's Jessica doing?"

"She's got some healing to do."

Scott shook his head. "I talked to a friend in Fairfax. Jess got a raw deal. I'm sorry I added on to that."

Nate nodded. "I'll tell her you asked after her."

27

TWO WEEKS after my mad dash down the mountain, I still felt raw from Scott's exposing me. "Exposing" is what it felt like anyway. They say love is the strongest force in the universe. I think it might be shame.

I was also ashamed of my idiotic response. I could have killed someone driving down the mountain like that. Just thinking of it made my stomach clench.

With all my failures, I found it amazing that Nate hadn't given up on me. He'd seen my craziness, but he'd remained steady. Like an anchor.

Still, I worried. Had Scott said anything to anyone else? Had Emily heard what I'd done? Susan? SAR volunteers were tough people, almost like cops. Once word got out, was I going to face the same kind of rejection from them as I had from my fellow LEOs in Fairfax? Would I have the courage to face them at the next callout?

Luke had slept in my bed every night the last two weeks, pressing his body against my legs, comforting me. He seemed to accurately read my stress levels. I could only imagine he was picking up some pheromone I was giving off.

Making myself a cup of tea, I found myself thinking. Every success in my life, including my agility career, all the awards I got from my work as a law-enforcement officer, and the accolades for finding Joey Washburn, every one was overshadowed by my enormous failure. I'd failed to protect my partner. He died on my watch. Something I'd done—my failure to cuff our suspect properly or my failure to pull completely off the road—had ended Lee Park's life. And now, his dead eyes haunted me.

There were a lot of other little failures, too, if I were honest. A lot.

I wondered, how did anyone ever balance the books? Was I doomed to live with the shame of my failures until I died? How could I carry that weight?

I'd always thought achievement was the key. After all, pride, or self-esteem was the coin of the realm in my generation and nothing feeds that like achievement.

It seemed to me now as I stirred honey into my tea that pride was a poor antidote to shame. Pride could not balance the books.

But what would?

I sat on the couch and thought about Nate, about the way he'd sat on the floor as I poured out my story. He was a good listener. And compassionate. I appreciated that.

I opened the drawer of the end table and took out the business card Nate had left me, the one for the psychologist. He said she had helped him a lot. Maybe that's why he was so steady. He'd been through this, or so he said. Yet, he seemed so well-balanced.

I fingered the card. Then I put it back and closed the drawer.

The thought of spilling my guts to another counselor filled me with dread. I could handle this myself, I decided. I just needed to move on. Let the past be past. Buck up, Buttercup.

After all, remember all your successes!

After that pep talk, I picked up the remote and flipped on the TV, zoning out on Netflix until I thought I could sleep, then I went to bed. That night in my dreams, we were not searching victoriously for a little boy. We were chasing a bad guy or being chased by him. In the end, I laid on my back in a little clearing, my face melting into the earth.

Luke found me, just as he had found Faith. And when he licked me, I woke up, tears on my face, and I wrapped my arms around my big dog like a scared three-year-old.

The next day, I pulled out that business card again. This time, I made the call.

28

FIVE DAYS LATER, on a sweltering hot July day, Scott Cooper held a meeting at BAU for everyone involved in what he now called the Caldwell investigation. Once word got out, he knew the press would come up with a catchier name.

The two analysts attended, along with the principal investigators in the Sandy Smith and Julie Mitchell cases, representatives from the appropriate local prosecutors' offices, and a couple of FBI agents.

Looking around the room before the meeting began, an odd thought popped into his head. He wished he'd been able to invite Jessica Chamberlain. Her ideas had broken the Sandy Smith case. She was smart, and she had a good investigative brain. He still felt bad about the abrupt way he'd spoken to her. And yes, he'd apologized, but he didn't think it had taken. He'd called her twice over the last couple of weeks, but she hadn't returned his calls.

Pushing those thoughts aside, he introduced himself and the BAU analysts to the assembled group, then having each officer explain his or her connection to the group. After that, the BAU people gave some introductory remarks. When they were finished, he passed out the questionnaires BAU had helped him develop.

"I've emailed these to you as well," he told the team, "but I wanted you to see what we're looking for. We need to study the victims in detail, as well as the locations they were last seen. On the sheets I passed out, you'll see lots of questions about the women—their habits, their personalities, their social contacts. Were they gregarious? The type of person who would automatically trust a stranger? Did they tend to be oblivious to their surroundings? And so on. We need to figure out how the UNSUB gained access to them.

"Please try to develop information through best friends or work associates—someone other than the parents. They often know less about their kids than anyone else."

Several people chuckled at that, but Scott knew from personal experience it was all too true. Neither he nor his parents had known about the boy his sister snuck out to meet.

A woman in the back raised her hand. "What aspect will you be concentrating on?"

"I'll handle the Caldwell investigation since she was found on federal property. I have agents out of Philly doing the interviews now. I'll also coordinate the ME reports and whatever information you feed me to see if we can find any link at all between these three women."

"Doesn't that seem unlikely, considering the places these women lived and, well, their educational and economic disparities?"

Scott drummed his thumb against his leg. "Yes, you're right. But we're going to ask all the questions anyway, just in case there's a link we're not seeing." He took a deep breath. "The second questionnaire focuses on location and time frame. We want to know how the subject picked his victims. Were these women targeted? Were drugs involved, or alcohol?

"So look at the location the victims were last seen and the

locations where the bodies were found. Discover everything you can about those places. Did anyone see them get into a vehicle? Anyone see someone on the roads nearest the places the bodies were dumped? Who owns the properties? Are there any hunting cabins or logging areas nearby? Work the time frame from about a week before the victims disappeared to a week after they were found."

"That's a lot of digging," an officer said.

"We need every bit of evidence we can find. That's the only way this case will be solved. Get what you can. Update me as facts develop. Don't talk to the press. And we'll meet again in two weeks."

After a couple more procedural questions, the meeting adjourned. As people shuffled out of the room, Scott could only hope someone came up with the key to this case before another young woman found herself staring into the eyes of this monster.

Scott's ASAC, the assistant special-agent in charge of his office, had assigned two other agents to help him. He'd get more later, he'd been told, if circumstances warranted it.

One guy he knew pretty well from the gym, Robert Hudson. An African-American from the Bronx, Robert had a reputation for being thorough. The other was a first-office agent, a woman from Chicago named Dana Danvers. She looked at Scott when the room was empty and said, "What do we do?"

"Sit down," Scott said, dropping into a chair. "Let's go through my list." The two agents found seats. "Here's what I need. 1. Any GPS information we can get from the victims' cars. Where they traveled, etc. 2. I want clear information on Sandy Smith's case. You know her car was found off the road. So did she just run off the road? Or did someone run her off? Did she survive the crash only to be abducted by this guy? Or was she badly hurt, or did she die in the crash, spoiling his plans?"

"Regarding Faith Caldwell, I want someone to go hang out at the coffee shop and ask customers if they noticed her. Jog their memories." He pulled pictures of Faith out of his briefcase and handed them to the agents. "Scope out the customers. I don't know who we're looking for, obviously, but I want to identify any guy who's big enough to kill a small woman and carry her a significant distance.

"Okay, now, her car was left on the shoulder of a nearby road. Local police impounded it and have gone through it. Make sure we have those reports, including the pictures. Had her car broken down? What made her get in the car with the UNSUB? Was she forced? Tricked? Was it a blitz attack? What?"

Robert and Dana were taking notes like mad. Scott kept talking. "We believe both Julie and Faith were dead when they were dumped in the woods where they were found. Was anything recovered on the scene that didn't belong to them? Was there evidence of premeditation, that is, precut bindings or gags, that sort of thing?" Scott looked up from his paper. "Basically, I want to know every blasted thing we can about these cases. And I want pictures of everything."

"Aerials?" Robert said.

"Good idea," Scott responded. "I'll ask aviation to fly over and shoot the sites." He ran his hand through his hair. "I want everything sooner rather than later."

Robert looked up, his brown eyes focused on Scott, his shaved head shiny under the lights. "I got the cars. Let me figure that out. Then I'll move on to something else."

Scott nodded. "Sure."

"What should I do?" Dana asked.

What could she handle? Scott wondered. She had short, dark hair and was about five-eleven, he figured. He'd heard she was a martial arts expert and could kick the guts out of anybody who tried messing with her. But she was also fresh out of the Academy. "You take the coffee shop. Go hang out there. Talk to the employees. Check out the regular customers."

"Got it."

"Let's go," Scott said, rising to his feet.

"Wait," Dana said, looking at her watch. "It's two o'clock. Should I wait until tomorrow?"

"What time was Faith at the coffee shop?" Robert asked. "That's your answer."

Dana shuffled through some papers. "Let's see..."

"Three-fifteen," Scott said, answering the question for her. "So go now and see who comes in for an afternoon caffeine hit."

Dana tossed her head. "Right."

She started to leave.

"Check in," Scott reminded her, "and clock your hours."

"Will I get overtime?"

Scott's eyes widened. He didn't bother to respond.

29

THE PSYCHOLOGIST RECOMMENDED by Nate was Sarah Pennington. A week later, I sat in her outer office filling out intake forms and wondering why in the world I had decided to put myself through this again.

Because I can't handle the anxiety attacks anymore. I need help.

Her office was on the first floor of an enormous, old Victorian house in downtown Charlottesville in an area populated mostly by University of Virginia students. It was summer, and many of them were gone, so I had no trouble finding a place to park. That would become a problem come fall, but I had no intention of continuing counseling that long.

A wreath of twisted vines and silk flowers hung on the door of the turreted house. A sign indicated it contained the offices of three other professionals—a dietician, another counselor, and one massage therapist.

Brown leather, split in some places, covered the chairs in Sarah Pennington's waiting room. They looked like she'd bought them at a thrift store. I tried not to be judgy, but really. A bubbling fish tank on a stand stood against one wall. On the other was a small, three-shelf bookcase that held a few self-help books, some magazines, and a bunch of brochures.

Apparently, a silent alarm or a video camera had alerted Ms. Pennington that I had arrived. A middle-aged woman with long blonde hair and a wide, open face popped her head out of the door to the inner office. "Jessica Chamberlain?"

I nodded.

"I'm Sarah Pennington." She handed me a clipboard, and said she'd be right with me.

Now here I sat, answering questions about my health, my purpose in making this appointment, my goals, and oddly, my religious beliefs. My health was good, and my goals were simple: I wanted to get rid of my bad dreams and end my anxiety attacks. (That's what Nate had called them, and I looked it up and figured he was probably right.) As for my religious beliefs, I sure hadn't come for a sermon, so I made that perfectly clear.

As I waited for my appointment, I thought about that last question. I saw too much organization in the universe and too much beauty in nature to think it all happened by chance, regardless of what brainiacs like Stephen Hawking said.

But my family didn't do church. I figured all religions were more or less the same. So if you were into that sort of thing, just choose one. The few times I had prayed, like when the Towers fell, nothing changed. So I'd decided I didn't need religion. I was on my own in life. Nate was not going to convince me otherwise.

A voice interrupted my thoughts. "Miss Chamberlain?" I quickly scribbled "none" under the religion question and stood up. "Welcome. Come in."

I wanted to do anything but walk into that office. Finally, I forced my feet to take those steps.

"Have a seat." She gestured toward a light-brown couch accented by a couple of bright pillows as she took her place in a classy, black-leather chair—an Eames knockoff I guessed. Beside her a bookshelf was crammed with weighty tomes, her old text-books maybe. The wall behind her held three framed posters, sayings of the sort you'd expect in a shrink's office. I didn't bother reading them. On her desk, which was to her left, my right, sat a six-inch wooden cross on a pedestal. It had a circle on it, right where the two pieces intersected. That was curious to me, but I was looking at the backside and couldn't figure out what that design was all about.

As I settled back, I noticed that next to the couch, to my left, was a huge basketful of stuffed animals, including a brown-and-white dog with floppy ears. I assumed those were for the kids she saw. But who knew? Maybe some adults were needy enough to want to hold them.

"What brings you here?" Sarah asked, fixing her gaze on me.

That's when I noticed her eyes. They were bright blue, like Nate's, and full of life. She couldn't be a relative, could she? I'd gotten the idea he'd seen her professionally. He wouldn't see a relative, would he?

I shook off my thoughts. Investigating Nate's social connections wasn't why I was here. Instead, I began telling my story, anger edging my words like fine steel on a knife. I was sick of my life being out of control, sick of the dreams, and sick of my fear. I was tired of worrying I'd fall apart at any moment, and I wanted a plan to end this mess I was in.

"Give me four points, five, even ten, and I'll do them," I said, sitting forward on the couch. "I'm very disciplined. Exercises, drugs, whatever—I just want all this to stop. I want my life back!"

Sarah had quietly listened, taken notes, nodded at times (in agreement, I presumed). She asked me about my home life, about my childhood, about my goals and ambitions, my friends, my beliefs, my social life.

Forty-five minutes later, I stood up to leave, proud I'd kept my composure and convinced I had been very clear. Sarah Pennington knew what I wanted.

"So tell me," I said, "what should I do? Give me a list; I'll get started."

Sarah looked at me, smiled, and said, "We're just going to keep talking for now."

I rolled my eyes. "I want to fix this quickly!"

"Our brains don't work that way," she said. "It takes time to work through things."

"I've spent enough time dealing with this mess!"

"I understand," she responded.

I jerked open the door.

"Jess," she added.

I turned.

"Expect things to get worse before they get better."

I drove home frustrated, wondering if I was wasting my time and money.

I had no idea that within three weeks, I would sit sobbing on that couch, clutching the brown-and-white stuffed dog as if it were real and could save me from the violent storm raging inside.

30

THAT APPOINTMENT with Sarah three weeks after I'd started left me shaking and anxious, scared to go on and afraid not to. I called Nate. He got me into this mess, so he could talk me off the ledge.

He came over, fixed tea, and listened as Sarah had, calmly and compassionately. At one point he told me to breathe, reminding me of the pattern—in for four, hold for seven, out for eight. After a while, he asked me a question. "Of all the people you're angry with, who is it hardest to forgive?"

"Myself," I answered without hesitation.

"Why?"

"I screwed up!" I yelled. "I deprived a woman of her husband, a son of his father. I let the bad guy win. And he's still winning."

Luke abandoned Sprite and climbed up on the couch with me. He draped his forefront across my lap, his head down, his eyes glancing around for whatever I thought was threatening me.

"What gives you the right to judge yourself so harshly? To condemn yourself?"

"If not me, who?" I exploded. Luke raised his head, then lowered it again. I knew the answer Nate wanted to hear. I just didn't want to say it. I began stroking my dog, thankful for the feel of his coat, for the rich colors, for the warmth of his body, for the diversion he provided.

Nate let some silence grow between us. My anxiety increased.

"That dog," he said, gesturing toward Luke, "he doesn't feel the same way about you as you do."

"He's a dog."

"You deprived him of his first owner."

"And I'm making it up to him!"

"Is that why you have him?"

His question stopped me short. I had to think about that. "No," I said, finally. "I love him." I leaned over and kissed the top of Luke's head. "That's why I have him."

"Ever make a mistake with him?"

"What does that have to do with anything?" I pushed back, trying to avoid the road Nate was leading me down.

"You're the one who asked me to come over," he said softly.

That was true. So I took a deep breath and said, "I lost my temper with him once, right after I got him. I had him off-leash in a park at dusk. I threw the ball toward the road, accidentally, and he went racing after it. I saw a car coming and screamed at him to come, but he didn't—he was focused on the ball. The car blasted its horn, and Luke stopped. But it scared me, and I was mad."

"And you ... "

I closed my eyes, momentarily, at the painful memory. "I jerked his collar, hard, when I got to him. I yelled at him. It was the completely wrong thing to do." I felt my face grow hot.

Nate didn't flinch. "What happened then? How'd he behave toward you?"

"He shook it off." Tears came to my eyes. "Three seconds later his tail was wagging." I pressed my cheek against the top of Luke's head. "I guess he forgave me."

"He gave you grace."

There was that word.

Something about that moment stirred Sprite, and she came over and climbed in Nate's lap. He was sitting on the floor, cross-legged, and he started stroking his dog's head. I sat mesmerized by his hand moving across her body.

Nate said softly, "Dogs see us for who we are. They don't expect us to be better than that. And they give us grace when we mess up."

"What do you mean, *grace*?" On another day, that would have been an angry snap, but today, vulnerability softened my tone.

"Grace is when you make a mistake, and the other person chooses to overlook it. It's forgiveness and forbearance mixed together. It's your dog loving you despite you mistreating him. It's … it's what God offers us through Christ."

I bristled. I groped for some way to redirect the conversation. "So this is when you tell me I need to give Scott grace. I need to forgive him."

"Scott, he's got his own burden to carry, a pretty heavy one."

I challenged him. "Like what?"

Nate bit his lip. He didn't take his eyes off Sprite. "It's his story to tell. Basically, his younger sister was murdered when he was seventeen." He looked up at me.

I blinked, trying to process what I'd just heard. "Wow."

"That's what's got him fixated on these murders; they're too much like his sister's. It's a hard road he's on too."

I swallowed hard, my throat tight. I thought about my little sister Brooke. I couldn't imagine losing my sister, as annoying as she can be. The weight of all the losses, of my dad, of Lee Park, of the three women, of Scott's sister, lay heavy on me. "How old was she?"

"Fifteen." Sprite wriggled into a different position on his lap. "There's lots going on in other people we cain't see. That's why givin' folks grace is a good idea."

I didn't know what to do with that, so I kept my face buried in Luke's fur.

"But sometimes, the hardest person to give grace to is your own self. You got to look outside yourself, to God. It's his love fueled by his grace that you need to receive."

"You pray for me, don't you?" I asked. There was bitterness in my voice.

"Oh, he's heard your name right much these last months," Nate said, grinning.

I shivered. I asked Luke to move, and I stood up. I'd had enough.

Nate got up too. "Want to go for a run?"

"No."

"Mind if I take the dogs out?"

"That's fine."

I just wanted to be by myself, away from Nate, away from the God-talk. In about a minute, I burst into tears and sobbed until my chest ached.

31

Scott Cooper stood over the walnut table in the conference room at his office, where he'd spread printouts from the Caldwell case. So far, they'd found absolutely no link between the victims, except for their general body type and hair color. They didn't know each other, didn't live near each other, didn't go to church together, hadn't dated the same man. They didn't even root for the same sports teams.

The only relevant thing they had in common was coffee. As far as Scott could tell, each one may have stopped for a cup of coffee before being abducted. But that didn't explain how the UNSUB actually abducted them.

Both Julie and Faith's cars had GPS units that tracked their locations. Faith's was already known—straight down I-95, around Washington, and off the exit in Prince William County, Virginia, where she stopped for a cup of coffee. Analysis of her GPS unit confirmed that. Her car was abandoned just up the road.

Julie had left Warrenton, where she'd stopped for coffee, and headed for 95 on back roads. Her car hit a tree on a two-lane road, about two miles from the woods where she was found.

And Sandy? Her car was too old to have a GPS, but Scott had

sent Robert Hudson on a hunt, and sure enough, security cameras at a different gas station—not Bobby's—showed her buying a cup of coffee about 10:25 p.m. the night she disappeared. Her car was found seven miles away.

He'd tasked Dana with following up on those leads, asking customers and staff if they'd seen the women or a big guy that same night. He'd told her to check security camera footage again as well.

The ME reports were consistent regarding body type. The three women were within an inch and a half in height and approximately ten pounds in weight of each other. Two, Julie and Faith, were strangled and had their necks broken. Sandy apparently died from a ruptured spleen. Plus, she had multiple fractures—ribs, arm, and ankle—along with a concussion. Scott's question was, did all that happen when her car rolled? If so, why did the UNSUB remove her from her crashed car?

One other forensic finding ... the women had not been raped, but none were wearing underwear. Did the UNSUB remove the underwear as a souvenir?

He'd asked the BAU people about that, and they'd factored it into their preliminary profile. They thought they were looking for a white male between the ages of thirty-five and forty-five, strong, probably into porn, and passive. He might have come across as a genial, helpful country boy.

There were only about a million guys who fit that description in the three-state area around Washington.

Dana was unsuccessful so far in developing anything more specific from the coffee shop leads, so he sent her on another quest. Remembering Nate's suggestion, he told her to check out woodchucks in the counties in Virginia around the crime scenes. Of course, she didn't know what a woodchuck was, but he explained it, and told her to pose as a homeowner inquiring about buying a cord of wood.

He could only hope she'd be able to pull that off.

Scott had one other thought, and for that, he called Nate. "Hey, Nate, what kind of knife do people use when they're whittlin'?"

"Well now," Nate said, "depends on how fancy you want to be. Most folks just use a pocketknife. The folks carving figures in wood, they're gonna use a whittlin' jack, like a Flexcut."

"Where do you find them? Outdoors stores?"

Nate laughed. "Walmart. Amazon. 'Bout anywhere."

Scott thanked him. They talked a little more and then hung up. He scratched his chin. Checking out whittlin' knives sold in the area would be a long shot but it might be worth doing.

There was so much to pursue.

Scott gathered up his papers and headed back to his own office, where he stashed them in an attaché case. He'd called Gary Taylor of BAU and asked if he could drop by about four. There were some facts he wanted to clarify, thoughts that kept him thinking late at night when he should have been sleeping.

Gary greeted him dressed in a white shirt and a tan, tweed-cardigan sweater over dark-brown dress pants. Scott suppressed a smile. The man looked like an academic, not a street agent, and he wondered about his background.

He was a good guy, though, and knowledgeable, and Scott gave him a pass on his soft clothes. After all, he spent all day studying criminals. It was his mind that needed to be tough, not his outfit.

"So what's up, Scott?" Gary asked. He gestured toward a chair across from his.

Scott sat down. "I've been thinking about the profile you all came up with. Something tells me this guy is an outlier, doesn't fit the mold."

"Why's that?"

"The wood shavings. The absence of rape. The clumsy way he's grabbing them contrasted with the aesthetic of their posing."

"So, what are you thinking?"

"I'm wondering, is he a psychopath? Or could he have been brain damaged—you know—by an accident or something? Did his brain development get stopped and now he has the physical drive to have a relationship with women but not the skills?"

"Those are good questions." Gary picked up a pen and held it in both hands while he thought. "There are a lot of things that can stop someone's social development. Brain damage, mild retardation, social factors like an abusive or alcoholic parent. Time in prison, actually. All those things can keep a person from developing social skills."

"So in the meantime, he's watching porn all the time and thinking that maybe he needs a woman who won't fight him."

"Like one that's small," Gary said. "Or even one that's dead. Then he poses her in an idealistic, Sleeping Beauty kind of way, because he's got this fantasy in his head."

Scott straightened his back. "And he sits there and whittles and fantasizes."

"Right."

"So, does he return to the site again and again?" Scott asked.

"Maybe, but only until the bugs and decay start in on the body."

"Because then she loses her ideal image."

"Yes." Gary scratched his chin. "Depending on the weather, that could only be a couple of days. The bugs get started pretty quickly."

"Right." Scott tapped his thumb on his leg.

"Serial killers are actually pretty rare. There's still a lot we don't know about them."

Scott rubbed his neck. "What I can't figure out is how he got these women to go with him. I mean, the others were on isolated rural roads, but Faith was abducted near the interstate."

Gary nodded, his eyes drifting to the ceiling as he thought. "I'd like to check out that location. Have you been there?"

"No, I haven't." Scott stood up. "Want to go now?"

"Sure. Now if I remember, according to her GPS, she stops for coffee, but when she pulls out of there, she turns right instead of left, heading away from the interstate."

"Right."

"So let's go to the coffee place first."

The Buzz Stop wasn't far from BAU, about twenty minutes up Interstate 95. Gary said he would follow Scott because it was late in the day and his home was up in that direction. His wife was expecting him for dinner at six-thirty.

The coffee shop stood by itself on the outskirts of the parking lot for a strip mall. A one-story building, its cement block walls were painted to look like coffee with swirls of whipped cream. A sign advertising locally roasted beans hung in the window.

Scott parked near the edge of the lot so he could scope out the whole scene. Gary pulled up next to him and climbed in Scott's passenger seat so they could talk.

Scott had a diagram of the store and parking lot on his laptop. "So we have Faith on the security camera walking into the store from the west side." He ran that grainy video. "The camera doesn't cover that part of the parking lot. So we don't know where she parked."

"But it probably was over by that line of cedars," Gary said.

"Right. Ten minutes later she comes out of the place and goes back around the building, sipping her coffee. Then we have her car leaving the lot."

"Let's see what we can find," Gary said.

They got out of the car and walked slowly around the building. Scott gestured toward the security camera. "It doesn't rotate, so this area isn't covered."

"Okay, then. He parks near her—"

"Because maybe he spotted her on 95 and followed her," Scott said, speculating.

"Or he was already in the lot, and she parked near him."

Scott nodded. He turned and looked up at the building. "There're no windows, so he had access to her car for like, ten minutes."

"What would he do?"

"He could get in it—hide in the back seat."

"He's a big guy."

"Okay, so he'd do something to disable it. Because he wasn't going to abduct her in this parking lot." Scott rubbed his chin as he fleshed out the scenario.

"Yeah, it's too busy."

"And at three o'clock in the afternoon, the stores in the strip mall are all open. There's lots of activity."

The two men stood there for a few minutes, trying to imagine what took place. Then they walked back to Scott's car to retrace her final drive.

Scott pulled out of the coffee shop's parking lot and paused at the main road. "Why'd she turn right?" he asked.

"There's no traffic light. Maybe there were too many lanes to cross and too many cars. Or maybe she got confused. There's no sign pointing you back to 95."

Scott turned right, drove up the road for about two miles, then pulled onto the shoulder at a place fringed with woods. "This is where her car was found." The location had been marked with a small, red, spray-paint dot.

The two men got out. "What happened to the car? What made her stop?" Gary said, thinking out loud.

Scott stared at the red dot. "The forensic report showed no problem with the car, except one tire was low on air."

"That'd be a pretty easy thing to make happen," Gary said. "And newer cars have low tire-pressure warning lights. That might be enough to make someone pull over."

"Especially, if she got encouragement from a driver behind her flashing his lights." Scott remembered reading about a series of abductions where the suspect pulled up next to a woman and gestured as if something was wrong with her car. She stopped on the shoulder and was never seen again.

"Okay, so she pulls over. Why not just wait for help? Or drive slowly to a gas station? Or call 911?" Gary asked. "I used to tell my daughters, you're a woman driving alone. That's enough reason to call 911 if you break down."

Would he remember to tell Mandy that, Scott wondered? She was only three years away from driving.

Scott shifted his thoughts. "Our interviews with her friends and family indicated Faith was a conservative young woman, not used to making long trips on her own, prone to thinking the best of people." He looked at Gary. "She still lived with her parents in a rural area near Lancaster. So probably not street smart."

"And she was driving to meet her maid of honor to shop for a wedding dress, so her mind wasn't focused on danger."

Scott frowned. "So she gets some indication there's a problem with her car. She pulls over here, and this guy pulls in behind her."

"Or in front," Gary said, "so it would be harder for her to just hit the gas and go."

Scott nodded. "He's low-key. Not slick. He just seems like a gentle giant, a good ol' boy who stopped to help. So she lets him. But why does she get in his truck? I'm picturing him having a truck."

"What was the weather like?" Gary asked.

The weather. Scott hadn't seen anything about that in the report. He pulled out his smartphone and began searching. He looked up as a rush of adrenaline ran through him. "Storms. Same as with Sandy Smith."

Gary nodded. "There you go. It starts to rain. It's November, so it's chilly. He invites her to wait in his truck or car. Then he kills her. The other drivers are distracted by the rain; they don't see it happen."

"Or, he disables her somehow. Drives off and ends up in the park. She doesn't know where he's going, and by the time she realizes what he's doing, it's too late."

Gary crossed his arms. "Let me think about that." He took a deep breath. "What do you say we get a cup of coffee?"

32

I KNEW on some level I was using Nate. He was my friend and mentor, but also my punching bag. I said things to provoke him. I challenged him and got angry at things he said just to make myself feel like I was in control.

He never gave up on me.

The day I had my last meltdown, he'd gone outside with the dogs. When he came back in, he told me he'd noticed some work that needed to be done on the house, something about downspouts and water runoff. He'd even called Bruce, right then and there, and volunteered to do it, an offer my busy landlord was happy to accept.

I knew it was just an excuse to be at my house. To keep an eye on me. I'd told him I was seeing Sarah Pennington. She was unearthing some ugly parts of my soul, and I was rattled. She'd been right when she said it would get worse before it got better.

I asked Nate where, besides the whole God-thing, his breakthroughs had come from. He had to think about that, because his faith was so entwined with his recovery. I was looking for something I could grab onto—a program, a list, a book. Something besides God, something practical.

I even used those words, and I saw by the way he looked at me that he thought finding God was the most practical thing a body could do.

But he didn't challenge me. He scratched his beard, his blue eyes focused on the carpet. "I think," he said finally, "that EMDR was good. Sometimes your brain just needs a reboot."

EMDR stands for "eye movement desensitization and repro-cessing therapy" and it's a physical technique some psycholo-gists use to do just that—reboot the brain. Sarah said she was going to try that with me after we'd made progress with some other stuff.

"In addition to that," Nate continued, "I'd say talking things out, regular exercise, and not isolating helped me the most. Of course, getting my dog Maggie made a big difference. But I don't know, Jess, sometimes you just need a different perspective. A change in the way you look at life. And that can come from anywhere at any time."

For me it came in a text from, of all people, Scott Cooper.

What was your dad's first name? he texted me one evening.

Why? I texted back.

He apparently thought texting was too slow. So he called. "Jess!"

I caught the excitement in his voice.

"What?"

"Your dad's last name was Chamberlain, right? What was his first name?"

"Michael," I said, curious enough now to share that informa-tion. "They called him Mike."

"He was with the NYPD, and he died on 9/11."

"Right." My heart beat hard. "So what?"

"I met someone who knew him!"

I sat down hard on the couch, suddenly dizzy. My throat felt like someone had stuffed a wad of cotton down it.

"I'm working with him at BAU on this case. He was a young

NYPD cop on your dad's squad. He was with him on 9/11! He told me stories ..."

My mind was so blown I could hardly understand what he was saying.

"... about your dad, and Jess, he wants to meet you. He said he'd love to meet you!"

"When did you find this out?" I put my hand on my brow.

"This afternoon."

"What's his name? His full name?"

He gave it to me and then said, "What are you doing tomorrow? Want to meet us for lunch? Or dinner?"

Tomorrow? Catching up on cases, maybe? Refilling my tissue supply? Trying to keep my gut in place?

I swallowed hard. "Let me check."

"Okay, but get back to me soon. He's traveling day after tomorrow. So let me know, okay?"

As I clicked off the phone, I heard Nate's voice in my head. *God works in mysterious ways indeed.* I walked over to my laptop. Luke raised his head momentarily, reacting to my swift move. I Googled "Gary S. Taylor" and scrolled through the search results.

He seemed legit. I found lots of academic papers, all on some aspect of criminal psychology. A bio showed his four years with NYPD and documented his MA from Columbia and PhD in psychology from the University of Virginia. He'd been with the FBI for fifteen years.

I crossed my arms over my chest and paced. What should I do? I wanted to know more about my father. Was Gary Taylor with him when he died? What was it like to work with my dad?

But I was worried. Would Scott tell him about me? Just thinking about that sent a rush of shame coursing through me.

I really wanted to meet Gary. But would I be able to get through it emotionally, with Scott right there?

I looked over to where my big dog lay on his bed. His eyes

followed me as I moved. It was like he was wondering if I was anxious, or were we going somewhere.

Scott said we could meet at a restaurant. Which meant no dog. But could Nate come?

Why had I even thought that? What was Nate, my babysitter?

Regardless, my thumb was already punching Nate's number on my cell phone.

He answered. I told him what was going on.

"What's hangin' you up?" he asked.

I told him.

"Seems like this would be a good time to confront that demon," he said. By that I knew he meant my own fear.

I swallowed hard. "Will you come with me?"

33

I CALLED Scott back and asked him if it was okay for Nate to join us. Sure, he said. He gave me the name of a restaurant and told me to meet them there at six o'clock the next day.

By three o'clock the next afternoon, I had showered, washed my hair, and laid three different outfits on my bed. What exactly did you wear to meet the friend of your deceased father? Luke watched me, his head cocked in puzzlement, as I held one up after the other and looked in the full-length mirror. The only clothes he cared about had to do with SAR.

Nate said he'd pick me up at five. The restaurant Scott had chosen was an Italian place with a terrific reputation, located about halfway between Quantico and my house. I might have opted for the Beef 'n Brew, but hey, Scott said he was picking up the tab so upscale was fine with me.

I'd already given Luke a good run. Brushed my teeth twice. Found my good sandals. Now all I had to do was pick an outfit and dry my hair.

I settled on a blue, summery print dress, not too girly, but a far cry from the jeans and khakis I usually wore. I brushed out my shoulder-length hair and put on a little makeup. Then I waited. And worried.

Would Scott tell this guy about me blowing my detective career?

I put Luke in his crate when I heard Nate's car pull up. I don't know which of us was more surprised when I opened the door. Nate had on dress pants, a really nice light-blue shirt, a blue tie with tiny pink stripes, and a navy sports coat.

His eyes widened when he saw me in my dress. "Hmm," he said. "You clean up good."

"I could say the same about you!"

Honestly, he looked great.

Villa Bellini sat perched on a little hill, surrounded by trees, in the foothills of the Blue Ridge. Made of flat, beige stone, the building had wooden trellises covered with vines and little lights inviting people in and a koi pond with a fountain out in front next to the path. The place looked like it was right out of Tuscany.

Scott and Gary Taylor were already there, waiting for us under the front porch. Scott's handshake with Nate morphed into a quick man-hug. That surprised me. He then turned to Gary, put his hand on his arm, and introduced him to us. "He's a profiler with the Behavioral Analysis Unit," he said. "Very smart."

Gary's eyes were fixed on me, and I swear, I thought I saw tears. "And you are Mike Chamberlain's daughter. I am so happy to meet you." He cradled my hand in both of his, looking at me with deep-brown eyes. Emotion flooded me. This man had known my father! I opened my mouth, but nothing came out.

Scott saw my paralysis and took over. "Gary, this is Nate," he said. "Nate Tanner. A friend of Jessica's. And my friend too."

Gary shook Nate's hand and then we all went inside.

Once we entered the restaurant, Gary turned his attention back to me. "Your dad was so proud of you. He talked about you all the time. How old were you when he died?"

"Twelve."

"And now here you are, all grown up."

The hostess interrupted, guiding us back to a candlelit dining room. The faux-marble walls were covered in murals and art reminiscent of the Renaissance. Lots of wood and rich red table-cloths added to the classy feel. I had to blink to remember we were in the middle of the Virginia countryside and not in Italy.

We sat down at a square table, with Nate on my left, Scott on my right, and Gary right across from me. I slipped my hand into my dressy little purse and fingered the icons I'd brought—my dad's badge and his pipe. After we ordered our food, I said to Gary, "So, you worked with my dad." I put the badge on the table.

His eyes fell on that badge. Reaching out, he picked it up care-fully, as if he were handling crystal, and he rubbed his thumb across the face. His voice cracking, he said, "Your dad was my sergeant, my mentor, and my friend. He was ... he was like a father to me when I was a young rookie cop. I will never forget him."

Stories began to flow out of him, typical cop stories of arrests, locker-room pranks, long nights of surveillance, working double-shifts, and boneheaded criminals and sometimes coworkers. As Gary talked, he fleshed out my dad for me, taking the outline I'd carried in my heart all this time and filling it in, something my mother never would do.

Our food came, rich and cheesy and warm, with crusty bread and crisp salads. Scott had ordered a bottle of red wine, a fine Sangiovese from Tuscany recommended by the waiter. I sipped it, clutching my dad's pipe with my left hand while listening to Gary's stories.

Just as he was getting to 9/11, he stopped short. "Tell me, Jess, what have you done with your life so far?"

I glanced at Scott, who was staring noncommittally at his food. How much had he said? I couldn't read him, so I swallowed, and gave Gary a Cliff Notes summary, beginning with the devastation I felt when my dad died, my mother remarrying, moving to Virginia, my younger sister. I outlined my high-school career, full of athletics, and, of course, Finn, and my college pre-law program.

I was still clutching Dad's pipe on my lap as I approached the next part. "I worked for the Fairfax County police for a few years," I said, my throat tightening. "I left after ... after a critical incident." The voice of shame screamed epithets in my head. I fought for control. "Now I work as a private investigator, and I do search and rescue with my dog as a volunteer. That's how I met Nate. He's a war vet, a former military dog handler, and he knows more about dogs than anybody."

"I'm the dog man," Nate said, grinning.

Perfect. Gary's attention shifted. "Really? Tell me about search and rescue."

The fear gripping my shoulders gradually faded as I listened to Nate's soft voice talking about SAR. He had so many stories— funny stories, sad stories, stories of bravery and perseverance. Stories in which he was never the hero: It was the dog, or the victim, or in one case, me.

I blushed as he told Gary about finding Joey Washburn, of my endurance and determination. "Grit" he always called it.

Then Scott chimed in, telling about my help with the Sandy Smith case. "She has really good instincts."

Gary looked at me, nodding his approval. "You are your father's daughter."

I felt a momentary rush of pride. But then I reminded myself that pride was not the antidote to shame, that self-esteem's ability to cover moral regret was inadequate. And so it was that night. Shame lurked in me like a dark pool, ready to suck me in and drown me.

The meal almost over, I ventured one more question. "Would you tell me about 9/11?"

Gary took a deep breath. I knew this had to be a hard subject for him too. In my mind, I coached him—*in for four, hold for seven, out for eight.*

"It was a beautiful day," he said. "Warm temperatures, bright blue sky, a perfect fall day. Your dad had agreed to meet me for breakfast at this coffee shop about two blocks from the World Trade Center." Gary paused momentarily and swallowed. "The girl I'd planned to marry had broken up with me the night before. Your dad, he was the kind of guy who would talk you through things like that."

Gary went on to describe hearing the boom of the first plane hitting, of their radios going off, of racing two blocks to the WTC. "Your dad, he had one thought—get people out of there."

They ran into the building, charging up the stairs, helping people down, warning people, directing people to safety, and as he spoke, I saw myself as a twelve-year-old middle school girl, suddenly sent home from school, huddled on the couch, watching my world destroyed.

"I was following your dad way up in the tower," Gary said, "when we heard a terrible roar. He turned, looked at me, and shoved me back down the stairs. The tower came down, right on top of us, and that's the last I saw of your dad."

Gary wiped away tears. The other two men sat like frozen statues. Then Nate said, "Now that's a brave man. And you too." Gary glanced at him, acknowledging his compassion.

"They never found him," I whispered.

"I know," Gary continued. "Your dad was a hero. I'll bet he got a hundred, maybe two hundred people out of that building. He never quit. And he saved my life for sure. He pushed me down those stairs, and I ended up in rubble, but not in the worst of it."

"Were you hurt?" I asked him.

Gary nodded. "I was trapped for a while. I just remember I couldn't breathe, didn't know where I was, and the pain was terrible. Eventually, firefighters got me out. I spent two months in the hospital and in rehab with a broken leg and some other injuries.

But I would have been dead if it were not for your dad." He paused. "All that time in rehab, I kept seeing your dad's eyes, boring into me, willing me to live."

By this time, tears spilled out of my eyes. Nate handed me his handkerchief. Then he looked at Gary. "And afterward?"

"I went through every emotion you could have—anger, grief, despair, rage, hope, guilt."

"Guilt?" I said, interrupting. "Why?"

Gary raised his eyebrows. "Because I didn't die with your dad." He closed his eyes momentarily. "Trauma is a strange thing. You feel things that aren't rational."

I felt Nate's knee bump mine under the table.

"I had a long period of counseling, which is what got me interested in psychology. I kept wondering what made people do evil things. Or heroic things. Because I'd seen them both." He gestured with his hand. The way he was talking, I halfway expected to see an anchor tattoo on him somewhere. "I wanted to know what was in the soul of man. Eventually, I went back to school and started working to get my advanced degrees."

Our server came by to see if we wanted dessert, which we didn't. Scott took the check, refusing our offers to pay for our own meals. I thought that was awfully generous. I wondered what he wanted in return.

"Thank you for telling me about my dad," I said to Gary, slipping the badge back in my purse, along with the pipe. I scooted back my chair.

"One more thing." Gary reached in to the breast pocket of his suit and pulled out a small black book, about the size of my Moleskine. I watched him, curious.

"That morning, when we had breakfast and I told your dad about my struggles, he shared something with me. I knew he'd been going through something personal..."

"What was that?" I asked.

Gary shook his head. "It doesn't matter what. He told me he'd

202 LINDA J. WHITE

actually gone to see the chaplain about it, a bunch of times, in fact.

"Your dad said the chaplain gave him this book, and it had helped him a lot, and the morning of 9/11, he gave it to me. I put it in my pocket to read later. Needless to say, I forgot all about it. Six months later, I ran across the plastic bag the hospital had put my clothes in. When I checked my uniform pockets, I found this." He gestured with the book. "I wanted to give it to your mom. By then I couldn't find her."

"She'd remarried. We'd moved," I murmured, feeling a stirring of emotion.

"I've kept this book all these years. Now I want you to have it." He handed me the book. "You can see your dad's signature on the inside. And every mark in there, every underlining, is his."

Opening the cover of that little book and seeing my dad's unique signature rocked my world. Stunned, I looked at Gary. "This was my dad's?"

He nodded.

I looked at the book again. It was a pocket-sized copy of the Gospel of John.

34

WE DROVE HOME IN SILENCE, Nate and I did. He must have sensed I needed to process all that Gary had told me. He couldn't have known I was in the middle to shifting all that emotion—my grief, my loneliness, my deep sorrow, even my confusion—to another place.

"You okay?" Nate asked as he pulled up in front of my house. "Need to talk?"

"No, I'm fine. Thank you for coming with me."

"You made it through. Good for you," he said.

"I'm glad you were there."

"It was right interesting," Nate said, and he gave me a quick kiss on the top of my head and left.

I went inside and let Luke out. What had my dad been going through that had prompted his visits to the chaplain? I had a feeling it had to do with my mom. I was determined to get to the bottom of it. My anger burned.

Luke needed a run, or he'd be restless all night. But I needed to call my mom. I decided to compromise. We ran for half an hour. And I chose to believe nine-thirty was not too late to call her.

She answered on the second ring. "Jess, how are you?"

"I'm fine, Mom. Listen, do you remember a friend of Dad's named Gary Taylor?" I paced as I talked.

"No, I don't think so ..."

"He would have been a young cop, an NYPD rookie."

There was a pause. "I may have heard his name. I'm not sure. Why do you ask?"

"I met him tonight." I told her about our mutual friend, about dinner, about the stories he told about my dad. "Did you know this, Mom? Why didn't you ever tell me exactly what happened? Why didn't you tell me he was a hero?"

"I guess ... I guess I thought it was too traumatic for a young girl."

"Oh really? You were protecting me? How about you were protecting yourself!" My voice was sharp, indicting. "Something else, Mom. Gary said Dad had been going through something personal. He didn't give me details. He just said Dad had talked to a chaplain about it. Any chance this had to do with you, Mom? Maybe, you and Frank?" I spit those words out. I might as well have been a cobra.

Even on my cell phone I could hear her sharp intake of breath. I struck again. "Tell me the truth, Mom. It's too late for lies."

Our conversation went downhill from there. She tried to tell me I had no idea what went on in their marriage. I suggested I knew more than she wished I knew. She tried to defend herself; I wouldn't let her. When I finally hung up on her, I was in a rage. It was like my mother had killed my dad, not 9/11.

As I stood in my apartment, shaking with anger, I recalled something Nate had said to me once. He said, shame runs so deep, it takes a strong emotion, like anger, to overcome it.

Anger was coming easily to me right now.

After I hung up, I paced around my apartment, and when I couldn't stand to be inside any longer, I went outside. Luke found a stick to chew, and I sank into an Adirondack chair and watched the stars.

The soft night air eventually modified my mood. I began thinking about my dad. I somehow couldn't imagine he'd be happy about the way I'd just treated my mom.

I slept badly that night. Luke eventually crawled into my bed to try to ease my restlessness. The warmth of his body against my legs anchored me, but still the images kept swirling in my head— my dad in his NYPD uniform, the towers falling, gray smoke billowing into the sky. My mom and Frank, and then, that rainy night when I let my partner die.

It was like the universe had created clips of the horror movie of my life. When I woke up, I was exhausted.

Nate called me later that day, wondering how I was doing after our dinner with Gary and Scott. I told him about the dreams, and he listened quietly. Then he asked, "What was the book Gary gave you?"

I hesitated. "I don't know, really. I haven't looked at it yet." That was a lie. I knew what it was; I'd read the cover. I was still shocked that it had been my father's. We were not a church family.

Probably because I needed to feel strong again, I told him about my phone call to my mom, about calling her out on what I assumed was her affair.

Nate's long silence suggested he didn't agree with what I'd done. And from the weight in my heart, part of me concurred.

"You coming to the training today?" he asked. It was for cadaver teams. But there wouldn't be any bodies there, just tiny fragments of human remains.

"No, I don't think so." I was avoiding him and the conviction I was feeling.

"We could use your help."

After a little more convincing, I finally agreed to come. "Sure, okay," I said. "I'll be there."

I'd been so caught up in my own drama I hadn't read the details of the training. When I arrived at the address, I saw it was a small house that had burned to the ground some time back. Only the chimney remained standing. A couple of charred lumps suggested they might have been metal cabinets once. A few bigger beams and timbers lay scattered about. Other than that, what had once been a family home was a heap of cinders.

No one had died in the blaze. We'd plant the human remains (a tooth and a small fragment of bone) after the trainees were out of sight. Nate began to speak. I suddenly wished I'd brought Luke.

I watched Nate stand in the middle of all that burned-out mess and explain about searching the remains of a fire. He talked about protecting your dog's feet with boots, about checking with law enforcement before turning over piles to potentially expose human remains. He spoke about what to do if your dog alerted, about good note-taking, and the importance of wearing good boots because of the possibility there'd be nails in the debris.

In the middle of his talk, I saw Sprite lean against him and put her paw on his foot. Just standing on a pile of burned rubble, smelling that smoke, was raising his stress level. She knew it, and now, so did I. Fire was not Nate's friend.

One day I hoped to be able to stand on the burned rubble of my life and function in a way that only my dog would know my stress, just like Nate.

Later, as Nate loaded up his car, some of the newer members came over and started asking him questions. He sat down on the edge of the Tahoe's cargo area and patiently answered them, all the while stroking Sprite who sat on his lap.

When they were all gone, I sat down next to him. "So," I said, "when will I get to the stage I can deal with my stress by petting my dog."

He laughed. "What are you talking about?"

"I saw the signs. The smell of that fire bothered you. But you still functioned." I slid off the back of his SUV, crossed my arms in front of me, moved a few steps away, and turned back to him. "That's all I'm asking for, to get to that level. I've tried to get you to help me, and Sarah Pennington, but you're not! You're not helping, either of you."

"In fact, you're getting worse."

"Right. And now you're judging me because I called out my mom—"

"Whoa, whoa. I didn't say anything about that."

"You didn't have to."

"That ain't me that's convicting you," Nate said, getting up and scooping Sprite into her crate. Even Nate had limits to his patience.

"Nate, I'm asking you for help! I need a way out of this." I kicked a little rock, searching my brain for a way to keep this conversation going. "You said ... you said shame runs strong enough it can only be covered by another strong emotion, like anger. So maybe that's why I got so angry with my mom." I tossed my head, proud of my confession. "So what else will do it?"

He stopped moving and fixed his bright blue eyes on me.

I threw my hands up in the air. "I want a plan!"

"There is one more thing."

"What?" I demanded.

"Tell you what," he said, closing the back of the Tahoe. "You read that little book, then I'll tell you."

I knew instantly he'd seen the title. The Gospel of John. Right up his alley.

It was an alley I refused to enter.

35

SOMETIMES YOU HAVE to go backward to move investigations forward. Scott Cooper knew that, and yet driving out to reinterview Sandy Smith's friends irritated him. It gave him too much time to think.

A big argument the night before had turned into a sleepless night. The problem? He'd called off Mandy's visit. Postponed it. He told his ex-wife he was in the middle of a big case.

You're always in the middle of a big case, Suzanne had snapped back. So, after trying to avoid the details, he finally broke down and explained why he didn't want Mandy here. Because this suspect was targeting women who looked like her.

"He's killed three, Suzanne. Three so far. And I don't want her at risk."

Even that didn't calm down his ex. Apparently, Suzanne had a new boyfriend and her plans didn't include having Mandy around those two weeks.

He'd hung up the phone, furious. Really? She'd rather have her daughter in danger than miss some whoopee time with her boyfriend?

"Aren't you going a little fast?"

Dana's question jarred Scott. He'd brought her with him to help with the interviews and also, he admitted, because he was asked to check her skills. He glanced down and realized he was doing eighty in a sixty-m.p.h. zone. He was also gripping the steering wheel so hard his hands ached. He eased up on the accelerator and relaxed his grip. "Yeah, sorry."

"So, Scott, I don't get what my part in this is."

"We'll be interviewing friends of Sandy Smith and Julie. When one of us is asking questions, the other looks for nonverbals. Some of the women may be more comfortable talking to you, or vice versa. We work as a team and learn what we can."

Dana sighed. "Hasn't all this been done before?"

Scott bristled. "What do you care? You're getting paid."

"I had plans for today."

When he looked over at her, he swore she was pouting.

Thirteen-year-old Mandy did it better.

The whole day continued that way. Scott felt like he was dragging an anchor behind him. The anchor analogy made him think of Nate and thinking of Nate made him remember what Nate said about the dogs who were good at SAR: *They've got to have a good play drive. Prey drive, some folks call it. They got to want to do the job and get that reward.*

So far, he wasn't seeing a lot of prey drive in Dana. He wondered how long she'd last in the FBI. One thing he was sure of, he wouldn't have hired her.

Just as they arrived back at the office, Scott got a phone call from Robert Hudson, who'd been checking on the victims' cars. He answered it as Dana got out, slammed the door, and walked into the office. "What do you have for me, Robert? It better be good."

"It is! It is good." Robert paused. "So I was talking to my brother, who's a mechanic, and he gave me an idea. So I went back and had the shop take the front grill off Faith's car. Somebody had punched a hole in the radiator, a small hole, near the bottom, but it would have been enough to drain the coolant while she was getting coffee."

"Yeah? Why didn't they catch that before?" Scott sat up straight and jotted notes.

"Guy was clever. He angled the awl or whatever he used just right. You had to take the grill off to see the hole. So then we looked at Sandy's car. The radiator had split when she hit that tree, so that's why the fluid was gone."

"And Julie's?"

"Bingo. Same little hole. Same technique."

"Wow. Good job!"

"They're analyzing it now to see if they can figure out what made the hole. But it's a definite link—between those two cases anyway."

That news was enough to inspire Scott to stay at the office late and write up the 302s on the interviews they'd conducted that day. He was nearly done before he realized he should have made Dana stay and do them. It would have been good discipline.

"I'd rather have it done right," he said out loud as he closed his computer. He stood to leave but had another thought. Keying in Gary Taylor's number, he composed in his head the voice mail he wanted to leave.

Much to his surprise, Gary answered. "You back from your trip?" Scott asked.

"Flight got in an hour ago. My wife has a meeting, so I thought I'd come into the office and get a few things done. What's up?"

Scott told him about the holes in the radiators.

"I wonder how many radiators he punched before he got his technique down?" Gary said.

That sparked a thought in Scott. "I wonder if we called a bunch of mechanics who'd fixed radiators in the past couple of years if we could find a pattern? A geographic connection?"

"That'd be interesting," Gary said.

As he clicked off his phone, Scott smiled. He was guessing Dana wouldn't find the task he was about to give her all that interesting.

As Scott drove home, he found himself thinking about Jessica Chamberlain. He wondered how she was dealing with what Gary had told her about her dad. Was she encouraged, or did it just stir up a lot of hard memories?

He almost called her. After spending the day with Dana it would be a relief to talk to a woman with a little, well, prey drive. But in the end, he didn't pick up his phone.

36

I SLOUCHED ON THE COUCH, a cup of tea steaming on the table next to me. The weekend stretched before me like the final walk of a condemned man. I could hear the rain pouring down and weathercasters predicted it would continue. Battlefield had postponed SAR practice, leaving me at loose ends. Nate said he was busy. In fact, I thought he was avoiding me. Since when were we unable to find something to do, even in the rain? But even Luke seemed to ignore me, lying on his side next to the wall, his mouth half-open. If he were a man, he'd be wearing a wifebeater undershirt and holding a can of beer.

It wasn't like I couldn't work weekends. With my job, I could work whenever I wanted. But the particular cases I had right now were best worked on Monday through Friday when people were in their offices and not in their homes.

Next to my tea sat the little black book, indicting me for neglect. I tried to think of something else I could do—another project, another phone call, another Internet search. But in the end, curiosity overrode my stubborn resistance.

After all, I rationalized as I picked it up, it wasn't as if Nate were making me read it. I was a big girl. I could make choices.

I opened the book, traced my father's unmistakable signature, and began to read.

At first, the thoughts seemed strange, almost like I was reading a foreign language I only partly understood. I couldn't put it together. What was he talking about, being born again? Raising up the temple in three days? Why were people so angry with Jesus? Why didn't he realize he was offending them?

I'd always pictured Jesus as meek and mild. Sort of effeminate. But the Jesus in this book was tough, almost abrasive at times. I didn't understand him.

I read about healings. Mercy. Loaves and fishes. Arguments. Bread. And then, the woman caught in adultery.

Oh, how I could see in my mind's eye that mob of men hauling that poor woman into the street. My anger rose, my jaw tight as I pictured it. Was she naked? Had she had time to even grab a sheet? And if she was committing adultery, where was the man? Why didn't they drag him out too? How dare they shame her like that?

I gripped that book, furious with those arrogant, abusive men. I knew I was about to judge Jesus based on how he responded to that poor woman. Because if he got it wrong, I'd know I couldn't trust him. Or Nate. Ever again. I braced myself for the lecture. The condemnation. The soul-baring, sin-revealing, heart-to-heart talk.

The mob of men threw the woman down on the street and challenged Jesus. He was surprisingly quiet. Then he bent down and wrote in the dirt. Wrote what? I wanted to know, but the book didn't say.

The men pressed him. He wrote again. And then finally he faced them and said the oddest thing: *Let him who is without sin among you be the first to throw a stone at her.*

Let the one without sin throw a stone.

And one by one, the men left.

My heart was pounding as I pictured this scene. Jesus, quiet as he was, conveyed authority. Those men could not stand before him. They slunk away like whipped puppies.

I could see the woman, cowering in the dust, full of shame. I could see her cringing, waiting for the lecture, the judgment, the harsh words, the mocking. I could see her looking up cautiously as he gently questioned her.

And I could imagine the compassion in his eyes as he said, *Neither do I condemn you: go, and from now on, sin no more.*

I'm very analytical. Three things hit me all at once: First, Jesus poured mercy all over this woman. He didn't condemn her. He was gentle and kind. Second, he gave her hope: *Go and sin no more.* What you've done doesn't need to define you. From now on, you can be different. Third, he told those men they had no right to condemn her. None.

And that both encouraged and convicted me.

I had been the victim, the woman thrown down and scorned in public, feeling naked and ashamed, abused by a bunch of men.

But I had also been a perpetrator. I had not only picked up stones against my mother, I'd thrown them. As if I had the right.

Oh, this little black book was a lot more unnerving than I ever imagined it would be.

That story worked on me all weekend. By Sunday night, I knew I had something I had to do. I left Luke in his crate, put the book in my pocket, and drove to my mother's house.

She was there. So was Frank. I wasn't sure they were going to let me in at first—they were so guarded when they answered the door. But they did, and we sat in the living room, and I apologized. It was difficult. Humbling. We all cried. But in the end, I felt like I'd laid down a burden. I hugged my mother, silently forgiving her and hoping she would forgive me.

Before I left, I showed her the book. She fingered it carefully and said she'd never seen it. I didn't ask her for any explanation. I just took the book back from her, put it in my pocket, and told her I'd come back soon.

The drive back that night seemed to fly by, I felt so light. When I got home, I took Luke for a run, then showered and went to bed. I felt happy. Happy. That was new. And I wondered if I'd discovered the second thing strong enough to overcome shame.

37

I SLEPT SOUNDLY until a callout triggered my phone just before 4:00 a.m. A young person was missing up in the mountains. No details beyond that. I called the incident commander and told her I'd respond. Then Nate called me. "You goin'?"

"Yes. You?"

"You bet."

"Want to drive together?" I was anxious to talk to him. I had so many questions.

"Might be handy to have two cars where we're going."

"You're right."

"But we can follow each other. That way, one of us gets into trouble, the other'll be there."

"Sounds like a plan."

We met thirty minutes later at a big gas station on Route 29. We got coffee, then Nate gave me more information. "Scott just called me. He's on this case too."

A flash of adrenaline raced through me. "This is one of his cases? Does he think it's connected?"

"Small female. Reported missing last night. Scott got the call about 9:00 p.m. When he got up here, he asked for us to be deployed. Sheriff's office isn't too happy about that—they got their own dogs. But Scott said he wanted our group called out. He phoned me to make sure that happened."

"So he's thinking this is the same perp?"

"He thinks there's enough similarities that it's got him worried. Thing is, he wants to find her alive this time, not laying in some forest with her neck broke." Nate paused. "Probably be best if we kept quiet on what we know."

"Okay." I shivered. Another young girl missing. When Nate showed me the map, I shivered again. The area was near my sister's college.

I decided to consider that a coincidence. Brooke was fine, or I would have heard from my parents.

We took I-64 over to I-81, then drove north. Thankfully, it had stopped raining, but the roads were still wet. A surprising number of cars had mixed in with the trucks on I-81 on this Monday morning. I'd heard people say folks commuted to DC from places like Front Royal and Winchester. I couldn't imagine it.

Nate called me as I was thinking about that. "They've got a search command center set up at the county sheriff's office. But they want the dog teams to report to a farm nearby. It has a yard we can pitch tents in and a big barn where we can get out of the weather. Even an outhouse."

"Yahoo!" I said, laughing.

"We'll get off this road up yonder about five more miles, then follow me. I've got the directions."

"Will do."

We arrived at the farm off Shady Creek Road at 5:30 a.m., just as the sky was getting light. The rain over the weekend made the yard around the barn a mess, but the owner, Hank Stanley, said we could pitch tents in the front yard or in the barn. Nate suggested we make that decision when it got toward evening.

The stalls in the barn were empty, so we let the dogs hang out in them while we huddled up. They were getting their snoots full of animal smells for sure.

Susan was once again the incident commander. By 6:00 a.m., she had muffins and coffee brought in. By 7:00, she was ready to brief us.

"Laney Collier, 19, was reported missing yesterday evening. She's a local college student."

College? What college? Brooke's college? How many colleges could there be up here?

Susan continued. "Her friends say she was at an off-campus party on Friday night." She pointed to a location on a blown-up area map. "They thought she was spending the weekend with her boyfriend, but her roommate saw him Sunday night, and he said he hadn't seen her since Thursday."

I was standing back too far to read the place names on the map but worry nagged at me.

Susan clipped a topographic map over the first map. "We're being asked to search this area." She pointed to a wooded area near an off-campus housing project. "We have four dogs present, but we're short on walkers."

"This here's a live search, right?" Nate asked.

"Yes."

"Why don't I walk with Jess? Leave Sprite for later and hope we don't need her."

"That's a good plan. She can stay near me at the command center," Susan said. "I'm giving you segments to search in two-hour shifts. We'll try to stick to that. Work two hours, rest an hour. This could be a long search. We want to stay fresh." She looked over the handlers. "Any questions? The sheriff's office is bringing us topo maps with the areas they want us to search marked. We'll set up the command center at this location, a small park near where Laney was last seen. The weather looks good for today, but there's wind coming in tomorrow night along with a cold front. The sooner we find this young woman, the better."

When Susan finished talking, I walked up to the easel she had set up, lifted up the topo map, and looked closer at the regular map. I used the light on my phone to see it better, tracing the marked location the girl had last been seen to the nearby college. There it was—Smithson College. My heart dropped.

"Something wrong?" Nate asked, coming up behind me.

"Brooke. My sister Brooke goes to this school."

"The missing girl's name is Laney."

"Right, but still..."

Nate put his hand on my shoulder. "We'll find her."

I checked my watch. How early was too early to call Brooke?

"All right people. First team, let's go!" Susan called out.

That would be me. And Nate. We put the dogs in our cars, but before I got in, I said to Susan, "I'll be there in a few minutes. I want to take a quick detour to orient myself on the way there."

"That's fine. It'll take us a few minutes to set up."

I followed Susan and Nate out of the farm property. When we got to Main Street, they went straight, and I took a right. I'd never seen Smithson College, even though my sister was in her third year there.

I knew the campus was small, much smaller than George Mason, where I had done my undergraduate work, but Smithy, as the students called it, was really tiny. Eight classic Colonial brick buildings, which I presumed held classrooms and offices, faced onto a central, grassy mall. At the head of the mall was what I guessed was a library. Dorms and administration buildings lay nestled into the hills around the mall.

I saw a few students walking on the campus paths, but no one who looked like Brooke. At a small college like this, you'd probably really get to know your fellow students.

No wonder I'd chosen a big school.

I plugged the park Susan had chosen for our search headquarters into my GPS and proceeded to drive there. I pulled up and parked and noticed a familiar figure talking to Nate. Scott, wearing his cargo pants and FBI raid jacket, stood pointing to something on a map. His whole body looked tense.

Sitting there in my car watching him, I suddenly saw him differently, not as an arrogant, aggressive, in-control man, but as someone haunted by his sister's death—a man who had to force all those feelings of anger, helplessness, frustration, fear, and despair behind a wall in order to function. I could imagine the shape that wall most often took was control.

As I said, hanging out with Nate was teaching me to see the world in layers.

I got out of my car and walked over to them. I thought I saw Scott's eyes change as he turned and saw me. I gave Hurting Man a smile.

"Thanks for coming out," he said.

"Glad to help."

"I was just telling Nate, we're canvassing the whole town. The campus is small—about four thousand students. The sheriff's office has the boyfriend and the roommate in for questioning."

"Her car?" I asked.

"It's still in the apartment parking lot where she lives. No damage. We're told she'd walked to the party." Scott looked at the mountainside in front of us. "This is going to be hard searching."

Indeed. The pocket-sized park was the only flat place around. The hills rose steeply behind and around it.

Nate touched Scott's arm. "We'll be fine. You take care of yourself."

I could hear my dog's tail banging against his crate. "I'd better let Luke out," I said. "He's ready to go."

Scott drove off. As Luke watered the bushes, I tried calling Brooke. No answer. I left a voicemail.

When Luke finished sniffing the bushes, I put his vest on. Then we gathered around the back of Susan's Explorer. She showed us the segment we were to search, a small creek valley that ran up the side of the mountain. "No one else has checked that."

"How about the bloodhounds?" I asked. I knew the sheriff's office had one, and so did the state police. There is no dog that can beat a bloodhound when it comes to tracking a specific smell. Their ability to distinguish one scent from another is unsurpassed.

But I'd put Luke up against any of them when it came to air-scenting—searching for any human in an area. He stood at my feet, looking up at me, tail wagging, ready to go.

Susan shook her head. "They used them starting at the apartment where the party was, the place Laney was last seen. But they didn't go up here."

"The hounds alert on anything?" Nate asked.

"One of them followed a scent to the curb and then lost it. They're guessing Laney got into a car there."

I hoped not. Too many ugly scenarios could follow that decision.

Nate looked up the mountain we were supposed to tackle. "Helmets would be a good thing," he said. "A fall could result in a clunk on the head."

I nodded. "I'll get mine. C'mon, buddy," I said to Luke, turning back toward the Jeep. His tail dropped, thinking he wasn't going to get to search. "I just need to get something, then we'll go."

The word "go" made his tail wag again.

"Okay, we're going to follow this creek up here to this outcropping. Then we'll work our way back," Nate said, pointing to the topo map.

Three minutes later, I said the magic word—"Seek!"—and Luke took off running, his joy spilling out as he swept back and forth through the woods searching for a scent.

The climb was hard going, even following the valley that little creek had carved. Trees towered above us, and more than once, I used a tree trunk to pull myself up the incline. Beneath my boots were rocks, running pine, mushrooms, and fungi. A couple of crows squawked at us, protesting our invasion, and once I heard the jungle-bird cry of a pileated woodpecker.

After twenty minutes, out of breath, my leg muscles shaking, I stopped. "This doesn't make sense," I said to Nate. "Who would come up here, much less drag a woman up?"

He nodded. "You're right. It's steeper than we thought. And rockier." He looked above us. The mountain got even steeper. He lifted his radio to his ear. I called Luke back to me, sat down on a rock, and waited.

Nate finished on the radio and came over. "We're gonna cross the creek and work our way back. I told Susan this is a no-go."

So we crossed over the water, stepping on stones to keep our boots dry, and I sent Luke to seek again. I was watching him race off when Nate suddenly grabbed me and jerked me back about two feet.

"What are you doing?" I yelled.

His arm around my waist kept me from falling. He pointed to a copperhead snake gliding off into the underbrush.

"He was ready to strike," Nate said. "Sorry for scaring you."

I shook my head, trying to release my tension. "I'm glad he didn't get Luke."

I watched the ground more carefully after that as we worked our way back to base. By the time we arrived, we'd shot sixty minutes of search time and a lot of energy.

"Not sure why they wanted us to search up there," Nate said. His kindness kept his comment understated. I'm sure he was as frustrated as I was.

I got Luke some water and a jerky treat, then put him in his crate to rest. Nate sat down in the back of his Tahoe, staring at a map. I sat down beside him.

"Susan's got another team about to go in over here," he said, pointing to a section of the map. "But I think the most likely areas would be here and here."

"Could be anywhere, though, couldn't it? If he got her into a car?"

Nate folded up the map. "I'll ask Susan if she'd mind if I go over to the search headquarters."

"Why don't I take Sprite back to the farm with me? She and Luke can relax until we need to go again."

Nate nodded. "Great idea."

He'd only been out of sight for about five minutes when a cruiser drove up. It was marked K-9 Unit, and I heard a roar of angry barking as the canine inside spotted or smelled Sprite. I quickly put her in my Jeep and closed the door.

The deputy who got out looked enough like a pit bull to raise my hackles. He ignored me and strode over to Susan. I couldn't quite hear what they were talking about, but it was easy to feel the tension in their conversation. I decided I could not abandon her right then.

"Officer? I'm Jess, one of the SAR handlers. Is there a problem?" I quickly read his nametag (D. Foster) and stood so I was facing him, hands on my hips. I kept my expression friendly, but I wanted him to know I wasn't intimidated.

"I'm just telling her you volunteers need to stick to the area you're assigned. We determine the search assignments, not you." He spit off to the side, then looked at Susan. "So I'll let them know the assignment wasn't completed."

"Wait, are you talking about the area we searched this morning?" I said, my voice rising. The look he gave me combined disdain and disinterest. How he did that, I'll never know. "Segment 30? Here?" I took the map from Susan's hand and held it in front of him.

"Yeah."

"My partner and I almost made it to the top, and determined

it not only was not safe to continue, it was fruitless to do so." I was on my toes. I hoped "fruitless" wasn't too big a word for him.

"That's not your decision."

"Safety is my decision. It's always SAR's decision. Furthermore, whoever set that search location doesn't know a whole lot about finding lost people." Okay, I should have left that last part out. But this guy was getting to me.

"If y'all can't do it, fine," he said. "I'll report that. But don't tell us how to do our business." He pronounced it "bidness," and I almost laughed. "This is a law-enforcement operation. We're in charge. You need to remember that." Then Deputy D. Foster scanned my body from head to toe and back again.

In an instant, shame flooded me. I felt like he was raping me with his eyes. My fists clenched.

"I'll tell 'em you couldn't finish." Then he turned and walked back to his cruiser, and I was left standing there, feeling naked and ashamed, my mouth open, unable to retort.

38

Scott Cooper stood in the conference room of the Jackson County Sheriff's Office looking at a wall on which was posted everything they knew so far about the disappearance of Laney Collier. She lived in a dorm on campus. She had a boyfriend. She was last seen Friday night at an off-campus party at which the alcohol flowed freely. An art major, she had a reputation as a party girl, a free spirit who could always be counted on for a good time.

After she left the party, information got murky. She'd told her friends that she was spending the weekend with her boyfriend, who lived in an apartment across town. So when she left, around midnight, they assumed that's where she'd gone.

Was she drunk? Scott had asked one of them. *Everybody was drinking,* the girl had responded. Now, staring at the wall, he wished that somebody, anybody, had looked out for Laney, had refused to let her leave alone, had protected her in that crucial moment.

Now, was she lying in the woods somewhere, staring up at the sky with sightless eyes?

Scott shook his head to dislodge those thoughts. He went back over in his mind what they were doing to find her.

The sheriff had called for volunteers, and hundreds of people were now searching sheds, woods, barns, garages, and other hidden locations for Laney. The state police bloodhound had tracked her scent out of the apartment, but then lost it.

They were interviewing everyone they could find who knew her—every resident of the dorm, people in her classes, folks who worked with her at the coffee shop where she had a part-time job —everybody.

There weren't many security or traffic cameras in the area where she was last seen, but a video tech was already pouring over the data they'd recorded. Laney's DNA, retrieved from a hairbrush secured from her dorm room, was being analyzed. Her credit cards and phone were being tracked live. Specialized agents were analyzing her social media and studying her cell phone calls and text messages.

Meanwhile, Scott was working the case backward from the evidence gathered from the other three cases, even though he wasn't sure Laney's was connected. So he had Dana, working from their Northern Virginia office, calling people who sold firewood in Jackson County. She was also calling mechanics who'd fixed radiators in the last year. He had Robert Hudson checking on the condition of Laney's car and running down information on every sex offender, every felon, in the area.

Scott hadn't revealed the details of the other murders to the local LEOs. He didn't want a deputy's cousin Jethro finding out about the whittling or the posing or the punched radiator in case cousin Jethro was the UNSUB. All they knew was that Scott was there to help them solve the disappearance of Laney Collier.

"Agent Cooper?"

The voice of the sheriff interrupted Scott's thoughts. He turned to face Bill O'Boyle. "Hey, what's up?"

"Laney's parents are here. I told 'em we'd brought the FBI in."

That was a bit of a twist on reality, Scott thought. The state police had asked him to come aboard.

"They'd like to talk to you."

"Sure," Scott said. A feeling of dread washed over him, but he followed O'Boyle back to his office.

Tim and Rachel Collier sat in two leather chairs facing the desk in the sheriff's small office. O'Boyle, apparently rattled by the presence of Laney's parents, forgot there were no other chairs until they were in the room.

"No problem," Scott said, stepping out to grab another seat. His chest tightened as he returned and settled into it. The mother, Rachel, had red-rimmed eyes and sat clutching a crumpled tissue in her hand. The father, Tim, held her other hand. His face looked hard as stone. Behind that face, Scott knew, lay a boiling cauldron of fear and anger and sorrow and regret. He had an instant flashback to two other devastated parents—his own.

Feeling sick, Scott began. "I'm Special Agent Scott Cooper," he said. "I'm sorry for what you're going through."

"You don't have a clue," Tim said, bitterness edging his voice. "What are you doing to find our daughter?"

Scott deferred to the sheriff, in part to be diplomatic and in part to collect himself. The coffee he'd just had wasn't sitting well with him. The tightness in his chest was creeping up into his shoulders and his neck.

He half listened while the sheriff outlined the search methodologies they were using. O'Boyle spoke slowly, almost casually. If he was doing that to keep Laney's parents calm, his technique was backfiring.

Mrs. Collier sobbed softly, dabbing her nose with the crumbled tissue. Mr. Collier perched on the edge of his seat like a hawk waiting for the mouse to move.

Finally, Tim Collier had had enough. He stood up quickly. With his hands on his hips, Mr. Collier glared at O'Boyle. "I don't think you could find your nose if you had a mirror." He turned to

Scott. "What's the FBI doing that'll get my daughter back? 'Cause this yahoo..." he didn't finish his sentence.

Scott looked straight at Laney's father. He saw the blaze in his eyes and rigidity of the tendons in his neck. He heard the anguish fueling the anger in his voice.

"Mr. Collier," he said, trying to ignore the golf-ball-sized lump in his own throat, "I believe the sheriff and the other law enforcement officers are working hard to get Laney back."

"She's been gone since Friday!"

"But she wasn't reported missing until last night."

"That's forty-eight hours!"

"Sir, I understand how frustrating this is."

"You couldn't possibly."

Anger flashed through Scott. He paused to collect himself. "Sir, the FBI is helping with evidence analysis, manpower, strategies, and in many other ways. I assure you, sir, we all want to get your daughter safely home." His neck felt frozen, the muscles were so tight. He turned toward Mrs. Collier.

"Ma'am, did you notice any changes in Laney's behavior lately? Either being really happy, or really sad, or secretive?"

Rachel Collier shook her head. "She was happy about going back to school. We're a conservative family, and well, sometimes our rules don't match what she wants to do."

"Yeah," Tim Collier added, "like staying over with that boyfriend. Have you talked to him? What's he got to say? Why wasn't he with her?"

Mrs. Collier touched her husband's arm.

"Yes, sir," Sheriff O'Boyle said, "we ran him through the wringer, we did. He had to work that night. Missed the party. Doesn't have a clue where she is."

She'd told a friend she was going to spend the weekend with him, Scott thought. So why didn't the boyfriend report her missing? Or call her friends to find out where she was?

He made a mental note to ask about that once the parents had left.

The tension had sucked all the air out of the room. If Scott had any excuse to leave, he would—in a heartbeat—but he knew he had to press through it. "Mr. and Mrs. Collier, here's what I suggest. Don't lose hope. I understand the sheriff arranged lodging for you. So stay together. Keep your phones charged. I promise you, we will not give up until we find Laney."

Tim Collier's face turned red. "If you think I'm going to hang out in some motel room while my daughter is missing, you're crazy." He took his wife's hand and almost pulled her to her feet. "I'm going to find my girl." He moved to the door. "And just so you know, I'm carrying." And with that, Tim Collier stormed out.

Scott stood up, his pulse pounding in his temples. He'd investigated other cases involving missing young women, but this was the first time he'd been in a small room face-to-face with the parents of one. It was like watching a terrifying remake of his teenage years.

As he tried to regroup, he realized the sheriff was talking to him. "... we'll find out if he has a concealed carry permit, and if he don't—"

Scott raised his hand. "Don't fight that battle yet." He ran his head over his brow. "I need to check on something, and then I want to meet with you and your lead detective." He checked his watch. "Say, fifteen minutes."

39

I WAS STILL MESSED up when Nate met me at the barn about an hour later. "How'd you do?" I asked, looking up from grooming Luke. He'd gotten a few briars in the woods, but I needed the rhythmic stroking as much as he did to calm me down. "How's Scott?"

"Never did see him."

"What?"

"They wouldn't let me in. I ain't law enforcement. What's more, they wouldn't even confirm Scott was there. I tried to leave him a message."

Nate's eyes flicked down to Luke, who had started licking my neck like crazy. I felt a flush of embarrassment as Nate read the signs of my emotional distress in my dog. I straightened my back. "So did you call him?"

"Called. Texted. He's busy." His eyes focused on mine. "So what's going on?"

There was no point in hiding. I told him about Deputy D. Foster and his attitude. I got more than a little dramatic.

Nate shook his head. "Sorry you and Susan had to deal with that." He looked at me with those blue eyes. "Folks in these small towns, they don't know how to handle stuff like this. They're in over their heads, and to them, we're just the dog people. Volunteers. Hardly to be trusted."

"If they only knew," I sputtered, "what it takes."

"I heard on the radio they got the whole town searching now. Hundreds of people— college kids, hunters, moms. They're all out in the woods looking for this girl." Nate made a clicking sound with his mouth. "The deputies got no clue how to handle it."

I tossed my head. The truth is, I'd been on the other side as a law enforcement officer. I'd kept my cards close to my chest, viewed volunteers (and sometimes other officers) with suspicion, and limited what I said, even to family.

The word "family" triggered a thought. I pulled out my phone and checked. Still no message from Brooke. I texted her. *Call me, please. I'm in your area.*

"What are we doing now?" Nate said, breaking my chain of thought.

"Kelly and Ron are searching Segment 28." I checked my watch. "They should be about halfway through."

"Segment 28." Nate spread the topographic map out over the hood of his Tahoe and traced the marked segment with his finger. "Man, that looks like another rough area."

"Why aren't they using drones in those places?" I asked.

"Good question."

Nate took out a Virginia road map and laid it over the other one. As we were discussing better search areas, he got a call. Scott.

While Nate talked to Scott, I tried Brooke again. Still no answer. Was she avoiding me? Then I had another thought. Was she out searching?

I didn't like that idea at all. Instantly, images of the dead young women ran through my mind.

I sat down on a straw bale. Luke nuzzled me, shoving his nose under my hand until I petted him. I rubbed behind his ears, on his neck, and stroked him between his eyes. Soon, he flopped down, his head resting on my foot.

Nate clicked his phone off and walked back to me. "That was Scott."

"I figured."

"I told him we were being asked to search areas that weren't safe and made no sense." Nate sat down in one of the camp chairs we'd brought. "He said he'd talk to the sheriff."

"Did you tell him about Deputy Foster?"

"Sure. Thing is, Scott's limited too. They haven't officially linked this case with the others, so he's here on an advisory basis. He's not in charge."

"And the locals are territorial."

"Exactly." Nate stroked his beard, his eyes fixed on the floor of the barn. Then he looked up at me. "Something's going on with Scott."

I absorbed that statement for a minute. "What makes you say that?"

"Heard it in his voice. Felt it as he was talking."

Before I could pursue that further, Susan called on the radio. "Nate, we need some help." Her voice carried a bit of panic.

"What's going on?"

"Kelly fell. She's hurt."

"We're on the way."

40

AFTER SCOTT CALLED NATE, he grabbed a cup of coffee and met the sheriff and his chief detective, Grady Hunsaker, in the conference room.

He'd asked Tom, the state police investigator who had worked with him on the Sandy Smith case, to come in as well, but he was busy. As he sat down with the sheriff and Hunsaker, Scott fought to maintain his cool, to keep his jaw loose, and his tone moderated, to belie the anger and frustration that gripped him. He had to stay diplomatic, or the locals would shut down.

"So what do we have for a timeline for Laney on Friday night."

Detective Hunsaker went through the basics. "She was last seen about midnight."

"No text messages after that? Social media posts?"

Hunsaker shook his head. "I don't know."

"Have we done a door-to-door of the apartment building, of people who live on that street?"

"Yes, sir. Did that first thing."

"You should do it again." Scott scratched his jaw. "Cab drivers

—has anyone checked cab companies to see if any of them picked her up, or even saw her that night?"

"Ain't but one in town. Caters mostly to old folks and the college kids with no car."

"We need to check with them. How about Uber or Lyft? Do you have that here?"

The sheriff and Hunsaker exchanged looks. "We got a few people do that. Though why you'd get in a car with a stranger is beyond me."

"Does the college have a safe-ride program? Or a safe-student plan?"

"Don't know."

"That'd be good to check on." Scott went over some other ideas he'd had. "Any calls in the last couple of years about a guy acting aggressively toward women, approaching them in bars, that kind of thing?"

"You know how college kids are. Things going on all the time. Mostly, it's women coming on to these guys, dressing the way they do, and then wondering why they're hittin' on 'em."

Scott could feel he was losing patience. "Okay, look. Here's what I suggest ... we need the most detailed timeline we can get of Laney's last evening, I mean, the evening she was last seen." He thought again. "Make it the last day. Every phone call, every text, every Tweet or whatever else we can get. Instagram posts. Whatever. My tech people are working on that, but it all needs to be merged with what you've gotten from interviews.

"Then we want a detailed search of the area. I can bring the dog team. They might pick up on something of hers, a purse, a sweater, something like that. Anything we might be able to get DNA off of. We'll match that with what's on her hairbrush. We need to interview that taxi cab company, Uber, Lyft, and reinterview everyone at the party."

The sheriff inhaled deeply. "You must think we got five

hunnerd deputies. We got twelve, Agent Cooper. Twelve. And some of 'em gotta sleep now and then."

"Okay, look, I can get you more help. But we need to do this. Every hour we don't make progress, her chances of survival get slimmer and slimmer." He stood up. "Now, I want to interview the boyfriend myself. If that's okay."

Fifteen minutes later Scott was sitting in an interview room, along with Detective Hunsaker, across the table from Jared Lawson, Laney's boyfriend. The kid had been at work, but his boss readily let him leave. He'd been pretty useless anyway, distraught over his missing girlfriend.

"Jared, I want to remind you of your Miranda rights." He pushed a form over to the young man. "You have the right to remain silent, the right to a lawyer ..."

"Yes, sir. I understand all that. I got nothing to hide." Tall with curly dark hair, he looked strong, and Scott figured most young women would find him good-looking. Jared glanced at the form. "You want me to sign this?"

"Yes, after you've read it."

"No problem," Jared said, putting his signature on the line and passing the form back. "I just want Laney back safe."

"You from around here, Jared?" Scott asked. He always liked to get a read on the people he was interviewing before he got to the hard questions.

"Yes, sir, born and raised here."

"You go to the college?"

"On a basketball scholarship."

"But you still have to work."

"Yes, sir. My mom, she's real sick and they got no insurance. So my scholarship pays for school, and my job, it's to help out my folks."

"What are you studying?" Scott heard Hunsaker, sitting to his left, shift in his chair.

Jared didn't hesitate. "I plan to be a PE teacher. Hope to coach one day. That's my goal. That and have a family."

Scott nodded and leaned forward, resting his forearms on the table. "Jared, when did you last see Laney?"

"Thursday, sir. We had lunch at the college cafeteria."

"Did she seem normal to you?"

"Yes, sir."

"Nothing off?"

"No, sir."

"Had she talked about anything strange happening lately— some guy she didn't know approaching her, some car trouble, some weird interaction with a stranger?"

Jared leaned back in his seat. He took a deep breath. "They asked me that before, and I've thought about it. I don't remember her saying anything about a guy like that." Tears came to the young man's eyes.

Scott looked straight at that kid, reading his face. The kid looked right back at him. "When's the last time you had a text from her?"

"8:36 on Friday." Jared didn't have to look at his phone. "She texted me that she was at the party, having a good time, and she'd see me later."

"So what was the plan?"

"She was supposed to meet me at my apartment around midnight."

"How would she get there?"

"She could walk from the party to where her car was parked. Then she was supposed to drive over."

"Did Laney drink a lot?"

Jared nodded, looking down toward the table. "I got upset with her about that. But she said," his voice choked, "she said she was just having fun."

After a few more questions, every fiber in Scott's body told him Jared had nothing to do with Laney's disappearance. "Jared, when Laney didn't show up like you expected, why didn't you report it?"

"To who? Her parents hate me. And it didn't seem like I should tell the police, I mean, that could get embarrassing."

"Why? Why would that be embarrassing? Jared, where did you figure Laney was?" he asked softly.

Tears spilled out of the young man's eyes. "I figured she was with another guy."

"Voluntarily?"

"Yes, sir." Jared shook his head. "Laney's ... well ... she's a party girl, and sometimes..." He let his voice trail off.

"Sometimes, what?"

Jared took a deep breath. "She thinks I'm boring. So I figured she met somebody at the party and just took off with him."

Scott nodded.

"It's happened before, so, I didn't call the police. I figured she'd show up. We'd have our usual fight. Then we'd get back together."

"I understand. Thanks, Jared, for talking to us." Scott rose and shook the kid's hand.

"Well that was a sheer waste of time," Hunsaker said, after he left.

"Think so?"

"I know so."

Scott watched the detective leave. He'd just learned that Laney was the more outgoing and stronger person in her relationship with Jared. He was more dependent. She was a party girl prone to risk taking. And it wouldn't surprise Scott a bit if she had gotten into some dude's car.

41

Susan filled Nate and me in on the details when we got there. Kelly had slipped and fallen while crossing a rock face. She was injured. Her dog, a border collie named Pip, was missing. And her walker, Ron, didn't know what to do.

"Where are they?" Nate asked.

Susan read off the coordinates and then pointed to a spot on the topographic map. "I think this is it." She looked at Nate. "Should I call 911?"

"Not yet. Let me talk to Ron." He walked away, his radio at his ear. When he came back, his face was intense. He looked at me. "Will you go with me?"

"Of course."

"Does Pip like Luke?"

"Yes. They play."

"Okay, let's take him and see if she'll come to him."

It took us about ten minutes to get packed and ready to go. We were carrying an emergency stretcher, first-aid supplies, and Nate's climbing gear in addition to our usual stuff. I put extra water bottles in a pack on Luke's back.

After a brutal half-hour climb up a wet, slippery trail, my legs were shaking, and I was out of breath. When we finally reached the rock face where Ron waited, I put Luke on a down-stay until we could scope out the situation.

I looked around. The granite outcropping they'd tried to cross was wet and sloped down. Irritation rose in me. I could see how Kelly fell. We should never have been sent up that trail.

Kelly was about twelve or fifteen feet down a steep slope. Nate was talking to her, figuring out what to do.

"I could safely make it down there," I said, suddenly. I wanted to help, wanted to do more than just stand there. And it was just a slope ... it wasn't like I was volunteering to jump off a cliff.

"Going down ain't the problem," Nate said.

"I know! But I'm lighter than you."

"But Nate's got the EMT cert," Ron said. He was an older guy, around fifty, with gray hair and a grizzled beard. He'd picked up SAR later in life, and I could tell he was frustrated.

"It better be me," Nate said. "Let's rig it up."

Ten minutes later he had his ropes, carabiners, and anchors set. He got into his climbing harness. It seemed a lot of trouble for twelve feet, but when I saw how loose the rock was, when I saw Nate slip even with all that gear, I was glad he was roped up. He knew what he was doing. Nate climbed down to where he could assess Kelly's injuries.

While he did that, I took Luke and went looking for Pip. "Where's Pip?" I said to my dog. "Go find Pip." Would he understand that, I wondered?

We had no luck at first, but then I decided to use the emergency whistle. A lot of the dogs were trained to respond to that. Maybe Pip was one of them.

I heard Nate on the radio, talking to Susan. "She's got signs of a concussion, and I think her ankle's broke. Ron and Jess can help me get her back on the trail, then we'll head back."

That sounded easy, but it wasn't. Nate put an Aircast on Kelly's ankle. Using this cool emergency stretcher that folded into a neat, portable package, he set it up, helped her lie down on it, and roped her in. Then he rigged the anchored climbing rope to it. While he supported the bottom, Ron and I pulled her up to the trail. Her first words to me were, "Where's Pip?"

"We'll find her," I said. I unhooked the rope from the stretcher and threw it back down to Nate. Then I helped Kelly get more comfortable.

I straightened up just in time to see Ron give Nate a hand up. And then I saw Ron slip and Nate fall, and my heart leaped out of my chest.

"Nate!" I raced over and looked down. Nate hadn't fallen far, but when he looked up at me, I saw a bloody abrasion on the side of his face. "How can I help?"

"Check the rope and get out of my way."

"It's secure."

Nate pulled himself back up. "I shoulda done that in the first place. How's Kelly?"

"She's fine."

He looked at Ron. "You okay?"

"Yeah, sorry, I slipped."

Nate nodded. I could tell he was annoyed.

"Let me fix your abrasion," I said to him.

"I want to get her down."

"I know. It'll only take a minute." I grabbed some antiseptic wipes from Nate's kit and cleaned his wound. I felt bad when he winced, but I knew it was for the best. I could tell it was going to continue to seep blood for a while.

"All right, let's go," he said when I was not quite done. "Ron, you okay to carry the bottom of the stretcher?"

"Sure."

Nate looked at me. "You and me, we'll take the top." He called Susan on the radio. "It'll take us twenty to thirty minutes to get down. Have an ambulance waiting."

Kelly's hand was on her brow, her face twisted in pain. Nate tucked a blanket around her. "I don't want to leave without my dog!" she said.

"Don't you be worrying about the dog. We'll find her," Nate said. "Jess is gonna keep blowing the whistle." He glanced at me. "She'll show up."

I wasn't so sure about that, but I stuck that whistle in my mouth before I picked up the stretcher, and I blew it. I kept doing that all the way down that slippery, treacherous hill. Luke seemed to understand his job was to follow us, and he did that well, until about twenty minutes into our descent. Then, he took off.

I started to call him back, but Nate said, "Let him be." He'd switched places with Ron, who was having trouble supporting the downhill weight on his own as well as picking the best way down. Twice he'd slipped, and we almost dropped Kelly.

"Find Pip," Nate called out to my dog.

It was a little annoying that he was telling my dog what to do, but I went along with it this time. We were all exhausted, and Nate was hurt, and well, I just decided to ignore it.

But as we neared the bottom of the hill, I began to panic about Luke. He was nowhere in sight nor could I hear where he was. I blew the emergency whistle again, and suddenly, I heard him barking. It was his happy bark, and seconds later he came crashing through the forest along with a very dirty and bedraggled border collie. Pip.

"Good boy, good boy!" I cried. "Good dog!" Thankfully, we had just set Kelly down, and I was able to pound Luke's side and let him know how happy I was. I looked up at Nate. "How'd you know he'd find her?"

Nate shrugged.

The dog man strikes again.

The ambulance took Kelly off to a hospital about forty minutes away. Ron agreed to take Pip home, and Susan, Nate, and I went back to the barn, dirty, tired, and frustrated. We'd spent the day, the whole day, on searches that were not only useless, they were harmful.

"We're not doing this tomorrow," Nate said as we walked into the barn. He sank down in a camp chair. That's when I saw his face wasn't the only casualty—his left pants leg was torn, and I could see his knee was bloody.

"Hey, your knee's all messed up. Can I help you with that?" I asked.

"I'll get it in a minute. I just need to sit for a while. You okay with me checking out for a bit?"

"Sure, Nate. Whatever you need."

"A while" turned in to half an hour. He moved to the back of the barn, sat on a straw bale, and leaned his head back against the wall, his eyes closed. Most people would have thought he was just resting, but I knew what he was doing; he was praying. I guessed that was his version of re-centering, of practicing mindfulness, of processing his emotions. Sprite jumped up next to him and rested her head on his leg.

I left him alone, busying myself with figuring out where to pitch the tents, and petting Luke, all while fighting my own internal battles. I felt like the sheriff's office was toying with us, giving us busywork so they could be the real heroes, but this wasn't about being a hero. The stakes were higher than most of them realized. A young woman's life was at risk. I wished I were back in law enforcement, using my gun and my badge to find her. To protect and serve, just like my father. That had been my goal since I was twelve.

I felt a rush of shame as the reality of my old failure hit me again. I heard the accusations from the guys back in Fairfax, felt the sideways stares, and cringed at the jokes they claimed were just part of being a cop.

Overwhelmed, I sat down on a straw bale in the stall. Luke pressed himself against me, and I softly petted him. I could feel that little book in my back pocket. I thought about pulling it out to distract myself with the stories inside.

But something in me rebelled at that, and instead, I sat there, consumed by a mini-panic attack. It felt like a series of little electrical shocks, like miniature cattle prods or Tasers being fired at me. It unnerved me. Would I ever be whole again?

After a while, I heard Nate get up. He opened his first-aid kit and doctored his wounds. I would have helped, but I got the feeling he didn't want to be touched by anyone, even me, just then. I understood that.

So I checked my phone and found a barbeque place not far away. I knew Nate loved barbeque. So, I volunteered to go get us food.

"That would be right nice," he said, looking at me with those blue eyes. "Thank you."

Nate was back. Thank goodness. I felt my own soul settle.

I put Luke in a stall and climbed into my car, happy to be behind the wheel, happy to be in control of something. Willie's BBQ was about fifteen minutes away. The whole time I was driving, navigating those twisty back roads, I was thinking about Laney, keeping alert for any clues I might happen to pass.

But there was another thought lurking in my head. It was just outside my mind's eye, and it was bugging me that I couldn't figure out what it was, couldn't bring it into view.

I was about five minutes away from Willie's when I got a call from Nate asking me to pick up food for Scott too. "And we ain't sleepin' in the barn. He got us rooms at a motel. I'm texting you the address. Meet us there. I'll bring Luke and your stuff."

Well, that was good news. I was bone-tired and sleeping in a bed rather than on the ground sounded great.

I got double orders for the guys, ribs and pulled pork sandwiches, with coleslaw and fries, and a sandwich for me. I plugged the address Nate had sent me into my phone and found it was only ten minutes away. I was on my way there when I remem-

bered I needed to get oil for my Jeep. Fortunately, I saw a place
that was a combination country store and gas station. I pulled in.

The place was jammed with men. They all looked like
hunters, wearing camo and orange hats, or construction workers,
and they were buying beer and cigarettes and Skoal. Instantly,
uneasy shivers ran up my spine. I moved toward the back where I
guessed the auto supplies would be found if they had any.

They did. They had five different brands of oil of the grade I
used, all in plastic containers. I picked up one and started reading
it, wondering if I could mix it with what was already in the oil
pan. I finally just grabbed one and went to stand in line at the
counter.

There were four guys ahead of me. I began looking at the
impulse buys they'd put up front near the register, the trinkets
and keychains, candy and lighters. And then something else
caught my eye. On the shelf behind the register next to cartons
and cartons of cigarettes, were some sculptures—animal figures
carved out of wood.

My heart thumped. "Can I see one of those?" I asked when
my turn came.

"Which one?" The clerk, a grizzled old guy in his fifties,
growled at me.

"The eagle." I moved to the side and said to the guy behind
me, "You go ahead."

I took the carved figure in my hand. It was about six inches
high, unpainted, and beautifully done. Wings outspread, claws
extended, that eagle looked like it was just about to grab a fish or
a mouse.

I turned it over, expecting to see a Made-in-China sticker on
the bottom. But no, there were only the initials "JJ."

I stepped back to the register.

Keeping my voice level, I said, "Where'd you get these?"

The old guy huffed. "Local guy. He makes 'em. Name's Junior.

Says he's from around here. I don't know him. Comes in every Monday, and I pay him for what we've sold."

My heart jumped. "I'd like three of these please, the eagle, the dog, and the deer."

"They're twenty bucks. Each."

"They'd make good Christmas gifts, right?" I flashed a smile as I pulled out cash.

He handed me my change. "Next?"

I scooped up my statues and oil and left, my heart pounding.

42

Ten minutes later I arrived at the motel. Nate had texted me a room number. I put the statues in my jacket pockets, grabbed the food, and went in, my head still buzzing from what I'd found.

Scott answered the door. Nate rose to take the bags of food out of my hand, and Luke came over and nudged me. I should have felt welcomed and comfortable. Instead, my excitement over finding the statues dissipated. My nerve abandoned me. How crazy was I to think these little carvings had anything to do with the murders? I mean, more than one guy knows how to whittle.

So I did what I always do. I faked it and passed out the food. We ate and talked about the case we were on and the problems we'd had, and all the while, those statues were dancing like sugar plums in my head.

Scott shared his frustrations, and as always, Nate listened thoughtfully and gave encouraging advice. I, on the other hand, remained mute, about as useful as a carved figure sitting on a shelf.

We finished eating and cleaned up, but oddly, that image—me, carved and sitting on a shelf—kept nagging at me. Finally I gave in to my intuition.

At a pause in the conversation, I said, "This may seem crazy, but on the way here, I had to stop at a gas station." I told them the rest of the story, then I rose and retrieved the statues from my jacket pockets. I handed one to each of them, keeping the little dog for myself.

Scott was the first to react. "Wow, these are beautiful," he said, rotating the wood carving in his hand.

"Somebody spent a lot of time whittlin' to get this good," Nate said. He looked straight at me, and I could tell by the light in his eyes he thought I was on to something.

"As soon as I saw them, I couldn't help but think—"

"of the guy whittling in the woods." Scott finished my sentence for me. He rose to his feet. "Where'd these come from?"

I felt a rush of affirmation. I could tell from their energy, both guys were on board. I told them about the store, gave them the location, and provided all the information the clerk had given me.

"All right. Thanks! I'll get right on this," Scott said as he collected the other two statues. Then he turned his eyes full on me. "You've got good instincts, Jess. And look, I'll punch out anybody who gives you a hard time. You just let me know."

Masculine posturing usually irritates me, but that night, it felt good.

My room was right next to Nate's. He helped me get settled in, then we walked the dogs together in the grassy area behind the motel. I noticed he was limping a lot, although the abrasion on his face had stopped bleeding.

We agreed to get up at five o'clock, so we had time to eat breakfast and take care of the dogs before the sun came up. Hopefully, we'd have more logical areas to search. In fact, both of us had wondered about searching the area of the apartment where Laney was last seen. Maybe she'd dropped something—a purse, a cell phone, or a tissue—anything that might provide a clue. Luke was trained to find *any* person, but I thought he'd alert on a smell from a specific person as well.

The next morning at breakfast, Nate asked me if I'd heard from my sister. "Nope," I responded, "but that's not unusual. We don't talk a lot."

He scratched his chin, which made me think. Should I be more aggressive about touching base with her?

The head of the K-9 unit called Nate at six-thirty, bypassing Susan, the incident commander. Typical. He wanted to meet with us and when Nate told him where we were, he agreed to come to the motel.

Ty Washington's demeanor was as chiseled and tough as his body. He barely looked at Susan or me. When he saw Sprite lying on the bed in Nate's room, he rolled his eyes.

His demeanor and aggression didn't seem to faze Nate, who held his ground, insisting on giving input as to where we would search. "We been doing this a number of years, Ty," he said firmly. "I can tell you what makes sense when it comes to searching."

Finally, the two of them began poring over the maps, and they came up with three areas both agreed were worth searching—two near the college and one near Jared's apartment. Nate asked Susan to consent, which of course she did, and the two men shook on it.

My enthusiasm for having logical marching orders for the day was tempered by a panicky phone call I received from my mother.

"Jess, Brooke's missing!"

"Mom, what? What are you talking about?" I pressed the phone to my ear and walked away from the others. Out of the corner of my eye, I saw the K-9 officer leave.

"Your sister! I can't reach her. And I saw on the news about this missing woman up in Brooke's area."

"It's not Brooke, Mom. The missing woman's name is Laney." I took a deep breath, trying to relax. To be honest, the fear in my mother's voice was getting to me. "When did you last hear from Brooke?"

"I talked to her Thursday night. But she was supposed to call Frank this weekend! And she didn't."

"About what?" I didn't hear an immediate answer, so I rephrased it. "What was she supposed to call him about?"

"I don't know. It's usually about money, or her car, or something."

"Well, Mom, she probably just got busy. With midterms or something." Did they still have midterms in college? It seemed to me they were just giving out smiley faces these days. "I assume you've tried calling her?"

"Over and over."

I chose not to mention my own unproductive calls. "She probably forgot to charge her phone. Tell you what, Mom. Give me her address and any names you have—roommate, friends, any contacts. And I'll see if I can track her down."

"You'll drive up there? You have time?"

A little flash of guilt went through me. Obviously, I wasn't that great at communicating either. "I'm actually in her town already, with Luke. We're working on the search for the other girl."

"I had no idea!"

"Sorry, I didn't tell you. We got called out suddenly and well, I've been busy."

"I guess so."

Mom gave me Brooke's address, but all she had for contacts were first names. Seems like little Brookie didn't want Mom and Dad to know too much about her college life. I took what she had, though, and promised I'd find her.

I clicked off the phone and turned toward Nate, whose eyebrows were raised. "Brooke. My Mom can't reach her either."

Nate shook his head just once. "Kids going to college can be hard on a parent. Not knowing where they are and all." He looked at me. "What do you want to do?"

I'd already decided. "I want to do this first search, and then maybe over lunch I'll run by her dorm."

"Sounds like plan."

"Nate ..."

He turned back to me.

"How do you stay so cool when you're dealing with people like that guy, Ty?"

"What do you mean?"

"He was so dismissive of you, me, Susan, even Sprite. So arrogant."

Nate nodded. "He was that. Deal is, though, he ain't my boss. Ain't my father or my teacher. Got no right to judge me. So why should I care what he thinks? That's his problem." He bent down and patted Sprite. "You got to know who to listen to, who to believe. You don't want to give just anybody a key to your soul."

I thought about that as we packed up. In the past, I'd allowed just about anybody that access. I usually succeeded at what I was doing, so the accolades piled up and so did my self-esteem.

But that dreadful night, that dark and rainy night when a suspect we were bringing in killed my partner, when I totally lost control of a critical situation, that night wiped out all the gains in self-esteem I'd ever made. My heart was used to searching for approval from the people around me. Then what it found was condemnation. Criticism. Scorn. And instead of self-confidence and pride, shame had flooded in.

Nate had said only two things were strong enough to cover shame. The first was anger. The second ... my mind flashed back to the woman in the story. I realized I had stopped packing up and Nate was staring at me.

I looked at him, eyes wide. "The second thing strong enough to cover shame—it's love, isn't it?"

He smiled softly, his eyes crinkling. "Yep. The unconditional love of God." He didn't go any further. It was like he was inviting me, not trying to control me. And it almost made me want to pursue it further.

Almost, but not quite.

The first area we'd been given to search was partially wooded and part open, rolling hills. The other SAR team took the open part. Nate and I would search the woods. Luke trembled with excitement as I put his SAR vest on. "You ready to go, buddy?" I asked him. "Ready to go?"

"Go" was one of his favorite words. He danced around me.

Nate had a search plan worked out. We cleared it with Susan and were just about to set off when I got a text from my Mom. *Let me know if you find her.*

I was so focused on finding Laney right then that momentarily, I was confused. Then I realized Mom was talking about Brooke. *Will do,* I texted back.

"Ready?" Nate asked.

"Yes." I made Luke heel, unclipped his leash, and uttered his very favorite word. "Seek!" He bounded off into the woods, and Nate and I followed.

It still gave me great joy to see my smart dog doing what he loved.

For the next two hours, we chased after Luke. We checked out gullies, a couple of abandoned outbuildings, a small cave, and several streambeds. We crossed an old, broken-down fence, found a pretty meadow, and started working our way back again.

All the while, I was hoping we would not find a little clearing where a dead girl stared sightlessly upward.

On the way back, I called Luke to me and distracted him. Nate went ahead and hid so Luke could find him. You've got to let these dogs succeed as often as possible to keep them in the game.

Luke was elated when he found his second favorite person in the world. He came racing back to me, pulled the tug on my belt, and raced back to Nate, back and forth. When I caught up with them, they were engaged in a rowdy tug of war over a stick. "Good Luke, good boy!" I said and pulled his toy out of my pocket.

Oh, the joy that dog expressed over such simple things. I couldn't watch him without smiling.

"Makes your burdens feel lighter, don't it?" Nate said.

We walked out of the woods and checked in with Susan. We agreed to meet at our next location in ninety minutes. Nate would take Luke with him back to the motel. I was on my way to my sister's dorm.

I started out in irritated, big-sister mode. Leave it to Brooke to intrude on my plans. I would have loved to be able to have a relaxed lunch with Nate, maybe stretch out a little, before going on to our next assignment.

But no, here I was, tracking down my irresponsible half sister so my panicky mother wouldn't completely disown me. Brookie was the family treasure. I had to find her.

43

I HAD no problem finding her dorm, and no problem getting in—
I just walked in behind someone. College students are notori-
ously nonchalant about security, even when they're sober. I took
the elevator to the third floor and knocked on the door.

No answer. I walked down the hall and found an open door,
stuck my head inside, and said, "Hey, I'm looking for Brooke
Anderson. Have you seen her?"

Two students were lying on their beds, both staring at their
phones. "Who?"

"Brooke. She lives three doors down."

"We don't know her," one said.

*If you'd get your faces out of your phones, maybe you'd know your
neighbors.* "Okay, thanks."

Undaunted, I continued looking for someone, anyone, who
knew Brooke. Finally, I found a young woman on the second
floor. "We usually study together for our psychology class. But
she hasn't been around."

"When's the last time you saw her?"

"Last Thursday."

Okay, now I was starting to get worried. Friday was the day

Laney disappeared. "What's your normal study pattern? Do you have a set day and time? Do you text each other? What?"

"We just text and meet when we can. But we always, always study together for tests."

"And when's your next test?"

"Tomorrow."

A chill ran through me. "Do you have any idea if Brooke knows Laney Collier?"

"The girl that's missing? No, I have no idea."

"It's a small school," I said.

"Yeah, but you know ... you have your friends and you text and you party, but nobody really knows anybody."

"Does Brooke have a boyfriend?"

The girl shrugged.

"A part-time job?"

"I don't know."

"Where does she hang out when she wants to relax?"

"The gym? Or the coffee bar? I mean, everybody does."

Everybody and nobody. Sheesh. I walked away from that interview, shaking my head. How could there be such a gap between my peers and Brooke's in terms of friendships and connection? How could you live three doors down from Brooke Anderson and not know who she was? How could you study with someone and not have a clue about the rest of her life?

As I left the dorm, I texted my stepfather to get a description of Brooke's car, the model year and license plate number. I figured my mom would freak if I asked her.

Frank got back to me pretty quickly. I drove over to the admin building and talked to the assistant dean of students. She didn't really know my half sister but was able to give me the parking lot to which Brooke was assigned.

I went to that lot, which was near her dorm, and drove up and down every row. Her car was not there.

By this time, my concern was building, but my ninety minutes were nearly up. I drove to the second search site. Nate picked up on my stress right away. "You want me to do this with Susan?"

"And Luke? No." Luke was my dog, and it was my search. Despite my anxiety.

Nate had mapped out a plan, and we set off. This time we were given open fields, pastureland that belonged to a farm adjacent to the town. It was within a mile of where Laney was last seen, so it made sense.

Not only that, it was easier to search. There were hills, but we weren't climbing a mountain and we weren't watching for snakes. We were looking out for cow pies.

Not a problem. Except that Luke thought they smelled delicious and managed to roll in one before I could stop him. I'm sure he thought that masking his own smell would make finding the elusive human easier.

I was so annoyed. But watching Luke luxuriate in his find, rolling on his back, a silly grin on his face, made Nate start laughing, and once he started, I couldn't resist joining in. There's nothing like a dog for comic relief.

Two hours later we had searched that whole farm, including the barn, an abandoned smokehouse (more delicious smells), an icehouse, and around the farmhouse itself. There was just one place we didn't search, and that was the manure pit, a big, round concrete structure behind the barn. I stopped and stared at it, thinking that would be a great place to hide a body.

Nate came up next to me. "Could Luke sniff out a body with all that manure smell?" I asked.

"Possibly. Let's walk around it. That thing's about eight feet tall. He won't jump in it."

"He'd like to," I said, smiling.

"Yeah, that's his kind of spa. Let's just walk around, slow-like, and see what he does."

The manure pit was about twenty feet in diameter. As we walked around, Nate told me all about manure pits, about how valuable they were for collecting fertilizer for the fields, and how they helped keep pollution out of the streams, and how they were the devil to search if you had to go in one. "Lot of farmers been killed in these things. The gas gets 'em if they're not careful."

Luke didn't alert at all as we walked around it, so Nate declared the manure pit was most likely clear. Not a 100 percent, he said, but likely clear.

We walked down the farm lane to the road that would lead us back to Susan. There was no traffic, and I had Luke checking the ditches as we went. Working this search had taken my mind off Brooke, but the closer we got to our base, the more my missing half sister intruded on my thoughts.

Nate said he'd handle the debriefing with Susan. He could tell my mind was somewhere else. Besides, I had to clean off my stinky, smelly dog.

A lot of the manure had already dried on Luke's coat. So I started out with a curry comb, brushing out all that I could. And while I brushed, I thought.

As a licensed private investigator, I had certain abilities to get into a person's life. But my mind had already raced past those limited abilities. I was ready to track my sister down, but to do that, I needed official law enforcement help. Which meant asking my parents to report Brooke missing.

I had another idea first. I used enough dry shampoo on Luke to drown a cat, then sprayed Febreze in the back of my car. He kind of wrinkled his nose, objecting as eau de cow poop diminished. Then I put him in his crate and closed the back.

"I'll be an hour," I said to Nate.

He looked at me. "I'll come with you."

I decided to let him. He put Sprite in my car, and we took off. "What are we looking for?" he asked.

I gave him the make, model, and license plate number of Brooke's car. Then I drove, and he looked.

We started with the college, checking all the lots, then we

started going through the town. We saw two similar cars and stopped to check them out, but they weren't Brooke's.

Then we started on the residential areas. There were fewer cars, of course, so Nate decided to call local towing companies to see if they'd picked up her car.

No luck. No luck with any of it. Finally, frustrated, I pulled over, turned to Nate, and said, "Is it time to escalate this?"

44

NATE STUDIED MY FACE, then stared straight ahead while he thought.

Truth was, the best ways to track Brooke would be by pinging her cell phone or checking credit card usage. Only law enforcement could do that. The thought of going into that police station and interacting with a bunch of arrogant officers was about as attractive to me as walking into a manure pit. Still, I felt I had to.

"I think it is," Nate said, confirming my thinking. "Call Scott."

My anxiety level rose ten points.

Nate touched my shoulder. "You can do this."

I closed my eyes and nodded. "Yes. I have to."

But first I wanted to get cleaned up. I smelled like Luke, who smelled like poop. So I drove back to the motel. Nate took the dogs, and I took a shower. I got dressed in my most confidence-producing clothes and called my stepfather.

My head swam as I talked to him. I kept my voice calm, but I told him the information he needed to have on hand—her debit or credit card numbers, cell-phone information, and any other ID.

"I'm headed to the police station now. We'll be in touch so you can make the official report."

I called Nate before I left. Honestly, I could have just texted him, but I wanted to hear his voice.

"You want me to go with you?" he asked.

"No, I got this."

"You talk to Scott?"

"I had to leave a message."

He nodded. "Okay, then."

I walked out of my motel room and was headed for my car when Nate came rushing after me.

"Jess!"

I stopped. "Here," he said, pressing something into my hand. It was a tan stone, very smooth, like it had come from a creek bed.

"Stick that in your pocket and remember ... ain't nobody got any right to throw a stone at you."

I felt my face grow hot. It was like he'd been reading over my shoulder. I looked at him, incredulous. Then I regrouped. I certainly didn't want to have that discussion now.

"Thank you," I said, and I gave him a quick hug. Nate kissed the top of my head, just like my dad would have.

I drove to the sheriff's office and walked in. I faced the desk sergeant and told him what I wanted. Within minutes, I was sitting at an officer's desk in a bullpen. Waiting for him, I could feel the testosterone-driven energy of the place and hear the cop-talk surrounding me. It was all too familiar. Nausea licked in my belly. Words flung at me in Fairfax raced through my head. I stuck my hand in my pocket, grabbed that rock, and gripped it.

"What can I do for you?"

I looked up as Deputy Billy Daniels sat down. He was an older guy with gray hair and a paunch. I explained to him what I wanted and told him why I was in the area. Then I glanced around. I didn't want Deputy D. Foster surprising me.

"I heard y'all went home," Daniels said.

"One team went home because one of our volunteers got hurt,

but there's still five of us here."

"And you're this girl's sister."

"Half sister, yes."

He went on to explain how missing persons reports work. I already knew all that, but I listened as if I didn't. I filled out most of the form he put in front of me, then called my stepfather and connected the two. Anxiety gripped me. I ached because I was so tense. I wished Luke was with me.

I didn't have my dog, but I did have my rock. So I clenched it.

"We'll put out a BOLO on the car," I heard the deputy tell my stepfather. "That's the first step. After that, we'll see what happens."

I could imagine that fell on my stepfather's ears like a ton of bricks. I also knew from a cop's point of view, it was pretty realistic. Chances are my half sister had just changed her plans. Was with a friend somewhere. Had decided to take a road trip. Didn't want her parents or her boyfriend to know.

Happens all the time. No need to panic.

Except the deputy didn't know about the other girls lying dead in the forest. The deputy didn't know my little sister fit the victim description perfectly. The deputy didn't know he had a former detective sitting at his desk, a detective that had no intention of depending on a BOLO alone, a detective who wasn't about to let her younger sister become victim number four. Maybe five.

"Thank you, sir," I said, rising from the chair.

"We'll be in touch."

I made sure he had my cell phone number. As I turned to leave, I saw Deputy D. Foster across the room. He was engaged in conversation, but he'd seen me, and the sneer on his face infuriated me, even from twenty feet away.

I walked out angry. I was halfway down the sidewalk when I heard my name.

"Jess! Jessica."

I turned to see Scott Cooper jogging after me. "What?"

He flinched at the sharpness of my response. "What's going on? I'm sorry I haven't had time to respond to your message."

I glared at him. Then I remembered he wasn't the enemy. Plus, he was Hurting Man. Layers. I had to see things in layers. I closed my eyes for a second.

Then I told him what happened inside. "A BOLO isn't going to cut it. You know that and I know that. We need to go live on her credit card and trace her cell phone. It has to be done now, Scott. She fits the profile." To my surprise, I started to tear up. I quickly looked down so he wouldn't see it.

"I'm on it, Jess. I'm totally with you. But I need information."

"Here," I said, and I texted him what my stepfather had sent me. Tag number. Description of car. Credit-card number. Cell phone. I added my sister's full name and physical description.

Scott grabbed my shoulders and looked hard at me. "Don't worry. We will find her. I will find her. I promise."

"Thank you," I said, my voice cracking.

I drove back to the motel, but there was no way, no possible way, I could stay in that little room while my sister was possibly in danger. I knocked on Nate's door. I needed Luke.

Nate invited me in, but I told him I'd only come for Luke. One look at his face told me the man was tired, and I made the decision not to include him in my plans. He needed to rest. I couldn't.

So I stood at the door and gave him the Reader's Digest version of my visit to the sheriff's office. I kept my voice level and relaxed my jaw. I didn't want him to get a hint of what I planned to do.

Then I gathered my dog and his leash and harness and food and water bowls, and I went back to my room. I sat there in the dark, stroking my dog, hoping Nate would soon go back to reading the book I'd seen on his bed. Maybe even fall asleep.

About fifteen minutes later, I quietly left, sneaking away with Luke like a teenager.

I wasn't five minutes away before my phone rang. Nate. I

swiped IGNORE.

The first place I went was my sister's dorm. While driving, I tried to figure out how to proceed. I'd wondered if Lee Park had ever begun training Luke to track. To follow a specific scent.

It was a long shot. But then, we didn't know he'd been trained as an HRD dog until he found Faith Caldwell's body. I'd trained him as an air-scent dog—find any human.

Was it possible he'd also be able to track?

I was venturing into Lassie territory, I knew. Pretty unrealistic.

I walked into Brooke's dorm, hoping her roommate was in.

She was. Tara Grimes was in the room. But she had no idea where Brooke was. Said she hadn't seen her for a couple of days, but frankly, that wasn't unusual for Brooke. She had a lot of friends and slept in different places.

I got Tara's cell-phone number and put it in my contacts. Then I took the T-shirt that was lying on Brooke's bed. If Luke could track, that T-shirt would give him the scent.

I'd left Luke in the Jeep. I got him out now and showed him the shirt. "Find it!"

Those were the words I'd used when I was training him to find cotton balls soaked in birch oil. I let him sniff around the bushes outside of the dorm. We walked all the way around the dorm and up and down the street. Nothing.

Then I dropped the shirt behind a car when he wasn't looking, moved a little further down the street, did a U-turn, and said, "Find it!" His nose started working, and to my great joy, he found the shirt.

"Good boy, good boy!" I said, and I took out a tug and played with him.

Was that luck? I had no idea. I suspected teaching a dog to track reliably took a lot more time, repetition, and practice. Still, what could I do? My sister was missing and conceivably in danger. I had no time. And I'd try anything.

Next, we moved to the apartment where the party had been

held. Again, I showed Luke the shirt and told him to "Find it."

He spent a lot of time sniffing around the porch of that building. A lot of time. Then, when I suggested we move toward the street, he led the way. I waited to see which way he'd turn when the front walk met the sidewalk. First, he turned right, then he backtracked a few steps and turned around.

I wanted to believe he was following Brooke's scent. Maybe it was wishful thinking. But maybe it wasn't.

Twenty feet down the sidewalk, Luke took a sudden turn to the left. He crossed the grassy strip and got to the curb. He sniffed left and right, forward and back, and then he looked at me. I imagined he was saying, "This is where it stops."

Oh, my gosh, was Luke really scenting Brooke? My heart beat faster. I turned and looked again at the path we had taken. Was Brooke at the party? Had she walked out of the building? Is this where she got into a car? Was it her car?

Despite my excitement, I reminded myself to reward Luke. I made him sit and stay facing the other direction. I walked back and hid the shirt in some bushes. Then I told him to "Find it!" It took him like five seconds. He tossed the shirt in the air and caught it over and over, as if to say, "Man, this is easy!" Then we played.

We got back in the Jeep. I texted Brooke's roommate and asked about the party. She said Brooke often went to Friday-night parties, but she didn't remember her saying anything about that one. I asked her if Brooke knew Laney Collier. She didn't know.

Don't kids know to keep tabs on each other anymore?

That thought seemed a little hypocritical when I noticed I had three missed calls and two ignored texts from Nate.

I had a sudden, sinking feeling. If Brooke had been at that party with Laney and had left in a car, they could be anywhere. Despite Luke's good work, I was no closer to finding either of them than I was before.

I stared through my windshield. What should I do now?

45

STARING through the windshield into the dark night, I debated what to do next. I couldn't just drive around aimlessly. There was no point in that. I thought of calling Nate back, but I knew he'd be mad at me, and frankly, I didn't want to face that. I cared about him too much.

I finally decided to call Scott. I wanted to be sure he'd gotten on my sister's case.

"Hey, Jess," he answered. "I'm glad you called. Nate's been trying to get in touch with you."

"Oh, yeah, sorry. I accidentally left my cell phone in the car," I lied. "Can you give me any updates?"

"We've put out a BOLO on your sister and her car. We're working on going live on her credit card and tracking her cell phone. And Jess, that lead you gave us on those statues? It may be panning out."

"What?"

"We finally got the carver's name, Charles 'Junior' Jones. We're trying to track him down now. His address is a PO Box."

"Good," I said.

"Listen, I get anything more, I'll call you, okay? Just answer your phone."

I felt myself redden. "Okay, I will. But don't hesitate to wake me up."

There was nothing for me to do but go back to the motel. My dread increased with every mile as I thought of facing the wrath of Nate. But I deserved it.

I wasn't even all the way out of the car before Nate's motel room door opened, and he came out. "I'm sorry!" I hoped a preemptive strike would diffuse his anger.

He stopped short, looked at me, his eyes narrowed, and said, "That was a boneheaded thing to do. What were you thinking?"

I faced him straight on. "I needed to do something. I knew you'd tell me to stay here and wait. I couldn't."

"So why didn't you tell me so we could do it together?"

I lifted my chin. "I saw you were tired. I was tired, too, but I knew I couldn't rest. So I decided to go alone. I'm sorry."

He shook his head. "Get your dog and come to my room. I want to hear what you found out."

Thankfully, the wrath of Nate was tempered by mercy and forgiveness.

We went into Nate's motel room. He got Luke water while I used the bathroom. We talked for an hour. I asked him if he thought it was possible Luke was really tracking Brooke's scent from the T-shirt.

"I cain't say for sure. He's a smart dog though."

Luke thumped his tail when Nate said that. Honestly. You'd think the dog spoke English.

By 10:00 p.m. I was worn out, so we walked the dogs together and I took Luke back to my room. I promised Nate I wouldn't leave the motel without letting him know.

I broke that promise just three hours later.

First, my recurring dream woke me up. I hadn't had it in weeks. So why now?

I sat up, gasping for breath, shaking, my heart pounding. Luke came to me immediately and tried to calm me down. I let him up on the bed and stroked him while I tried to relax. I laid there, trying to figure out what had triggered my nightmare.

It had something to do with the sculptures. What had Scott told me? I went over our conversation in my head.

That's when it struck me. Adrenaline hit me so hard I jumped out of bed.

I didn't remember a lot about the night my partner was killed, but I did remember this— the suspect was a woodchuck. He sold firewood in the suburbs. His name was Charles Jones Jr. When I searched him, I found an unusual knife. A carver's knife, maybe? And the woman he was choking before we arrested him was small and blonde.

Seriously? Seriously?

I paced. I worried. I tried to put the facts of that night together, but it was like trying to put together a jigsaw puzzle with some of the pieces missing.

After Jones asked us to leave, we heard screaming. We reentered the house and found him choking his girlfriend. We arrested him, cuffed him, and put him in the car. I remembered it was pouring down rain. The roads were slick. I was driving when I heard a strange sound. I turned and saw Jones choking my partner. I reached for my gun, and then there was a terrible crash.

I began shaking, an anxiety attack creeping up on me like a wildcat in the grass. Could Charles Jones Jr. really be Junior Jones?

I checked my watch. It was 2:00 a.m. I hesitated, but then I clicked open the contacts app on my phone. I could not believe that after nearly three years, I was calling my police captain in the middle of the night.

Obviously, I woke him up. "Jones is a common name," he said.

"I know it's a stretch." My phone beeped, signaling another call coming in. I looked. It was Scott. "I'm working with Scott

Cooper, an FBI agent out of the Northern Virginia office. He's calling me now. I gotta take it. If you find out anything—"

"I'll look into it in the morning." He paused. "It's good to hear from you, Jess. Even if it is two in the morning."

I clicked over to Scott's call, desperate to catch it before it went to voicemail.

"Hey, we found your sister's car," Scott said.

My heart jumped.

"It's on State Route 676, about a mile past Route 741, just beyond an abandoned gas station," he said.

"Any houses around?"

"Nope. It's a rural, wooded area, kind of in the middle of nowhere."

What would she be doing there?

Scott continued. "We're finishing up here, then we're taking it to a secure garage for more analysis."

"What about the dogs? Have the dogs searched the area?"

"The K-9 officers want to wait until morning. They said it's too dangerous to work these woods at night."

Baloney. "Okay, thanks for letting me know."

"You'll tell your parents?"

"In the morning." I clicked off my phone. My bed was waiting, but I knew there was no way ... no possible way ... I'd fall back to sleep.

I got dressed. I gathered up Luke's things. I grabbed my SAR pack. And I snuck out of that motel again despite my promise to Nate.

GPS is good for finding an address, but a vague location like Scott had given me was harder. Fortunately, I had a paper Virginia map. I pulled it out and traced the curly path Route 676 took as it wound through the mountains. I found the intersection with Route 741, started the Jeep, and drove out of the parking lot.

As I drove, my mind raced ahead. If they'd already picked up the car, how would I tell where it was? Would they have left crime-scene tape? I doubted it.

I shouldn't have worried. As I passed the abandoned gas station, I saw Brooke's car was gone, but my headlights caught the reflection of two marked sheriff's deputy cars. One of them was marked K-9.

I drove past them and pulled off on the shoulder, hoping against hope that Deputy D. Foster was not the K-9 officer. As I got out of my car, angry barking erupted.

I had to find Brooke. And two sheriff's deputies stood in the way.

Making sure the K-9 was contained in a car, I took Luke out of the back of my Jeep. I leashed him up and showed him Brooke's T-shirt. Then I stuck it under my jacket and walked toward where her car had been.

"Can I help you?" one of the deputies asked, moving to block my access to the site. He had that command-and-control tone I so hated. It was Deputy D. Foster.

I felt Luke tugging on the leash. I decided to be direct. I reminded Foster I was with the volunteer search and rescue team. I said it was my sister's car they'd found, and I wanted to see where it had been parked. I told them I was worried about her.

"There's nothing to see."

I silently wished I had my badge and gun. "I'd like to look, if you don't mind. I won't touch anything or move across the crime scene."

"Let her look," the other guy called out. "It won't hurt anything."

After a second, Foster stepped aside.

I moved ten feet closer to the marked crime scene and cast my flashlight over it. Foster was right—there was nothing to see.

But there was lots to smell if you were a dog.

Luke did his job. Soon, he began pulling me toward the woods.

Would Brooke have run into the woods? Or been forced into them?

Quickly, I reviewed my options. I'd left my pack in the Jeep, but if I went back for it, the cops would get suspicious. I shouldn't go into the woods on my own, but I wanted to follow Luke. I could call Nate or Scott once I was away from the cops.

"I guess he's gotta go," I said to the deputies. "Thanks for letting me see that spot." Impulsively, I moved into the woods before they could stop me. "Be right back!" I said when they called out to me.

But I wasn't going to be right back. I was going to follow my dog. Luke had his nose to the ground and barely deviated from the tiny path he'd found. I was thrilled he was tracking something, but I was also growing more nervous by the minute. First, with the thought those cops might try to follow me, and second, with the fear of what lay ahead.

Had my sister come down this way? Would I find her in the woods? Who else would I find? Did Brooke see Laney get abducted and try to follow? Was she searching for her and got lost in the woods?

A strong wind had come up, and it whistled through the trees. Now and then I heard a limb break and crash to the ground. A few white clouds, illuminated by the half moon, raced across the dark sky. I had the feeling the whole world was adrenalized like me.

Luke pulled me like he was after a steak. Then I heard a text come in.

"Stop, Luke. Hold up," I said. I was so out of breath. I tugged my phone out of my pocket and looked at the screen. It was from Scott:

Your sister's car is intact, but she was definitely at that party. Left right after Laney.

Fear ballooned in me. Where was she? In front of me? Or not? Was Luke really following Brooke's scent? Was I crazy to be following my dog through these woods when she could be ... I shuddered.

The thought of my parents' reactions if it turned out I was chasing the wind while Brooke was in danger somewhere else nearly made my knees buckle.

"Dear God!" I whispered. I didn't honestly know if that was a prayer or just an exclamation of profound horror and confusion.

I knelt down and Luke came to me, licking my face and nuzzling me. "Sit," I said, and so he did. "Luke, focus." I pulled my sister's shirt out of my jacket. "See this? See it?" I moved it toward his nose. "Get a good whiff, Luke, because there's a lot riding on it."

Then I rose to my feet, showed him the shirt again, and said, "Find it! Find Brooke."

He took off. Thankfully, he was still on leash or he would have quickly been out of sight. He raced forward, nose to the ground, maintaining the course we'd been on. Fifteen minutes later, he suddenly stopped.

I almost ran over him. "What is it? What do you have?"

Luke sniffed off the little path, then pawed at something in the leaves. "Wait. Sit." I directed my flashlight beam to where he had been pawing. And there, in the middle of a hundred dry oak leaves, lay my sister's phone in its instantly recognizable case.

"Oh, no," I groaned, dropping to my knees. My first instinct was to pick it up. But then, I didn't want to mar any fingerprints on it. It was evidence, and as a former detective I knew how important it was to maintain its integrity.

But what should I do? "Good boy, oh, good boy." As I petted my beautiful dog, I ran through the options. But there was really only one.

I called Scott. "I got your text."

"Where are you?"

I took a deep breath. "Luke is following a scent trail down from where Brooke's car was parked." My voice shook. I closed my eyes and confessed. "I'm in the woods, about fifteen minutes west of where Brooke's car was found."

"Who is with you?"

"Luke."

"Just Luke?"

I knew it took a lot of restraint for Scott not to yell at me.

"Stay put. I'll be there in twenty minutes. Okay? Jess?"

Luke was already pulling me further down the trail. If my sister was there, and she was alive, I wanted to get to her. I had to get to her. Before …

"I can't." My voice was barely a whisper.

Scott started to say something else, but I clicked off my phone.

46

Scott Cooper stared at his phone in disbelief. Had Jess really hung up on him?

He ran to find the lead detective. "Who's standing by at the site where Brooke Anderson's car was found?"

Grady Hunsaker stared at him, taken aback. "I told 'em to go home 'bout ten minutes ago. No sense guarding grass."

"We need somebody back out there right away." Scott keyed in a phone number.

"Why?"

"Just get somebody moving, and I'll tell you in a second."

Scott's gut felt like he'd swallowed a thousand shards of glass. "Nate!" he said. "Where are you?"

"I'm on Route 656, trying to find Jess," Nate said. "She took off again. Do you know where she is?"

Scott gave Nate the short version. "I'm afraid she's going to do something on her own."

"That's likely," Nate responded. "Hold on, I see her car parked up ahead."

"I'll be there in fifteen minutes!" Scott replied.

"Looks like there's a farm lane an eighth of a mile before where Jess's car is parked. I'm going into the woods," Nate said. "I don't think I should wait."

47

I KNEW I had to mark the location of Brooke's phone. I hadn't brought my SAR pack, just my GPS and a flashlight. I marked a waypoint in my GPS, then I took off a boot, removed a sock, and dropped it on the phone. After I put my boot back on, I pulled Brooke's T-shirt out of my jacket again, gave Luke a good sniff, and said, "Find it! Find Brooke, Luke!"

He took off. I tripped once and nearly lost my grip on the leash, but I held on, got up, and we kept going. Ten minutes further on, we came to a clearing. I made Luke stop, and I marked the place we'd left the woods on my GPS. Just for good measure, I grabbed three rocks and piled them up.

Part of me was relieved to be out of the woods. Part of me was trying to see what was ahead. I had switched off my flashlight. As my eyes grew accustomed to the dark, I could see a big building, a barn, about fifty yards ahead. A smaller outbuilding was behind it, and up on a nearby knoll, a farmhouse.

There were no signs of life except for a dim light on the front of the barn. As I moved around, trying to get a better view, I saw a truck parked nearby.

Luke wasn't finished following the scent. Frustrated at the

brakes I'd put on our search, he barked three times. "Shhh. Quiet."

I texted Scott. *I found a clearing and an old farm. Barn, outbuildings, house. One small light. Truck parked outside.* Then I gave him the coordinates.

It took two hands to text. I was lying on the ground on my belly trying to be as invisible as I could. I had Luke's leash secured under my elbow ... I thought.

I heard a noise, looked up, and saw a door at the back of the barn open up and light spill out. Luke took off running.

"Luke!" I cried and started to scramble to my feet.

A hand grabbed the back of my jacket and pushed me to the ground. "Leave him be."

Astonished, I turned and looked at Nate. "How'd you get here?"

"While you were in the bathroom earlier, I turned on location sharing on your phone. I've learnt I got to keep my eye on you."

A kaleidoscope of emotions swirled through me. I was embarrassed, chastened, and happy all at once. "I've got to get Luke."

"He'll come back on his own."

When I looked up, the door had closed, and Luke was racing back. I grabbed his leash. Then I turned to Nate. "I think my sister may be in there!" My breath came in short gasps.

"Scott's coming."

"I can't wait for him! That guy could be killing her!"

"You have to wait."

But brutal images flashed through my mind, and I panicked. "No!"

Just then we heard a noise behind us. We turned as two cops emerged from the woods. D. Foster was one of them, and he had his Malinois, who erupted in barking when he saw Luke. I tightened my grip on my dog's leash and stood up.

The cops were out of breath. "What's the story here?" a deputy with the last name of Martin asked.

"I think my sister may be in there. I think she's in danger." I pointed toward the barn.

"I just see that one light."

"I think I saw a door open, there in the back."

"I'll check it out," Foster said, and he and his dog started toward the barn.

"There's more help coming," Nate said. "Might be smart to wait."

"We got it."

Deputy Martin muttered something under his breath as Foster walked away. Then he gestured toward the east. "Look." A line of cars with their lights off, at least five of them, were edging their way down toward us.

I was so anxious about my sister that I was trembling. My heart sank as I saw Foster head toward the front of the barn. Didn't he hear me say I'd seen a door open in the back?

The clouds streamed by and exposed the half moon. I could see Foster near the barn. I saw him let his Malinois off-leash, and I saw the dog racing around toward the back.

Good. But Foster must have thought entering through the double doors in the front was a better idea. I saw him slide the double door open a crack and saw him disappear inside.

Nate squeezed my arm. That's when I realized he'd been holding on to me this whole time. He gestured toward the cars. They'd stopped and were parked five abreast, blocking the egress from the property. I could see officers getting out.

"Let's head over there," Nate said. I knew he was trying to keep me from doing something stupid.

But before we could move, there was a tremendous explosion. We turned just in time to see flame and smoke erupting from the barn.

Both of us started running toward the barn. Martin did as well. All I could think about was my sister. My sister! Fear made my tired legs pump hard.

The fire blazed in the front where Foster had entered. I raced toward the back, just in time to see a small vehicle—a Gator or a Suzuki Sidekick—disappearing over the hill. Luke saw it, too, and pulled the leash out of my hand.

I thought I could see people in the Gator. Two, maybe three. I turned to tell Nate, but he was gone. And I knew in an instant what he'd done. While I'd headed for my sister, he'd gone to help the deputy. He'd run straight into danger. Fire danger.

I hesitated a second, but even I knew there was no way on foot I'd catch the vehicle I'd seen. My dog was disappearing over the hill, but Nate—with his war wounds, his aversion to fire, his anxiety—was also in danger.

I ran to the front of the barn. I got there just in time to see Nate dragging that deputy toward the open barn door. I ran in, grabbed the guy's other arm, and together we extricated him. Coughing and choking, I turned just in time to see Nate run back into the inferno.

Why?

The dog, of course. Nate was after the dog.

I went in after Nate.

The fire was so intense, it felt like the flames of hell. Whatever was stored in there—hay, straw, fuel—was burning hot. That barnwood had been drying for a hundred years and was ready to burn.

I could hear Nate ahead of me, coughing. I saw his back through all the smoke, then I saw him bend down. When I caught up to him, he had the dog in his arms. He also was choking on smoke.

"Here," Nate said, shoving the dog toward me.

I assumed he'd follow me. I got the dog to where Martin was crouched over Foster. I put the dog on the ground, and I turned back to Nate.

He was nowhere to be seen. Why hadn't he followed me?

So I went back in the barn. By this time, I could hear the

shouts of the other officers. I moved toward where I'd last seen Nate, covering my face with my sleeve, peering into the thick, gray smoke.

Then I saw him. He'd collapsed.

"Nate!" I yelled.

Before I could get to him, there was a flash of light, a loud boom, and the barn exploded again. I covered my face. And when I looked up, I saw the unthinkable. A part of the barn wall had fallen on Nate. He was trapped!

"Help!" I yelled. "Help us." Two shouts were all I could manage. I bent down and found Nate struggling to breathe. His eyes were wide open. He was terrified.

I grabbed a sturdy hay rake and tried to move the burning rubble off his leg. He was panicking. I knew he didn't have enough air for that.

Scott showed up. Scott and two others. "He's trapped!" I said.

By now, the thick smoke had us all coughing and gasping for air. One of the guys grabbed the hay rake from me.

"Get that!" Scott said to the second man, gesturing toward a metal rod.

I crouched down and tried to calm Nate. I knew he'd pass out if he couldn't slow down his breathing.

I grabbed his hand. "We got you, Nate. Breathe. Breathe, Nate. We're going to get you out."

He squeezed my hand and released it. Then he squeezed it again and this time, did not let go. Out of the corner of my eye, I saw they were using lengths of wood and the hay rake and the rod to move the large beam that had fallen on him.

"Nate, hang on. Hang on!" I said, my voice breaking. I saw the agony in his face, the wild fear in his eyes. "Please, Nate, breathe. Breathe like you taught me." I couldn't remember the breathing pattern, but it didn't matter. It was obvious he was too panicked for that.

"Move him now," I heard Scott say.

I grabbed Nate's arm, and another guy grabbed his other arm, and we pulled him out of that rubble while his screams rang in our ears.

We carried Nate out of the barn and laid him on the grass a safe distance away. I knelt down next to him. I couldn't look at his leg. "Breathe, Nate. Come on," I urged. "Breathe!"

"I got him." An EMT dropped down next to me.

I moved to give him room. As I stood up, I saw another EMT bending over Foster. I watched, coughing, as the EMT placed a mask over Nate's face. Beyond him, the lights of an ambulance flashed.

"Jess!"

I turned and saw Scott leaning over, hands on his knees, trying to catch his breath. And then I thought of Luke, and my sister, and that Gator that had disappeared over the hill.

"Scott." I had a coughing fit. I stumbled over to him and told him what I'd seen.

He looked at me, his eyes watering from the smoke. "C'mon, let's go."

I looked back at Nate. "I can't leave him!"

"They've got him. There's nothing more you can do right now."

I knew Scott was right, but I was shaking with fear for Nate.

"Let's go," Scott said. "Show me where they went."

Reluctantly, I turned to leave.

48

SCOTT GRABBED a couple of other deputies and commandeered one of the Ford Interceptors, a smaller SUV than Scott's Bucar. We drove to the back of the barn, where I'd seen the people leave, and continued toward the woods. We were both coughing and hacking, and if I hadn't been so adrenalized, I think I would have passed out.

My mind was split two ways: Ahead of me was my dog and maybe my sister. Behind me, was Nate. I couldn't get his screams out of my head. I felt like I was leaving half my heart with him.

As we drove, Scott dropped a bombshell on me. "Your old police captain called me on the way here."

I turned to him, incredulous.

"We think this guy, Junior Jones, may be the same Charles Jones Jr. you had a run-in with three years ago."

I felt my neck tighten. "Wow. So I was right."

Scott continued. "We got an address. We're getting a search warrant. He's about the same age, he's a woodchuck, he lived in Fairfax with his girlfriend three years ago, and the girlfriend fits the profile. A Fairfax detective is tracking her down now to see if she can help us."

I couldn't believe it. The same guy we'd found choking his girlfriend, the guy who killed my partner, the guy on the run for three years—this was the guy we were chasing?

As we drew closer to the woods, we saw an opening and a path that led down from there, a path too narrow for the Interceptor. We piled out, and the deputy driving grabbed the shotgun. "Split up," Scott said. "Jess, you're with me."

As the deputies moved off, Scott said, "You have a concealed carry permit?"

I nodded.

"But you're not carrying?"

"No."

About fifty feet down that trail, we found the Gator, overturned in a ditch. Then I heard something crashing through the woods. My heart jumped. I whistled, and my dog Luke came running, his leash trailing behind him. "Luke! Oh, good boy!"

"You go back now," Scott said.

"What?" I stared at Scott, incredulous.

"You got your dog. Now go back before one of you gets hurt."

I raised myself to my full height, which admittedly wasn't much. "My sister is still in these woods." My words were clipped. "There is no way I'm leaving 'til we find her." My heart drummed in my chest. Were we going to have a fight right here in these woods?

Scott glared at me. I braced myself. My jaw tightened. Then I saw the slightest relaxation of the skin around his eyes, and I took advantage of it. "Let's do this together, Scott. Together."

He hesitated. "All right," he said. "But take this." He handed me his backup weapon. I hadn't had a gun in my hand for three years. It felt good.

"Luke can find any human," I said. "You want me to ask him to?"

"There's a risk to him," Scott said. "Jones could be armed."

"I know."

"Your call."

Of course, I didn't want Luke shot. But the woods were deep and dark, and I thought he could help us find this guy, or my sister. I settled him, got him sitting at heel, removed his leash, and said, "Seek!" He didn't have his vest on, but apparently, in his mind that wasn't a requirement.

Luke took off running, and we did our best to follow. Neither of us had much lung capacity left. Three minutes later, Luke ran back. I wasn't wearing a tug on my belt, so he reverted to his original indication and jumped up on me. Fortunately, Scott was behind me and caught me. "He's got somebody," I said. "Let's go!"

We followed the dog until Scott suddenly grabbed my arm. He thought he could see someone ahead. Then we heard a man cry out, "Get off! Get away!" Luke had found somebody and that somebody was afraid of my dog.

Scott motioned for us to split up. He'd go left, and I'd go right.

Luke came back, confused about why I wasn't going straight to the "human" he'd found. I motioned for him to heel with my hand. That was the first time I'd ever used the hand signal alone, but he did it. I clipped on his leash. I wanted him close.

I listened carefully. I could still see Scott about twenty feet from me. We diverged further and circled.

Thoughts raced through my mind. I still didn't know where my sister was. I was terrified Nate would die. I had to get the guy Luke had found. Was it really Charles Jones Jr.? The man who killed those women? The man who killed my partner?

The wind was still high, and the woods dark as pitch. I could smell the humus, the dampness from the rain. An owl took off from a nearby tree, his wings whooshing through the air, making me jump. I stayed low, trying not to cough, trying to pierce the darkness with my watery eyes.

Suddenly, to my left, I heard Scott say, "FBI, put your hands up!"

Clutching my gun, I moved closer, Luke with me. I saw him look at me, then look at the man, then back to me again. He'd never seen me in a tactical situation.

"I didn't do nothing!" Jones said.

That voice! Suddenly, I saw images and heard sounds from three years ago. My heart beat harder.

"Hands up!" Scott yelled.

I crept low. I saw Jones, a muscular guy wearing overalls and a jacket. He was looking away from me, but he had his hands up. Still, I raised my gun, my heart beating so hard I was afraid he could hear it. I didn't notice Luke's leash slip from my grasp.

Then, horrified, I saw Scott stumble. He stepped in a hole, or tripped over a log, or got tangled in a bramble. He fell and this man reached inside his jacket. "Junior Jones!" I yelled.

He turned to me, surprised. My flashlight caught metal, and I squeezed the trigger three times.

Luke leaped on Jones just as I fired. The two of them went down in a heap. Had I shot Luke? Had I shot my dog?

Scott scrambled to his feet. We both raced toward the man and the dog.

"Luke, Luke!"

The dog rolled over and got up. I grabbed his collar. Scott took control of the suspect who groaned loudly. I heard Scott call on the radio. "Suspect's down. I need a medic."

Meanwhile, I ran my hands over Luke's body, searching for blood, searching for wounds. He was licking my face and wagging, like he was so proud of himself.

"Jess!" Scott shouted. "Is he okay?"

"Yes, I think so."

"Come here, then."

I raced over to Scott. He had his knee on Junior Jones's back. "You cuff him," he said, holding out his handcuffs. "This is your collar."

When Scott handed me those cuffs, I saw something in his eyes—respect. A frozen part of me thawed. A wall crumbled. I grabbed those cuffs and put them on tight. Really tight.

49

"WHERE'S HE SHOT?" I asked.

"Looks like his arm," Scott said, shining his flashlight on the suspect.

I'd aimed for Junior Jones's center of mass—his chest—but when Luke knocked him down, he'd twisted, and one of my bullets caught mostly his shoulder and upper arm. How my other shots missed Luke, I'll never know.

I'm guessing Nate would call it grace.

I turned Charles Jones Jr. over. When I saw his face, not only did I remember him, he remembered me. "You!" he said.

"Yes."

"I didn't mean to kill him. Honest! I was scared. I was trapped. I had to get out!"

I swear I saw tears in his eyes. I grabbed his shirt at the collar. "Where are they? Where are the women?"

He shook his head. "They got away." And he began crying. Crying.

But I wanted more information. I got ready to exert pressure.

Scott touched my arm. "Go. Take your dog."

Just then, his radio squawked. "We got the girls."

Girls. "Ask what their names are."

Scott repeated my question into the mic.

"Laney Collier and Brooke Anderson. They're scared but fine."

Tears of relief flooded my eyes.

"Go see your sister," Scott said. "I got this."

Exhaustion had turned my legs to spaghetti. They couldn't carry me out of those woods fast enough. But minutes later, I was standing in the field looking at my sister in the light of a blazing barn.

We both cried. We held each other so tightly I thought we would melt together.

I released Brooke, pulled out my phone, and called our mother. Then everybody was crying.

I blew my nose while Brooke talked to Mom. I turned to the deputy who would accompany Brooke and Laney to the hospital. "Where will you take them?"

She gave me the name of a hospital forty-five minutes away. "It's the closest one."

"Our parents will meet you there," I said.

Brooke handed me back my phone, and I told our parents where to meet her. When I clicked the phone off, she gave me another hug. "Thank you, sis. I hoped you'd find me. You and your beautiful dog." She bent down and hugged Luke.

"What were you doing? How did you get here?" I asked her.

"I saw Laney leave the party really, really drunk. And I felt like someone should keep an eye on her. Maybe give her a ride. So I followed her out. She could barely walk. But before I could catch up to her, she got into this guy's truck." Tears streamed down Brooke's face as she told the story.

"I was scared for her! So I followed them. He turned down this lane, and ... and ... I figured if I followed on foot it might be better. So I pulled off the road and went through the woods. He was going really slow. I could see his headlights."

"Did you think of calling the cops?"

Brooke shrugged. "By the time I did, I'd lost my phone."

"I know where it is. Luke found it," I said. "So what happened next?"

"I saw a light in the back of the barn and crept back there. I saw him walk up toward that house. I ran in. Laney was all tied up. I tried freeing her, but he came back!" She started sobbing. "He caught me too!"

I pulled a ragged tissue out of my pocket and handed it to her.

"But you know what? He couldn't figure out what to do with two of us. I mean, he's kind of simple."

"Oh, Brooke!" I hugged her again.

"I'm okay, sis," she said. "He didn't do anything to us. We were just terrified he was going to kill us."

Moments later, after more tears and hugs, I watched her climb into the deputy's Interceptor. My crazy, brave little sister.

But now that she was safe, my mind shifted to Nate. Honestly, he had really never left me. I needed to find Nate. But the heat from that fire and the brightness of the flames reminded me that I didn't even know if he was alive.

I saw the sheriff and tried to ask him, but he was surrounded by firemen and deputies and either didn't hear my question or ignored me. Then I saw Scott. He and a deputy were walking Junior Jones out of the woods. Our eyes met. He grabbed another deputy to help with Jones and came to me.

"What's up?"

"I want to see Nate. I need to find Nate." I felt tears forming again.

His voice was gentle but firm. "Jess, I don't want you to drive. Do you hear me?"

I nodded, too tired to fight.

"I'll have someone take you."

"Luke..."

"Could another SAR team member take him?"

"Yeah, sure. Susan." I was so compliant I barely recognized myself. "Susan can take care of him and Sprite." Then I thought of something. "I need his crate."

"Give me the gun. I'll have a deputy drive you up to your car. You can put Luke in the crate, and the deputy will stay with him until Susan comes. Dana will meet you there."

I handed him his backup weapon, which he put in an evidence bag. "Don't worry, it was a good shoot. Jones had a gun too." Then, he picked up his radio and called Dana.

I turned to my dog. The light of the fire flickered in Luke's beautiful eyes. "I love you. You're a good, good dog." Luke thumped his tail. "You need to stay with Sprite for a while, but I'll see you soon."

"You saved two women, nabbed a fugitive, and probably saved my life," Scott said. "You've had a good day, Jess. I agree with Nate. You've got grit." He hugged me, and he probably meant it to be a quick hug, but I held onto him even when I felt his grip loosen. I needed his strength right then. I was so scared for Nate. As I looked over his shoulder, my smoke-stung, teary eyes were filled with the light of that barn fire. And in the middle of the flames, so hot they were white, I swear I saw a cross.

FIFTEEN MINUTES LATER, I sat in the front passenger seat of my own Jeep, flying down Interstate 81. Thankfully, Dana had been smart enough to find out where we were going before we left. Nate had been transported to the same hospital as my sister, but then he'd been airlifted to the Level 1 trauma center in Charlottesville.

We pulled off at the first truck stop so I could get cleaned up. Dana suggested I buy something to eat, but nothing appealed to me. She finally grabbed a yogurt and a fruit smoothie and shoved them into my hands.

"Put something on your stomach," she said.

It's not just men who can be pushy.

Still, I knew she was right. I drank the smoothie as we got back on the road and found myself drifting into much-needed sleep.

It was a good thing. When we got to the hospital, Dana handed me my car keys and took off. She said she'd take an Uber to the state police barracks where she'd get a ride home.

I walked into that hospital alone and terrified. I didn't know if Nate was dead or alive, but bright images of the agony he'd been in played in my mind. I practiced my breathing. In for four, hold for seven, out for eight. Then I went to the information desk.

The volunteer finally tracked Nate down. He was in surgery. So at least he was alive. She told me where to find the surgical waiting room, where I identified myself to the receptionist. A few minutes later, a nurse appeared with a clipboard in her hand.

When I joined Battlefield, I had to fill out a medical emergency form. SAR is dangerous. I used my mother as my emergency contact. I had no idea that Nate had designated me. Of course, he had no family. But still.

So there I was at the hospital, exhausted and brain-dead, staring at a form authorizing a surgeon to amputate Nate's leg.

"Just if they need to," the nurse said.

I was horrified. Losing a leg would be a huge adjustment for Nate. It would mean a whole new type of rehab. A lot of pain. The end of SAR, probably.

But he would be alive. He'd still be here. He'd still have Sprite, and she would have him.

More to the point, I'd have him too. We all would. The world without Nate was unimaginable to me.

My confusion must have been apparent. "I'll be back in a few minutes," the nurse said, patting my hand.

Was I being selfish? Condemning him to another round of terrible pain? Would Nate want to live with one leg? Would he be able to do the things he enjoyed? Would he be able to work?

Conflicted, I did something I'd never done before—never imagined myself doing. I prayed to a God I didn't believe in on behalf of my friend who very definitely believed. *Help me know what to do. Help me make the right choice. For Nate, who loves you.*

I sat there for a few minutes. And then I signed the form.

Why? Because something Nate said to me came to mind. *Sometimes the devil will try to convince you life ain't worth livin'. That's a lie, a damnable lie.*

After the nurse left with the signed form, I tried to get comfortable on the waiting room couch, snuggled in the corner, using my jacket as a pillow. At the truck stop I had changed into the relatively clean jeans in the back of my Jeep. As I scooched around, I felt something in the back pocket. I pulled it out. It was my Dad's little black book.

I was too tired to read it, too stressed to deal with its contents. But I curled around the hand that held that little black book and let the memory of Dad and his mysterious connection to the Gospel of John comfort me. Soon I fell asleep.

NINETY MINUTES LATER, the nurse woke me. The surgeon would see me in Consultation Room 1. Shaking with nerves, I used the restroom, washed my face, and found that room.

"Your friend," Dr. Chichester said, "sustained a severe crush injury plus third-degree burns on his lower left leg." He showed me an X-ray on his laptop. There was no piece of bone in Nate's lower leg that was larger than a dollar. Most were smaller than a half dollar. Even his ankle was broken. "I consulted with a limb preservation specialist, but he agreed. The combination of the crush injury and the serious burns, well, it made it impossible to save his leg."

My heart sank.

"The good news is, his injuries were localized. He has a few other burns, but nothing that would need hospitalization. His lungs are compromised from smoke inhalation, and we'll have to watch his kidney function, but I think there's a good chance he will fully recover."

"He'll need rehab—"

"Of course, and eventually, a prosthesis, but a lot of people are living these days with amputations."

I thought of his friend, Peter Turner, the double amp.

The whole time the surgeon was talking to me, I was either coughing or suppressing a cough. He finally cocked his head and said, "Were you in that same fire?"

"Yes."

He took a deep breath, something at that moment I couldn't do. "Tell you what. It'll be about two hours before you can see him. How about you go down to the ER and get yourself checked out? Smoke inhalation is nothing to fool with."

I could see myself sitting in the ER waiting room a lot longer than two hours. I hesitated, but he anticipated my objection. "I'll call down and grease the skids," he said. "You won't have to wait."

True to his word, Dr. Chichester got me in and out of the ER in record time. Armed with a new inhaler, orders to drink lots of fluids, and symptoms to watch for if my lungs got worse, I caught up with Nate in ICU.

Heavily sedated, he lay on the bed intubated, with multiple monitors, an IV in his right arm, and an empty space under the covers where his lower left leg should have been. Tears came to my eyes when I saw that.

I pulled up a chair, took his left hand in mine, and began to tell him how brave he was, how much I admired him. I told him we were all safe, including my sister and Laney.

While I was sitting there, Scott kept texting me updates. The girls were fine, at least physically. My parents were with Brooke. Deputy Foster was injured, but he'd make it, and so would his dog.

Jones was in the hospital but well enough to be interviewed.

Apparently, he never got over the relationship with the girlfriend from three years ago and kept trying to recreate it. Of course, the girls he abducted were resistant, terrified, and so they ended up dead. Detectives found carved statues in his house when they searched it. Jones was, as Brooke had said, of limited mental capacity. Paranoid after killing the women, he had rigged the barn with explosives in case the cops came after him.

I told Scott about the doctor insisting I get my lungs checked, and I suggested he do the same. "Smoke inhalation is nothing to fool with," I said, quoting the doctor.

Scott said he would. His last text message brought tears to my eyes. *I'll come to you as soon as I can.*

AND SO BEGAN A VERY intense period. Nate was sedated heavily for four days. They were trying to give his lungs time to heal.

Scott showed up as promised on the second day and visited frequently after that. We talked quietly in Nate's ICU corner. He told me all about his sister, and I told him about Lee Park. We both cried. That's when I realized how much this man lying in the bed had changed us both.

On the fifth day, they decided to lighten up on Nate's sedation. I was holding his hand when his eyes opened. He looked over at me and squeezed my hand. Then he frowned and raised his eyebrows, and I knew he wanted to know what had happened.

I told him about the barn fire and his compromised lung function. "That's why you're intubated. They want to make sure you're getting enough oxygen." I told him about Brooke and Laney and the dogs and Scott. I mentioned Foster and his dog. "You saved them," I told him. I did not tell him about his leg.

But he knew. Later that day he kept shifting his hips in bed, restless. The nurse told me the doctor was on the way. Thank goodness.

Dr. Chichester stepped through the curtain and introduced

himself to Nate. I moved, and he came and stood next to Nate's bed, right where I had been sitting.

I knew what was coming.

The doctor told Nate about his injuries. He said his lung function had improved, and they would try taking out the breathing tube tomorrow. "You'll be able to talk and eat normally." He said lots of other positive things. Then he calmly told Nate about his leg.

I held my breath, but Nate seemed to take the news in stride, closing his eyes as he listened.

"I expect you to make a full recovery," Dr. Chichester said. "Eventually, you'll get fitted for a prosthesis and get back to your normal life." He patted Nate's arm. "You're a strong man, I can tell. You're going to make it."

Nate nodded.

As Dr. Chichester left, I went back to Nate, taking his hand in mine. I saw a single tear slide out of Nate's beautiful blue eyes. "You'll figure it out, Nate," I said. "You'll be okay. You still have your anchor."

He squeezed my hand. Then I felt him tremble.

I didn't know what to do. If he were in my place, he'd pray, or sing, or say wise, encouraging things.

I had none of those resources. But I did think of one thing that might get his mind off his leg. I said, "Nate, you want me to read to you?"

His eyes lit up, and he nodded.

I only had one book.

I pulled the Gospel of John out of my back pocket, lingering over my father's signature. I turned the page and began reading. And as I suspected, as the words flowed out of my mouth, Nate's trembling stopped. He held my left hand while I held the book in my right. I read through that confusing first chapter, on past the born-again business, and on to that poor adulterous woman. I kept looking up to see if Nate was asleep.

He wasn't. He squeezed my hand, encouraging me to continue. And somewhere between Jesus raising Lazarus from the dead, and "I go to prepare a place for you," (a verse my father had underlined) something changed in me. Like the man born blind, I began to see. It was fuzzy at first, but then it became clear, and suddenly, I knew what I was reading was true.

The person most shocked by that was me.

OVER THE NEXT FEW DAYS, Nate made good progress. He got moved to a regular room and started physical therapy.

I took my role as Nate's designated medical emergency contact seriously. I watched as a physician assistant taught him how to clean and dress his stump, in case I ever had to do it for him. (Yes, at first I wanted to throw up, but by the second or third time, I was used to it.) I listened carefully as the prosthetist talked to him about an artificial leg. I advocated for him when he decided to wean himself off the heavy-duty pain meds. I cheered him on in physical therapy.

I also watched for depression, which is common after limb loss. Mostly what I saw in Nate was a gritty determination to recover and gratitude for the people who were helping him.

His doctor told me privately that attitude was a significant determinate of recovery. "I've seen people give up the will to live," he told me, "and just die. I don't believe your friend will do that."

When I told Scott that, he told me about an FBI agent, badly wounded in a gun battle, who said later, "If you lie down to die, you *will* die."

I believe that now.

One day, however, Nate had a setback. He had been exercising, walking the loop around the nurses' station on crutches, when someone emerged from a patient's room and plowed right into him. Nate fell, landing on his stump, sending waves of agonizing pain through his whole body. Then he couldn't get up, and the frustration and pain overwhelmed him.

I arrived just as the staff was helping Nate get from a wheelchair back in bed. The nurse told me what happened. Nate couldn't talk. He was focused on dealing with the pain, his brow furrowed, his fists clenching and unclenching as if he was trying to let go of it. When he finally asked for pain meds, I knew he had to feel defeated.

Over the next few hours, Nate drifted in and out of sleep, moving restlessly in the bed. Twice I saw his body jerk and his eyes fly open, as if he was having a mini panic attack. I could imagine it: the fire, the pain, his leg, the terror of it all enveloping him again. Finally, I couldn't stand it anymore. I left.

When I returned an hour later, I carried a gym bag in my left hand. I strode past the nurses' station without making eye contact, and walked into Nate's room. He opened his eyes. I unzipped the bag and put a wiggling, happy Sprite in bed with him.

"Sprite!" Nate said. "Hey, girl, hey girl. How are you? Oh, baby girl!"

The two of them were a sight. Sprite wagging her tail like crazy and turning in circles, licking his hands and face, Nate petting her all over, tears in his eyes, grinning for the first time that day. "Thank you!" he said, shooting me a glance..

"You're welcome." I sat down in the chair, a wide smile on my face. The dog man needed his dog. Obviously.

After a while, Sprite settled down, lying with her body pressed up to Nate's, her head resting on what remained of his left leg. Nate's hand moved over her body, petting her. A nurse came in to check on him and startled at the sight of the dog. "Oh, my!" she said, raising her eyebrows.

I tensed up. Was she going to kick the dog out? I got ready to fight.

"This here," Nate said, his hand stroking Sprite's head, "is better than any pain med or any anti-depressant you have."

"Well, then," she said, smiling, "I'll make sure this therapy is noted and authorized in your chart."

The tension left the room. From then on, Sprite became a regular visitor.

Nate also had a steady stream of human visitors—Emily, Susan, and the rest of the SAR group, including, surprisingly, Kevin. Friends from work, people from his church ... I had no idea he was so popular. Even my parents came, along with Brooke. He spent most the time telling them what a wonderful person I was.

I still hadn't told him, or anybody else, about the change in me. I honestly didn't quite know what to do with it.

But one day, I was hanging out in his room while Nate and Sprite slept after physical therapy. I spied his Bible on the side table, picked it up, and opened it to where he'd placed his bookmark, at Acts 12. I wanted to read what he was reading. I needed to know more.

So I began, and I soon became absorbed by the crazy stories. James killed. Peter arrested. An angel shows up. Chains fall off. And then I almost laughed out loud when a servant girl left Peter standing at the gate, she was so shocked to see him.

When I looked up, Nate's eyes, crinkled with amusement, were fixed on me. "What are you reading?" he asked innocently.

For some reason, I felt embarrassed. I closed the book. And then I finally told him. "Somehow I began to believe," I said. A tremor of fear ran through me. What was I getting into?

"Aw, Jess," he said. He sat straight up and swung his leg over the side of the bed. "Come here." Tears filled his eyes. He hugged me. "This is the best news!"

"I still have a lot of questions," I said, hedging my bets.

"That's okay. Can I pray with you?"

I said yes.

It didn't kill me.

SCOTT ALTERNATED between visiting Nate and taking care of his house, cutting the grass and making sure the garden was kept up. I slept there some nights, with both dogs. I thought Sprite would like being in her own home.

I started seeing Sarah Pennington again, as her office was near the hospital. But things were different this time. I no longer expected four steps to a better me. I was learning about processing shame and grief. I was learning about giving and receiving love. Surprisingly, I found receiving harder.

Nate progressed well. Because he lived alone, doctors decided he should go from the hospital to the rehab center next door for a while. That gave us time to execute a plan of mine. Working together along with members of Battlefield SAR and some friends of Scott's, a group of us built a ramp from Nate's driveway to his back door, one he could easily navigate with crutches, a wheelchair, or a cane. I couldn't wait to surprise him.

But then I had another idea as well. I talked to Scott about it over lunch one day, and he was all in. He told me if I'd do the research, he'd take some time off and carry out the plan.

A couple of weeks later, I was at the rehab center next to the hospital, watching Nate as he did PT. I'd brought Sprite, and she was scampering around him, encouraging him as he used parallel bars to walk with his temporary prosthesis.

I was so excited I could barely suppress my smile.

"What's got into you?" Nate said as he wiped the sweat off his face.

"Nothing," I said.

"Track down one of your fugitives?" he suggested.

I decided to go with his idea. "Yes, I did. Somebody who's been missing a long time."

He insisted on walking back to his room instead of letting me push him in the wheelchair. Nate could be a stubborn man. The slow pace nearly killed me. Eventually, we arrived, he got back in bed, Sprite jumped up next to him, and I adopted a pose in the chair that I hoped looked relaxed.

"Don't you need to get home to Luke?" he asked me.

I had to think fast. "Sprite and Luke played so hard before I came I think he'll be out for a while."

He didn't quite buy that. I could tell by his look.

Finally, I heard Scott's characteristic *tap, tap* on the door. He stuck his head in. "You up for a visitor?"

"Sure," Nate said, petting Sprite with his left hand.

Scott walked in. He was a tall man and broad-shouldered, and he easily blocked the view of the person behind him. Once he was inside the room, he stepped aside.

Nate's eyes shifted as the second person entered. I stood up, unable to stay in my chair. His eyes got wide and his mouth dropped open. He sat up straight in bed. Sprite alerted too. Nate looked at me, then back at the woman. She stood next to Scott, tears in her eyes.

"Laura?" he said. "Laura O'Brien?"

"Nate," said the woman in his wallet, and she went to him and wrapped her arms around him. "It's been so long."

She was still beautiful, still had her long, dark hair. An elementary school librarian, she wore tailored slacks, a light-blue silk blouse, and a little beige jacket. She'd never been married, despite what Nate had heard, and hadn't moved more than thirty miles from home; that's how I'd found her so easily. When I'd contacted her and told her why I was calling, she'd cried.

"Are you sure he'd want to see me?" she'd asked.

"Oh, I'm quite sure," I'd told her.

Now, looking at the tears in Nate's eyes, I knew I'd guessed right. He still loved her. I whipped out my phone and took some pictures.

Nate looked at me. "You are a rascal!" he said, but his grin said the opposite.

I pocketed my phone and moved back next to Scott. "Good job," he said, and he put his arm around my waist and gave me a side hug. It felt like the most natural thing in the world.

We watched the two old friends for a few minutes, enjoying their happiness, laughing as Sprite tried to lick them both. Then Scott nudged me. "Let's take the dog for a walk." So I called Sprite and leashed her up.

As we walked out of the building, I saw a poster on the wall I'd not noticed before. It read, "Your scars can give someone else hope." And I thought of the dog man, and his beautiful scars, and the twisted road he'd been on, and still was on, and I thought of his tattoo in memory of Peter, and of Laura, the long-lost love he now embraced.

Peter's scars had given Nate hope, and Nate's scars had given me hope. And not just any hope, but a hope that I thought might overcome all the sorrows and pain and failures and shame of this life. Hope that is an anchor, an anchor that is love.

Scars that give hope. Welcome to my world.

-THE END-

ACKNOWLEDGMENTS

For an author, writing a book is a labor of love. But as in birthing a child, it's not done alone.

I'm so grateful to the members of Dogs East, a volunteer K-9 search and rescue group in my area. They let me observe their training exercises, answered my questions, and later, several read my manuscript to correct any misconceptions I had. (Any mistakes that remain are mine.) Thank you especially to Sharon Johnson and Jessica Burnside for their particular help.

Until I connected with Dogs East, I had no idea what a huge time commitment SAR involves, or how much training these volunteers undergo, or how much equipment they need to buy. Called out at all hours of the night and day in all kinds of weather, their contributions to the community are remarkable but go mostly unnoticed, except by the families they help.

Dru Wells, retired FBI agent, provided assistance with the Bureau aspects of the book, and as usual, caught some other errors as well. Thank you, Dru, for so generously sharing your knowledge and wisdom.

My daughter, Becky Chappell, did a great job with the initial edit of the manuscript. Then she began helping me with my website, memes, and social media, all while juggling her growing family. Finally she undertook the job of actually publishing the book. Her sharp eye, design sense, and cheerful attitude helped me immensely. I'm so grateful for you, Becky!

I appreciate Barbara Scott's work on the final edit for Dread. Her comments and corrections made it a better book, and her encouragement buoyed my spirits. As always, my agent, Janet Grant, of Books & Such Literary Management, gave me wise advice along the way. And thank you to fellow author Erin Unger, who challenged me to write in first person. I love it!

After my husband died in 2017, I wondered if my writing days were over. I prayed about that a lot. As words began to flow, I received my answer, and I praise God for the opportunity to write for Him again.

Finally, thank you readers, for joining me on this journey.

Soli Deo gloria

ABOUT THE AUTHOR

Linda J. White is a former journalist and author of multiple FBI thrillers. Her books have won the HOLT Medallion and have been finalists for National Reader's Choice Awards. Her husband was a video producer-director at the FBI Academy for decades. Mom of three, grandmother of five (at last count), Linda lives near Quantico, VA. A speaker and Bible study teacher, Linda also enjoys working with her Shetland sheepdog, Keira, and spending time with her grandkids.

Website: lindajwhite.net
Email: lindajwhitebooks@gmail.com
Facebook: LindaJWhiteBooks
Twitter: @rytn4hm

ALSO BY LINDA J. WHITE

Made in the USA
Las Vegas, NV
12 January 2025

16289543R00184